THE REPUBLIC OF CEDAR KEY

MICHAEL PRESLEY BOBBITT

WAYWARD WRITERS PRESS

Contents

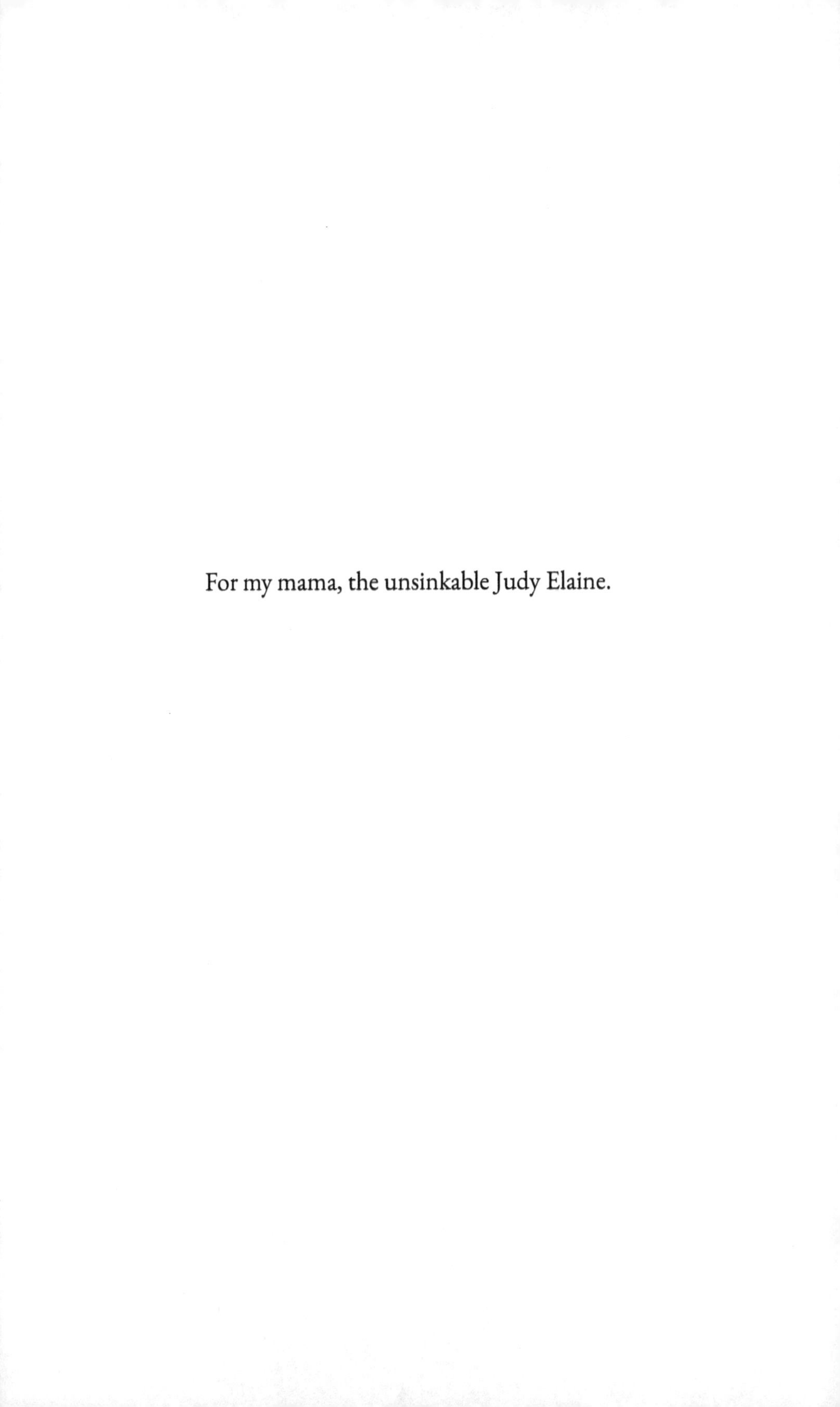

For my mama, the unsinkable Judy Elaine.

1

THE NEW OLD WORLD

We are water, born from the sea. The anchor that binds us to the land runs no deeper than the dust beneath our feet. Island living is hard to root out of the blood when it takes hold; once surrounded on all sides by the mothering of water, lulled to comfort by the movement of the tides, no other place could ever feel like home again. So it was for the people of Cedar Key in the old world and the new.

In the quarter-century since the island's horizon exploded in a dazzling fugue of splitting atoms and human stupidity, change had overwhelmed the Earth. It came quickly at first—a de-industrial revolution waged and won in a microsecond of piercing light—then slowed into the glacial meter of progress that would set in for countless generations. Life was better and worse than it had ever been, and memories of the old world were harder to conjure with each passing year. Details faded quickly. The big ideas held on longer, but they were slipping away now as well. There had been no discussion about the annual 4th of July parade ending, but years of radio silence from the American government had slowly eroded the island's bedrock of patriotism until, eventually, people just stopped showing up. Everyday technologies from before the flash were now indistinguishable from sorcery, and the Information Age was a dream that seemed as far away from them as Alpha Centauri.

In the fifty-first year of his mayorship, more than half of which had elapsed after the great experiment of humanity failed around the world, Hayes David awoke one cool September morning and decided it was simply time to step aside. He was tired, and his body was older than the seventy-three years on its odometer. The right ear that was shot off in the Second Battle of Cedar Key had barely affected his life, but the little toe he lost in the Two-Day War on the Suwannee River had hitched his giddy-up significantly. The inconvenience of it grew into an arthritic impediment as the years piled up. There had been an election every year as usual, but no one ever stood to oppose him. The other four seats on the town council turned over with regularity, but the weight of the top job was more than anyone else wanted to bear.

Thomas Buck didn't want to think about the island without his best friend Hayes at the helm. "You sure about this, buddy?"

As they rocked in chairs on a front porch he had built with his father, Hayes replied, "I used up all my good ideas, Thomas. I haven't had one for years now."

"That's not true. We've held it together here pretty good as far as I can see."

"Maybe so," Hayes replied. "But it's just time. Luke or Ryland or one of the other young'uns needs to take a turn."

"If you're sure about this, then okay. But I don't like it."

"I'm sure," Hayes said without a break in the slow rocking that set the languid tempo of the conversation.

The two men had developed a kind of shorthand that made the long-winded discussions from their younger years largely unnecessary.

They were opposites in so many ways. Hayes' legendary anal-retentiveness was the perfect foil for the writer Thomas' cavalier free-wheeling, but they cared for the island with similar devotion and had defended it alongside each other into the twilight of their lives.

The old mayor's intuition was prescient. He could not have known the extent of the challenge the island was about to face, or indeed that it was coming at all, but the many years of relative peace he had helped to create would soon be threatened in a way that would demand the vigor of a younger leader. It was, in fact, Thomas' son Luke who stood for consideration in the special election, himself meeting no opposition but vowing to take the job only if a majority of the four hundred and twelve islanders voted for him.

On the day of the flash, Luke Buck had been twenty-three years old. His wild blonde hair and wiry frame cut a striking figure at the helm of his 16-foot boat, *The Big Skiff Energy*. He and his best buddy, Ryland Beecham, each lost a mother on that awful day. This unspoken connection bound them together almost immediately as they hunted in the scrublands on the other side of the Number Four Bridge in the early months of the new world. In short order, they developed a partnership as strong as that enjoyed by Thomas and Hayes, and it paid dividends in whitetail deer, squirrels, hogs, armadillos, and the kind of emotional support the modern world had taught men to avoid.

It was on one of their hunting trips across the channel, while stalking a deer through dense morning fog, that Luke met his wife Kinsey. An armed standoff between the boys and a girl from Sumner seemed primed to end in tragedy until Luke managed to talk everyone off the ledge. The moment he saw Kinsey's avalanche of red hair spilling out of her camouflage boonie hat, he was smitten. As he and Ryland dragged the deer out of the woods for her—one she had taken down with three fast, skillful shots while the boys hesitated—Luke was transfixed by the incongruity of her delicate features and icy composure, and knew then he would follow her anywhere she went. Instead, Kinsey was happy to let him lead as they fell in love over the coming weeks in equal, life-altering measure.

Now, as he stood to become Cedar Key's first new mayor in a half century, forty-eight-year-old Luke maintained a boyish quality, due partially to the trademark Buck smirk inherited from his father and in larger part to the energetic enthusiasm with which he approached even the most menial of tasks. If Ryland was the calm voice of reason in the friendship—and he was—Luke was the *hold my beer* vanguard of any foolhardy endeavor laid before them.

What Luke sometimes lacked in caution and forbearance, he made up for in relentless effort. If he were to be mayor, he decided when Hayes first approached him about resigning, then he wanted to learn everything there was to know about the job. He shadowed the old mayor for the last week of his tenure, asking questions and taking notes on how the levers of power were pulled and pushed on the island. Having no son of his own, Hayes' friendship with his best friend's boy had grown into a kind of paternal love that was meaningful to both men in ways mostly unspoken but clearly understood. Hayes took Luke door to door throughout that last week, using the time to tell every islander in person about his decision to resign, so that they could hear it directly from him, and to give his personal endorsement for Luke's candidacy to replace him.

Like his father, Thomas, Luke was a dedicated, almost fanatical student of history, even minoring in it for fun during his business studies at the University of North Florida in Jacksonville. He took a special interest in the wild, hard-scrabble history of Cedar Key, from its earliest beginnings when Timucuan Indians roamed the estuaries, through its antebellum days, the railroad era, and into the modern age. After the flash, Luke spent much of his adulthood writing, by hand, the history of the island in the years after the end of the world. He had played a critical role in much of that history, alongside his father and the old mayor whose influence permeated every aspect of life on the island. This made him a primary source on which he could confidently, if not objectively, rely. In the practice of writing down the story of the island, the deeds noble and inglorious of the people who had willed its continuance despite unreasonable odds against it, Luke felt connected even to the neighbors with whom he had few close interactions. As he recorded their stories, he grew closer to them.

While the town voted on election day, Luke took another walk with the outgoing mayor, taking in what additional wisdom he could as the potential new responsibilities began to weigh on him for the first time. Fog had rolled in from the mainland and blanketed the island in the kind of misty gray that made the open Gulf blur into oblivion. With the road ahead of them and the backwaters on either side in soft cinematic focus, the moment and the conversation were imbued with more importance than either man had intended.

"I was thinking about that mean old yankee lady today," Luke said.

"Which one?" Hayes asked with a grin.

"The college professor from Pennsylvania who hated everybody."

"Oh yeah, Miss Margie. She was a peach."

"Did my dad really throw a dead alligator in her yard? What was that all about?"

"Allegedly," Hayes said, laughing. "I'm not saying he definitely did it, but if he did, it's not like he killed the gator or anything. It had been run over and was sitting for days out on the highway when he . . . I mean, somebody . . . just threw it in the back of their truck on the way into town from Gainesville one day. I don't know how they managed it. It had to be 7 feet long and 150 pounds, and it smelled like a corpse."

"He didn't get into any trouble?"

"The investigation into the matter wasn't what you'd call *robust*," Hayes said gleefully. "The Chief and even the state boys knew she had it coming."

"I never met her in real life," Luke said. "I guess she died pretty soon after everything went to hell. But my dad told me all about her . . . how she called the cops on her neighbors all the time and filed formal complaints about the crab traps and boats everywhere on the island."

"That's her," Hayes replied. "She even sued the city, more than once, when I wouldn't do anything about her complaints. She was relentless in trying to make Cedar Key something it wasn't."

"Why do you think that was?" Luke asked.

"Hard to say. Some people are just miserable and want other people to be miserable with them."

"But she had to have seen the crab traps and the boats and all the rickety docks the first day she drove into town. It was a working waterfront, and it'd been that way forever. Why go through all the trouble to buy a house and move here if she didn't like what she saw?"

Hayes smiled at his young friend as they walked on. "After years of dealing with folks mad at the city or me or the other council members for one thing or another, I learned a hard truth about people. There's something stupid in human nature that makes us see what we want to see, not what's actually there. She probably liked the sunsets and the seafood, like everybody else. But she was arrogant enough to figure she'd set us straight and change the things she didn't like."

"How'd you stop her?"

Hayes shrugged. "I just kept saying no."

Luke laughed. "Just that easy, huh?"

Hayes replied with an unexpected note of sternness, "It was almost never easy. And it won't be any easier for you. But sometimes the most important thing you can do is to say no. I had to do it all the time, especially when no one else would. Listen, Luke, if you need to be liked, then this isn't the job for you."

Unsteadily, Luke answered, "I don't especially need to be liked, but I'm still not sure I'm the man for the job. It just didn't seem like anybody else was gonna step up."

"They weren't. But you did. And you're as solid a boat captain as we have in the fleet. That's plenty to get my vote."

"Thank you, Mr. Hayes. That means a lot to me."

The older man shook his head. "After all these years, how many times do I have to tell you it's Hayes? Just Hayes. You're not a kid anymore. Hell, you're older now than I was when we met."

The younger man's face settled into a calm self-assurance as he replied, "I don't like things to change any more than you do, Mr. Hayes."

"Fair enough," Hayes relented with a warm smile. "In the old days, all I cared about was trying to keep this island from changing into every other coastal town in Florida. But the truth is, Cedar Key's been constantly changing from the beginning. We were a timber town until they cut down all the cedar trees and didn't replant them. We were a railroad town until the railroad moved to Tampa. Then we were a mullet town until they banned the nets and a clam town until the bombs fell. It's useless to try to stop things from changing. They're gonna change, sure as the weather.

But the guts of this place, the way we look after each other, have got to stay the same, Luke. That's the thing worth digging in and fighting for."

"I hadn't thought about it like that," Luke said.

"Well, do with it what you want. You're about to be the new mayor, and I'll be the old mayor and glad on both accounts."

They had walked the length of the island by then, arriving at the Number Four Channel and the narrow wooden bridge built to replace the one the islanders dynamited to keep the outside world away in those first frantic months of the new world.

"End of the road," Luke said.

"The road keeps going," Hayes replied wistfully. "But everything past here is nowhere."

"Dang," Luke said, looking dramatically into the nowhere. "That's pretty good. Did you just come up with that, or you been holding onto that little nugget till just the right moment?"

Hayes rolled his eyes so hard he nearly had to pick one up off the ground and put it back in. "Smart ass."

Luke slapped the old man on the back, and they turned for home.

When they returned from their walk, the votes were counted and tallied. Three hundred and fifty of the four hundred and twelve islanders had voted for Luke, who took the oath of office from Hayes in the city park to the cheering of a large crowd.

Cedar Key is a Southern town. It is situated on a collection of barrier islands extending five miles into the Gulf of Mexico off the western coast of Levy County. It was an hour's drive west from the University of Florida when driving and universities were things that still existed outside of memory and stories the newest islanders found too fantastic to believe.

In the early days after the flash, the island's challenges were acute and immediate. A dozen clam farming boats were exposed on the water when those first kilotons fell on the Duke Energy Power Complex, thirty-eight miles across the Wacassassa Bay in Crystal River. The plant's twin hyperbolic cooling towers, remnants from a decommissioned nuclear reactor, were gone in a quintillionth of an instant, a tiny part of an atomic chain reaction happening on horizons around the world. In all, twenty-seven men and two women from the island fleet were caught in the haunted wind of the fallout and overwhelmed with radiation. The poison withered them into nothing over a few to several days while loved ones tried in vain to care for them. The elderly and infirm all across the island began falling shortly thereafter when medicines ran out or went bad in the unrefrigerated Florida heat. In those first terrible months, death and life and the in-between blended together like the glassy Gulf and placid sky on a cloudless afternoon.

Thereafter, especially in the first year, the islanders heard almost nothing from the outside world. Isolated as they were on an island dangling off the coast of the peninsula, it seemed for a time as though everything beyond the Number Four Bridge had simply vanished. If they hit the civilian power plant in Crystal River, when so many more strategic targets existed in the state—the US Central Command at MacDill in Tampa, the Navy bases in Jacksonville, the Eglin and Tyndall Air Force bases and others—surely some sequence of events had triggered the nightmare total war scenario seared into every Cold War kid's mind from an early age. Over time, the silence in the skies and on the waters became more terrifying than the falling of the bombs. As they continued to bury their neighbors, learning quickly that digging a grave by hand is not as easy as it always looked in the movies, the islanders made peace with the fact that no one was coming to help.

When the dying slowed, those who seemed likely to live got on with the hard business of living. Hand pumps were installed on a handful of private wells, providing a temporary source of drinking water until, months later, the water tower was miraculously brought back to life with solar panels and golf cart batteries. Wood gasifiers created a fuel that could power boat motors and electric generators. Front yard gardens sprang up all over the island, augmenting the always abundant crabs, clams, and mullet.

The annual arrival of the white shrimp in the waters around Cedar Key created not only a temporary abundance of food but also a reason to enjoy living in the midst of survival. Millions of enormous, nearly translucent shrimp, some larger than the palm of a hand, arrived fairly reliably every year in early July. A kind of religious zeal developed for the event, such that its occurrence eventually overshadowed the 4th of July completely. It was easy to see divine providence in so rich a gift from the Gulf, and by contrast, the failure of the nation the old holiday heralded was as self-evident as the rights America had been founded to protect. When big ideas fail, more tangible truths rush to fill the void. The white shrimp were a truth that could be seen and touched. Especially against the backdrop of a world so inarguably forsaken, they became as bedrock to the island's spiritual life as the Ten Commandments or the Christ story.

Just as something approaching a rhythm of daily life began to set in, invaders came from the mainland community of Sumner, kicking in doors and killing Folksy, the island's Episcopal minister. By the time the crew of outlaws made it to the little bridge in front of Fannie's Café, an impromptu citizen army lay in wait for them. A rain of bullets and arrows piled bodies one upon the other on the bridge until the threat was ended. The next morning's retaliatory strike in Sumner killed Little Don Meade, the outlaw leader who organized the attack, and a dozen more, some co-conspirators, some who were innocent onlookers caught in the melee. The vengeance the islanders collectively dispensed discouraged future attacks, but at a cost each would pay privately in still moments for the rest of their lives.

A year after the flash, a prodigal son returned to Cedar Key following two decades in the Coast Guard, commanding a fleet of vessels and threatening the stability and resources of the island. Isaac Skipjack had lost his father young in a cloud of island controversy, then sought and earned the love of a surrogate in Mark David, a hard waterman with a kind heart and the respect of everyone who knew him. When their connection was torn asunder by a misunderstanding as simple as it was tragic, sending Isaac across the Number Four Bridge for good, prolonged pain dug into both men and never stopped hurting. Isaac's invasion was thwarted at the cost of lives on both sides, but the old man and the boy he had grown to love were able to make peace at the end.

Thereafter, despite an array of challenges big and small, peace had largely prevailed on the island. Life slowly became more difficult as short-lived items like batteries, solar panels, and other hodgepodge technologies wore out or broke beyond repair. One by one, outboard motors powered by wood gasifiers fell silent. For a while, several broken motors could be torn apart and put back together into a single functioning motor, but eventually, the years and attrition were too much to overcome. Thus began a new age of sail in Cedar Key, gone since the days when the dread pirate Blackbeard first mapped the main channel between Way Key and Atsena Otie, and the notorious Jean Lafitte was rumored to have buried treasure on Dead Man's Key.

Miss Bette, the old mayor's mother, began sewing sails when the last outboard motor failed. She was eighty-three when her first sail was fitted to the *Cogency,* Hayes' bay boat that served as the island navy's flagship. By her ninetieth birthday, she had outfitted the entire 25-boat navy using a variety of makeshift materials, and now, at a spritely ninety-three, she oversaw a half dozen apprentices who would preserve and pass on her critical skill set.

So it was in the 26th year of the new world, on the 9,161st day since the cataclysm of man, on that bright, electric February morning, when life had found its footing again as solidly as the shifting sands of the island could ever allow, that a dragon appeared in the sky above Cedar Key.

2

KINDLING

In February of 1517, Francisco Hernández de Córdoba landed in Cape Catoche on the Yucatan coast like a bolt of lightning, dazzling the humid, tropical afternoon. To the Maya warriors observing from a flotilla of canoes, the Spanish were dreadful in their splendor as the sunlight gleamed off their steel armor and swords. The majesty of their caravel ships, adorned with elaborate riggings through square and lateen sails, was as terrible to behold as the feathered serpent Kukulcan, Maya god of the wind, rain, and storms.

The early interactions between the Spanish and the Maya were surprisingly cordial. The Maya civilization was as good as dead when Spanish ships first appeared on the horizon, but neither side knew it yet. Over the coming few weeks, the Spanish would make their way more than a hundred nautical miles down the Yucatan coast, arriving in the city of Campeche on St. Lazarus' feast day. They were met admiringly by the local chieftain and a large crowd of residents. The Spanish commemorated the moment with a grand gun salute that mystified and terrified the Maya.

Córdoba and his men were led to the city proper, and a feast was thrown in their honor. Here, it was time for the Spanish to be awestruck; in Campeche, they saw more than three thousand limestone dwellings, numerous shrines, a small pyramid, and a spectacular Maya temple. After an elaborate meal of fruits, game, maize, and fowl, the Spanish were invited into the temple, a tower-like stone structure with an idol carved at its top featuring the 40-foot-long Kukulcan devouring a fierce lion. Historian Bartolomé de las Casas would later write of the temple, "Everything was awash in the blood of men who had been executed or sacrificed there." Despite the terrifying imagery and the hard evidence of Maya brutality, the Spaniards were entreated by great hospitality to sojourn in Campeche for two days, resting and eating their fill while the Maya took measure of the foreigners in their midst.

While continuing south along the Yucatan coast, many of the cheap water containers on the Spanish ships failed. Driven by extreme thirst, Córdoba and his men stopped at a town called Champotón, where they were surprised to be greeted harshly by armed Maya as they tried to replenish their fresh water supply. Nightfall came earlier than the Spanish expected, and they were forced to spend an anxious night away from their ships as Maya warriors amassed in the darkness.

The morning broke terribly for the Spaniards, who found themselves surrounded by warriors adorned in cotton armor, fearsome headdresses, and faces painted black and white. They were armed with bows and arrows, slingshots, spears, and massive two-handed swords. With the Maya war captain shouting for his men to target the Spanish captain, frenzied, bloody combat ensued. Within a half hour, more than half of Córdoba's men had fallen. He himself was riddled with arrows as he called for retreat. The Maya pursued, pushing the European invaders into the sea and back to their ships. Spanish losses were staggering—55 dead, 2 missing, 52 injured. Francisco Hernández de Córdoba had suffered the biggest defeat since the

Spanish first landed in the New World. He would make it back to Cuba in time to die there of his wounds.

The Maya didn't know they were living in the New World, or that their civilization's high-water mark had come and gone. For the warriors along *La Costa de Mala Pelea*, the Coast of the Evil Battle, Spanish Dragons were racing away from them, disappearing over the horizon from whence they came.

It was the sound. The sight of the impossible machine hovering over the island was puzzling, unsettling, a cause for wonder; the sound ignited panic. Booming, mechanical noise covered everything, sending islanders scurrying for cover like ants caught in a ray of sun focused through a cruel child's magnifying glass. The youngest islanders had never heard anything like the deafening groan of the Blackhawk helicopter slowly landing on the beach at the city park. Older folks who could remember a time when flying machines were common had lost their memory of the sounds, and they, too, were struggling to comprehend the scene before them.

Luke Buck had been the mayor for less than two months, and during that time, the biggest issue he had faced was a gang of raccoons that kept beating up the old tabby cat that Fire Chief Johnson kept at the station as a mouser. As soon as he heard and saw the helicopter, Luke started running toward the park. As he passed the Island Hotel on 2nd Street, the oldest building on the island, he could see a cloud of white sand from the little beach being kicked up from the wash of the helicopter's rotors and blown against the condo units adjacent to the park. When he rounded the corner of 2nd and A Streets, Luke could just make out his son William on the other side of the artificial sandstorm, paddling a kayak in from the bay, heading toward the beach as well.

The younger Buck was twenty-four years old—tall, broad-shouldered, inquisitive, and feral—the third new world baby to be born in Cedar Key. For him, the machine landing on the beach could just as well have been a three-headed Hydra or the Millennium Falcon, such was the fantastic unreality of its appearance. By the time the Buck men made it to the park, Hayes and Thomas were rounding the corner as well, slower but every bit as determined to meet the potential threat. The four men shielded their eyes from the stinging sand as the helicopter began to power down. While they waited for the rotors to slow and stop—a length of time that seemed to be repeating on a loop—other islanders began arriving in numbers, all straining to look into the darkened windows of the terrible machine, waiting anxiously to see who might emerge.

By the time the door began to open, a dozen rifles were pointed at it, though all but a few had been without ammunition for many years. The figure that emerged was too magnificent to believe. The crisp creases of his Army Green Service Uniform, the full breast of medals, and the shimmering silver stars on his shoulders were jarringly out of place and time, as though King Arthur had appeared on Mars pulling at the reins of a flying horse. In all the commotion of that morning, the sudden time-shifting jolt of the helicopter's arrival and the lone figure emerging from it, nothing so unnerved the new mayor and the old as the pair of oxidized silver letters on the general's lapel. They were small, unassuming, and powerful. Luke Buck furrowed his brow in disbelief as he mouthed a questioning *U.S.?*

The United States was a relic that hurt to think about. For most of the 20th and the early part of the 21st centuries, United States power was unmatched. Its influence permeated the world, and the brute force of its economic and military might wore down even its most determined enemies. When the government of the United States fell so dramatically silent on the day of the flash, it was as though the sun had gone dark in the hearts of its citizens. The possibility of its failure had been absent from the American psyche since at least the War of 1812, so its seeming demise over a single February day had unmoored its people from two and a half centuries of identity.

From the magnificent general came an underwhelming voice. "Hello, there," he said, high-pitched and airy, "I apologize for the dramatics, but I wasn't sure your little bridge would hold my trucks."

"What trucks?" came a voice from the crowd.

"The ones holding with my men on the other side of the channel, waiting for orders," the general replied.

Tension rushed into the scene, and Luke strained to decipher if the general's words were meant as a threat.

"I'm Luke Buck, the mayor of Cedar Key. What's your purpose here, friend?"

"Yes, yes," came the almost feeble reply. "I am a friend. I come with news of the war and to ask for your help."

Filtered as they were through twenty-five years of silent isolation from the rest of the world, the general's words might as well have been Greek or Swahili or just idle noise. Luke looked toward his father, and then to Mr. Hayes, finding no guidance in their expressions as confused mumbling rolled through the gathered crowd.

"Well?" asked the general.

"Welcome," Luke said at last, hesitant but friendly. "Come on down and let's get acquainted. You'll have to forgive our reception. We don't know anything about a war, and we haven't heard so much as a whisper from the government or military since the world ended."

"The world goes on," replied the general as he climbed carefully down from the helicopter, testing each step before applying his full weight and reaching always for something to grasp. "Is there someplace we can talk, Mr. Mayor? There's a lot you need to know."

Finally, the old mayor intervened. "Luke, why don't we take our new friend here to my dock and talk by the water?"

The new mayor nodded, and without being asked, Hayes, Thomas, and William followed a short distance behind Luke and the general on the walk toward the old clam docks along 3rd Street.

"What do you make of this?" Thomas asked, keeping his voice low.

"I don't know," Hayes replied.

"Me either," Thomas said with a shake of his head.

William was incredulous. "Seriously? That thing just came out of the sky . . . like, it *flew* here, and you don't have anything else to say about it? How does that even work? This seems like a big damn deal, don't you think?"

Thomas had learned to fly small planes when he was about his grandson's age and could give a serviceable explanation of how they operated. The concept of lift was easy enough to explain—air being forced over and under the surface area of the wings lifting a plane off the ground—but he wasn't sure anyone really knew how helicopters worked. A helicopter's main hope and dream in the world, he had always been convinced, was to fall out of the sky.

Thomas put his arm around his grandson as they neared the dock. "Yeah, son. This does seem like a big deal. Your daddy has been thrown right in the fire with his new job."

"He'll be fine," William said.

"We'll help a little, if we can," the old mayor said with a smile.

With the rest of the town preoccupied by the helicopter and the general, Rolf Alvarez, III, headed quickly toward the Number Four Bridge. The moment he heard about men gathered on the other side of the channel, he slipped away from the crowd and moved with urgency to meet what he viewed as a second, immediate potential threat. He was the quieter third member of a dedicated friend group that included Thomas and Hayes. The three friends had fought alongside each other in the Second Battle of Cedar Key, the mainland strike on Sumner that eliminated the outlaw Little Don, and the fierce naval battle on the Suwannee River that settled a two-decade misunderstanding between the old mayor's father and Isacc Skipjack. Years later, when Rolf's wife, Jenny, the longtime island postmaster, failed to return from a routine kayak trip to the long-dormant clam leases, hoping to find a few stragglers for a surprise anniversary dinner, it was Hayes and Thomas who led the search. As the days turned to agonizing weeks with no sign of his bride, Rolf eventually settled into the loss, steadied by his ever-present friends. In matters of war and peace and everything in between, theirs was a triumvirate on which the island continued to rely.

In the old world, Rolf retired from the United States Army as a 38-year-old First Sergeant, having served with honor and distinction. The highlight of this service was his participation in and frequent domination of the Army's perennial combat fighting championships. For a man dispossessed of height and bulk, he was nevertheless a vicious, sublime maestro when conducting his chosen art of violence. He had been such an efficient and reliable killer in the early conflicts of the new world that his island neighbors began to refer to him as the Angel of Death. The name made Rolf proud and uncomfortable at the same time, especially when Thomas and Hayes used it with the kind of relentless mockery that only close friends can deliver.

Now, at a fit but slowing 68 years old, the roughly two miles from the city park to the Number Four Channel would take him some time to cover. He had covered this distance in as little as ten minutes and forty-three seconds during his fastest timed run, when turning forty ignited an early midlife crisis that Rolf met with intense physical training. It would take him twice as long now, and his knees would hurt terribly thereafter, but this was a price he was willing to pay.

Rolf had moved his family into the old Crofts house, adjacent to the channel, when the Crofts succumbed to the difficulties of those early months after the flash. The widow's walk atop the second story of the sprawling yellow house made it a strategically advantageous forward operating base for the island. From its height, Rolf could see well into the mainland in one direction and all the way back to Fannie's café in the other.

Even before he reached the side yard of the house, Rolf could see the line of trucks on the other side of the channel and countless armed men amassing on the far side of the bridge. While Luke was distracted by diplomacy with the general, Rolf began to implement long-established defensive protocols without hesitation or authorization. The old soldier did not need orders to recognize an invasion when he saw one. Moving with stealth and determined malice, he slipped unnoticed beneath the island side of the narrow wooden bridge. Palm fronds, sticks, dried bark, and other kindling were piled tightly under the bridge along the twenty or so feet of land leading to the water. A La Niña in the Pacific that year had led to an unusually dry winter along the Gulf Coast, such that the kindling was a tinderbox waiting for the slightest excuse for transmogrification into leaping, burning life.

Rolf used a fifty-year-old flint-and-steel contraption to send sparks into the brush pile, which almost instantly ignited. In seconds, flames were licking at the pine supports of the bridge and jumping excitedly through the narrow spaces between the top boards. In minutes, before any of the men on the bridge could discern what was happening, an angry, raging fire exploded across the bridge, growing with such remarkable speed that Rolf had barely made it back to the house and up to his mounted rifle on the widow's walk before an impenetrable wall of smoke blocked his view of the soldiers and theirs of him.

Back at Hayes' dock, the conversation with the general was just beginning when Thomas saw the billowing column of smoke rise above the backwaters. Hayes saw it, too, and without consideration for the fact that he was no longer in charge, instantly gave the order.

"All hands, all hands, general quarters. Put the word out. Condition One. Invaders at the bridge."

"Wait!" the general yelled, but already the islanders were racing to their boats.

3

WHITE NOISE

There were two chiefs in Cedar Key, and they were both Johnsons. Michael and Hallie Johnson were the children of Hayes' pretty, abrasive sister, Lida Maria. The Johnson patriarch had been working near their home in Tampa on the day of the flash and was never heard from again thereafter. His wife and children, as they often did, were spending a weekend on the island with the rest of the David clan when the flash across the bay tore their family apart, along with much of the wider world. Hallie was sixteen years old, and Michael had just turned eighteen when they lost their father. Now in their early forties, they had spent more years in the new world than the old.

Like his father, Michael was quiet, decent, and competent. Like her mother, Hallie was fierce, loving, and mean. When Fire Chief Roberts and Police Chief Jenkins, heroic figures in the island's history, each decided to retire within a few weeks of one another, the Johnson kids were the most reasonable replacements the island had available. Michael was already volunteering with the fire department when Chief Roberts announced his intention to resign. They spent a few months training closely together to ensure Michael had mastery of the new firefighting techniques that a department from a hundred years prior would recognize.

When Hallie began her training with Chief Jank Edwins, she was already an expert marksman and possessed of a rough athleticism at odds with her feminine face and disposition. She was five feet eleven inches tall in bare feet, but a foot taller to her adversaries. On her high school basketball team at a preppy Christian private school, Hallie had been the enforcer, delivering elbows, hard picks, and hip checks with the lean mercy of Old Testament God. She kept a quiet aloofness toward strangers, but those she let past the barrier found a friend on whom they could rely and a quick-witted contrarian whose implacable moral compass strangely enhanced her sneaky sense of humor. As a leader, she inspired fear and devotion in fluctuating proportions, but regardless of the motivation, those in her charge generally did what she told them to. Her last name was Johnson, but Hallie was a Cedar Key David in every respect.

The island's two chiefs were about the same height, but Hallie's force of character amplified her stature such that folks distinguished between them by calling her *Big Chief* and her brother *Little Chief*, to her great delight and Michael's begrudging acceptance.

For several years after the flash, when wood gasifiers kept outboard motors running, the Cedar Key Navy would have descended on the Number Four Channel with remarkable speed. Now, like everything else in the new world, the boats were moving slowly. The wind was favorable for the sail from the 3rd Street canal to the burning bridge, but just barely. While Hayes and Luke led a sluggish charge through the backwaters, Big Chief assembled an emergency 50-person militia and began a quick march down State Road 24 toward the building column of smoke.

Unlike the rifles aimed at the helicopter earlier in the morning, the various firearms being carried by the militia were all loaded, as were the guns on the navy's boats. In the aftermath of the island's last major conflict in the short-lived war on the Suwannee River, the town council proposed, and the islanders voted to accept a plan to pool and stockpile most of the island's ammunition for the common defense in case of attack. There had been no such meaningful attack in more than two decades. This left the island armed more heavily than most other places, though the finite nature of their ammunition supply meant that even the best marksmen among them had seen their skills diminished by a lack of shooting practice. Both the militia and the navy trained regularly in the care and handling of their arsenal, including every aspect of firearm deployment except the actual act of firing. The two forces moving toward the bridge from land and water might have been rusty in matters of actual war, but they were armed to the teeth.

On the slow sail toward the burning bridge, Thomas stood next to his best friend, as he had done so often for so many years, at the helm of the flagship *Cogency*. "Why would the general pretend to be friendly if he knew his men were invading while he talked to us?"

"I don't know," Hayes replied. "It was either a distraction or something happened at the bridge we don't know about."

"I wouldn't put it past Rolf to pick a fight," Thomas said. "But he worked as hard as any of us building the bridge back. He wouldn't burn it if he didn't think he had to."

Hayes held firm to the wheel that controlled the improvised rudder on the 25-foot Morgan bay boat. "If the goal was to invade and take us out, why not just open fire with the Blackhawk? That thing could have wiped us out quick."

Thomas replied, "The real question is why that Methuselah-looking general was flying the thing himself. He had to be two hundred years old. Wouldn't a general from a real military have a pilot to fly him everywhere? That dude could barely walk."

"None of this makes sense," the old mayor replied. "Who'd Luke leave behind to keep tabs on the general?"

"Big Chief took him to City Hall for safekeeping and left a few of her team to guard the helicopter."

"Good," Hayes replied. "I like our chances against trucks at the bridge, but we'd be in trouble against that thing."

The fleet moved quietly past Dog Island and Scale Key, where, remarkably, hundreds of white PVC poles still marked the boundaries of some of the 2-acre submerged land leases where tens of millions of clams used to be cultivated. As they approached the bright white sand of Cedar Point, the old mayor nodded his head in affirmation when he noticed Luke signaling for several boats to turn north at the Point, and calling for the remainder to follow him around the backside of Live Oak Key.

"You see that?" Thomas asked proudly.

"He's always been sharp on the water," Hayes replied as he signaled an acknowledgment of the new mayor's order and waved for the breakaway formation to follow him. "We'll hit them hard from the island side of the bridge while Luke and the others swing wide and box them in along the other shore."

The adrenaline rush of the maneuver and the quickening of the blood as the coming engagement took shape in the sailors' minds worked against the somnolent pace forced upon them by the indifferent wind.

"Holy shit," Thomas said, wide-eyed and impressed when the full bridge finally came into view.

The fire burned like a second sun, amplifying the already bright morning and casting the legion of men on the mainland side of the channel in dramatic, smoky relief.

Hayes, annoyingly calm as ever in the impassive manner of his father and David men through the ages, replied coolly, "Yep."

Rolf had initiated the protocol for invaders at the bridge, but the primitive signal had been unable to convey the full story. The smoke and frenzy of the moment made an accurate count impossible, but from the perspective of the men and women on the boats, there seemed to be a vast army stretched out before them on the mainland. In all, just over a thousand uniformed soldiers held armed formations on the road and the land adjacent to it, occupying the ground where the Battle of Station Four had transpired in February of 1865. Then, Confederate Captain J.J. Dickison, the famed *Swamp Fox of Florida*, drove away a significantly larger Union force in the waning months of the American Civil War. Out-manned and out-gunned, but fighting to expel invaders from their home, the local army had triumphed.

The history of the field on which the invaders were gathered was not lost on Hayes or Thomas, but the comparisons were apt in generality only. Whereas the Swamp Fox faced a two-to-one disadvantage, the islanders in the boats and those marching along State Road 24 with Big Chief would each be offset by six or seven seemingly well-trained and provisioned soldiers across the channel.

Big Chief's militia made it to the burning bridge just as the first wave of boats negotiated the last of the skinny water between Cedar Point and the Number Four Channel. For all the momentum of the effort to meet the threat signaled by Rolf's inferno, the specifics of the situation forced a sudden stalling of the action. Luke, who was seldom given to restraint, sailed his formation past Ludlow Creek, along the Wacasassa Shore, and emerged within a hundred yards of a force so overwhelming that even he was forced to halt.

"What do we do, Dad?" William called from behind a mounted rifle at the bow of his father's boat.

"Nothing yet, son. Jesus, where did they all come from?"

"No way that many people fit in those trucks. They marched here from somewhere. Do you think it's really the U.S. Army? Is this what they looked like?"

"It's sure as shit some kind of army," Luke replied while signaling for the boats in his charge to halt alongside him. He could see the *Cogency* making its way toward him, grim and beautiful against the backdrop of the flames and smoke, his father and the old mayor as steely on the water as they ever were.

"Paw-Paw and Mr. Hayes will know what to do," William said with some measure of relief in his voice.

To his credit, Luke nodded in agreement, feeling undiminished by seeking counsel from his elders, a quality lacking in most leaders through-out human history. As they waved at the approaching boat and waited, calm descended on the otherwise chaotic scene. The army along the bank of the channel and extending down the two-lane road seemed fixed in place, resolute and threatening in its stillness. The crackling hum of the great fire became a soothing white noise that pushed against the tension while a half dozen Roseate Spoonbills patrolled the muddy bank of the channel in idle leisure, picking off juvenile shrimp and clumsy fiddler crabs during a brunch unhurried by human crisis. A pair of mated ospreys worked together to slash and peck at an interloping third osprey intruding on their territory, while a fat, waddling raccoon made a long track of bumbling paw prints along the edge of the mangroves on the island side of the channel. The mullet were jumping, the tide was moving the water, and the official business of the Gulf carried on while the islanders paused to consider the dire circumstances laid before them.

"Well," Hayes said as he pulled alongside the new mayor's boat, "what do you think?"

"I was hoping to ask you," Luke replied. "But here's how I see it. I don't think the boats give us much of an advantage. I don't know why they haven't opened up on us already, but until they do, I don't think we ought to provoke them into it. The marsh along both sides of the road would keep them bunched up where they'd be easy to hit, but there's so many of them I think they eventually win a shoot-out."

"Agreed," Hayes said.

Buoyed by the old mayor's approval, Luke continued, "The only cards we have to play are the general we're holding and that helicopter. If he's a real general, then maybe we have some leverage to stop an attack, even if it's just long enough for us to figure out what our next move is."

Even in the heaviness of the moment, Thomas indulged a moment of fatherly satisfaction because his boy was holding under pressure. "What's the move, son?"

"Mr. Hayes, you take charge of all the boats. Muster them together close enough to their side of the channel that you can keep an eye on their movements, but far enough away that it's at least a hard shot for them if they start firing."

Hayes replied, "I'm on it. I'll put most of the fleet behind those mangroves next to the old fishing pier, and we'll rotate a couple boats to stand watch in the channel."

Luke nodded. "I'll have Big Chief and her crew meet up with Rolf at the Crofts place and set up some kind of defensive position. Dad, come with me and William to see the general. He might feel more like talking if there's another old guy there."

"Yes, sir," Thomas replied with a note of over-enthusiasm meant as a light-hearted jab at the idea that an election gave his son any authority over him.

Oblivious, Luke said, "The wind's against us, so we'll have to walk. Your knees up for it, Dad?"

"Alright, that's enough, I'll run circles around you even now, son."

Both men smiled because they knew it wasn't true, and it hadn't been true for a long time.

"Follow me, gray hairs," William said, pushing past them both and heading back toward town at a brisk pace.

When Big Chief and her militia arrived at the Crofts house, Rolf was already busy fortifying his side of the channel. The kindling under the bridge was not the only established protocol for times of trouble. A couple decades of peace had given the old soldier plenty of time to think up, try, abandon, and retry countless measures to employ if war ever came for the island again. Having experienced the horrors of war in the old world and the new, Rolf prayed often for peace because he was a good man and wished for suffering to be absent from the lives of his friends and neighbors. If there was to be violence, however, Rolf was a cultivated, efficient conduit for it. The monotony of daily life wore on him more than most other men; idle peace sat heavy on his wide shoulders and frittering mind, compounding the effects of passing time and age. The moment he first laid eyes on the columns of men across the channel, a youthful spark sprang up in his belly even before he lit the kindling under the bridge.

Big Chief found Rolf at the water's edge, unspooling rolls of barbed wire along the shore.

"How can we help?"

"Hey, Hallie. We need to dig in as best we can. The bridge being gone won't hold them off for long. They'll figure a way across eventually. There are a bunch of shovels in the shed. Let's get a rotating crew of folks to dig foxholes along the front and side of the house. Have them pile the dirt up in front of the holes."

Big Chief replied, "No problem. Okay if I keep a watch stationed on your widow's walk?"

"That's a great idea. Probably best to keep two up there at a time. Not sure how much they'll be able to see now, but once the fire dies down, they'll have a clear view of the whole army across the channel."

"Army? How many are there?" Big Chief asked, having seen only smoke and fire in the direction of the mainland.

"I don't know. Hundreds at least. Maybe more. Way more than we can handle anyway."

"Let's get to work then," Big Chief said as she turned and headed back toward her team to give orders.

Rolf called after her, "Let everyone know that the worst thing anyone can do right now is to fire their weapon unless we are under immediate, close-in attack."

"Roger that," said the tall, determined chief.

"No accidents," Rolf emphasized. "We're as good as dead in a head-on fight. Every minute we can buy without an attack gives us a shot to figure out what to do."

The smoke from the burning bridge continued to create a visual barrier between the island and the mainland as the militia fanned out across the Crofts property, State Road 24, and the old Florida Fish and Wildlife research station just across the road. Rolf rolled out stockpiled barbed wire until the outline of a makeshift military camp began to take shape. A dozen islanders took turns on the shovels, digging holes in the sandy soil along the water's edge and near the house. Others used what materials they could scrounge to create makeshift breastworks where they seemed most likely to impede potential invaders.

The crude fortifications being hastily created on the island side of the channel would have been useless just twenty-five years prior, as easily bypassed as the Maginot Line in World War I. Before the flash, a burning bridge would have done little to stop an advancing army, but in the technological declivity of the new world, a short expanse of water, some barbed wire, and holes in the ground were as meaningful as the Walls of Jericho to citizen soldiers facing a thousand-rifle foe on the other side of a fire.

The uniformed multitudes across the channel seemed unaffected by the end of the world, operating trucks and carrying the advanced weapons of a legitimate first-world military. For the time being, at least, they did not seem to have boats, and on this thin detail rested the hopes of the defenders. Even without consideration for the helicopter that had shaken apart the morning and a quarter century of island stability, some among the militia turned quickly, forgivably, to despair. To a people whose lives had evolved from modern convenience to the preindustrial struggles of their ancestors, the force across the channel was as terrifying as the first caravels in the Yucatan.

The islanders went about what work they could to prepare for what may come, but no one, save for maybe the Angel of Death, felt good about their chances in the coming fight.

4

THE GREAT LIBRARY

Compared with all that had been lost along with the smokestacks across the bay, the various silver linings that arose in the aftermath were often hard to see. One of the first to appear, however, was the rapid rise in literacy on the island. With long days and slow time to fill without television, video games, and the Internet, the islanders naturally turned back to books.

The Cedar Key Pubic Library had held out against almost yearly calls in the old world for its closure. Critics in the wider county government cited the high operational costs of operating a standalone facility so far removed from the rest of the county, and the lack of return on investment for such a small population. In addition, the old library building was located on a relatively low spot on 2nd Street, which made it susceptible to flooding. Every time a hurricane kicked up in the Gulf with an eye toward the Nature Coast, trucks would have to come from the mainland to load up all the books on the first floor of the library and ship them to higher ground in Chiefland or the county seat of Bronson.

When Hurricane Jonah surprised the islanders in the first year of the new world, owing to the loss of modern weather-forecasting technology, there was insufficient warning to move the books to higher ground.

Waist-deep water had rushed down the town's main street, washing away most of the bottom three shelves of the library's collection. Then librarian Nance Stephenson spent painstaking months thereafter sorting through every flooded book she could find, trying to salvage what she could to little success. Most of the loss occurred in the children's section, which was something of a lucky break since the library at the Cedar Key School, which had not flooded, had a large collection of children's books.

Over time, the island's private libraries became as valuable to Cedar Key as the library at Alexandria had been for the ancient world. Blue-collar families had defined Cedar Key's identity for generations, but in the few decades leading up to the flash, a fair number of artists and academics had moved to the island, usually in retirement. Arriving with them was a treasure trove of books spanning the whole of human inquiry. The net result was a significantly larger number of books per capita on the island than in most other places. Of all these collections, none was finer than Thomas's library in his house at the corner of E and 3rd.

When Thomas first arrived in Cedar Key several years before the flash, he did so on the heels of a lost marriage, with his tail between his legs and licking emotional wounds that were trying their best not to heal. Cedar Key had been his weekend getaway for the two decades he lived and worked in Gainesville, where he had developed a relatively wide following as a playwright. When he saw his wife Annie driving away from their home for the last time, with his beagle coonhound looking back at him dolefully through the open window of the silver SUV, the turmoil in his gut sent him scrambling away from the world he had built for her, away from the chickens, goats, and donkey they hilariously kept in a bid to feel like farmers, away from the five acres that seemed like a kingdom to him, away from the little farmhouse and the ridiculous inflatable hot tub on its side porch where they would sit together on chilly mornings as the steam rose around them and into the overhanging branches of the massive live oaks that had first drawn them to the land, away from a life he wanted to go on forever, toward the island and the Gulf because there had been nowhere else to go.

The circa 1884 E Street house was in disrepair when Thomas saw it on the day of his retreat from Gainesville. He made a fair deal on it and got to work bringing it back to life. His first project was to knock down a wall in the narrow central hallway of the house, eliminating a bedroom and creating a large open space for a library and music room. In this room, he built a dramatic staircase leading to an attic he converted into a sprawling new bedroom and bathroom. The angles of the two-section staircase in the open space were striking, framing in a warm, inviting area for an antique piano his son Luke could play, and books upon books upon books. In his early days on the island, before his life-altering friendship with Hayes and the other Davids pulled him from his malaise, Thomas spent most of his days in the library, seeking solace from characters in the great works of literature. Raskolnikov whispered that rebirth would only come by confessing his own sins in the marriage; Joe Christmas cajoled him to brood on and strike out against an unfair world; Quixote and Ahab—each in their own way—pointed to the divine purpose of adventure, and Yossarian reminded him that climbing a tree naked was a perfectly reasonable response to trauma.

The deeper Thomas immersed himself in his treasured collection of books, the more books he ordered for delivery. In a few months' time, he had lined the tall walls of the library from floor to ceiling with bookshelves he made himself from narrow slabs of live-edge cedar and cypress purchased from a homespun sawmill on the side of the road near Chiefland.

By his first Christmas in the old house, there was little space remaining on the shelves. Three lifetimes of books surrounded him on all sides of his favorite room, elevating his mood by their mere presence.

In the new world, Thomas opened his library to everyone on the island. His three copies of *Ender's Game*, including the signed first edition, were perpetually on loan to teenage readers, along with the *Hunger Games* books and Tolkien's legendarium. Joseph Heller's *Catch-22* was seldom on the shelf for more than a few days, and the leather-bound *Complete Works of Mark Twain* were especially popular with older readers. In addition to the histories and biographies, Luke Buck had his perception of war colored in by the firebombing of Dresden in Vonnegut's *Slaughterhouse-Five*.

In Thomas' magnificent library, Faulkner and Hemmingway were finally friends, Wolfe and McCarthy found middle ground between the poetic and the sparse, and Proust and Joyce remained as wonderfully incomprehensible as ever, while Fitzgerald and O'Conner compared notes on Jazz and sweet tea. On the handmade bookshelves, and in the minds of island readers, the great writers and stories had not only survived the end of the world, they were more alive than ever.

The melancholy that led to the creation of the E Street library, as it would come to be known in the new world, would, over time, seem an utterly reasonable price to have paid for such a treasure.

When Luke arrived at the City Hall building with his father and son, they found the door to Big Chief's office being guarded by Dale Warble, the former golf cart rental king of Cedar Key.

"He in there?" Luke asked.

Dale replied, "He is. The old coot has been banging on the door and hollering almost nonstop."

"About what?"

"Just going on and on about needing to get to the bridge before something bad happens."

"It's happening," Thomas said. "There's an army on the other side of the Number Four. If Rolf hadn't set the bridge on fire, we'd be overrun."

Dale was incredulous. "An army?"

William replied, "I've never actually seen an army in real life, but if I had to describe what I thought one looked like, all those men with the guns would be it."

Dale then asked the question that would sow division between friends and neighbors, and draw an ideological line in the sand that demanded a side be taken.

"Is it the American Army?"

"They're dressed the part," Thomas replied.

"So there might still be an America?" Dale asked with something approaching jubilance in his voice.

"Unlikely," replied Luke. "And if so, where the hell have they been for the last twenty-five years? Don't you think we would have heard something by now?"

Dale was uninterested in the details. For him, the possibility of a big idea was too appealing to risk killing with examination. "Who cares?" he said, wide-eyed and elevated.

"I care," Luke replied sharply. "The America I remember ended when they let all this happen."

Dale pushed back. "You don't know any more than the rest of us about how it all happened. Or why."

"Does it matter?" Luke snapped. "Feel however you want about America. I like the old stories, too. I've studied them, maybe more than anyone here except my dad. But what does any of it count for if it couldn't stop the world from killing itself?"

A pall of silence moved between the men at the door to the chief's office. Luke was immediately self-conscious about his outburst. He meant and felt everything he said, but knew that he had created unnecessary conflict with his friend Dale, whose only sin had been to indulge in a little hope. Worse, everyone in the room had witnessed a failure in leadership, had seen him take a strong position on an issue—maybe the biggest issue the island had faced in as long as he could remember—without having all of the facts pertinent to it.

"I'm sorry," Luke said. "You're right. I don't know anything more than you do. But a guy flew here today on a thing no one thought existed anymore, and there are enough men at the channel to maybe take the island from us. Or maybe they are exactly who they appear to be, and this is the good news you imagine it to be, Dale. I promise we'll sort it out."

Dale was a naturally amicable man; the magnanimity in Luke's apology was enough to instantly smooth the waters between them.

Thomas said, "Let's see what the old man in there has to say."

Big Chief's office was a time machine. The walls and desk were still adorned with the certificates, medals, and knick-knacks lauding former Chief Jank Edwins' long career at the helm of the Cedar Key Police Department. The framed newspaper front page announcing the Miami Hurricanes' 2001 National Championship still hung obnoxiously on the wall behind the desk. Chief Edwins delighted in his contrarian fandom of a team that could unite even the bitterest of rivals—The Florida Gators and the Florida State Seminoles—in the kind of pure, simple hate that made college football in the South so wholesome and wonderful. Since Cedar Key was only an hour's drive from Ben Hill Griffin Stadium where the Gators played their home games, a significant percentage of islanders were faithful to the Orange and Blue. A respectable minority wore the Garnet and Gold of the team in Tallahassee, but only scoundrels, malcontents, or yankee transplants could stomach the low-moral perfidiousness required to root for the team in the pastel-colored coke binge of Miami. Chief Edwins was a Levy County boy, but comfortably met two of the three criteria to be a Hurricane.

The general, a West Point man, was sitting in Big Chief's chair when Luke and the others came into the room. He sprang to his feet with more spryness than seemed possible given his seeming frailness earlier in the morning.

"Thank goodness you're here," the general said in a state approaching panic. "What's happened with my men? Did you provoke them into a fight?"

Luke was put on a hard edge immediately by the general's tone and insinuation. "You've got a lot of nerve talking to us about provocation."

"I don't follow," said the general.

"What's to follow?" Luke replied. "You flew a gunship here, and now you've got us under some kind of siege at the channel."

The general was either a gifted actor or genuinely puzzled by the mayor's position, because his face contorted into realistic confusion. He said,

"I told you we were friends, that I was here with news. Then just when we started talking, all hell broke loose, and you took off after my men."

Thomas wanted to intervene on his son's behalf, to push back against the general's Pollyanna assessment of the situation, but he didn't have to.

"Bullshit," Luke said, expressionless, as he looked into the general's eyes, seeking a tell or flinch or some indication of his real intentions.

The general was a blank page. "Well, if you're determined to be discourteous, we're not going get very far, young man."

Luke flexed the muscles in his jaw imperceptibly, but so hard he could feel his teeth grind. His inclination to snap back at the general gave way to a calculated exhalation, long and focused.

The general indulged the silence for several heavy moments before announcing, in a tone bordering on forceful, "I need you to take me to my men so I can settle whatever dust you've kicked up before people start getting hurt."

Luke was angry at how easily the general seemed to rattle his cage. The undercurrent of implied threat was clear to him, but he wondered if the others felt the same way. His son William was oblivious to the tension, smiling aimlessly in his usual way, ready always to follow his father and Paw-Paw into the breach without hesitation or grumble. Dale stood smiling in the open doorway to the office, listening in, transfixed by the general and everything he might represent. Thankfully, Luke caught a supportive glance from his father and could see in his face the same disconcertion weighing on him as well. Something about knowing his father understood his mistrust of the general was calming to the mayor, who steadied his mind for the moments ahead.

In a direct but unagitated tone, Luke said, "I'm not taking you anywhere until we sort out who you are and what you want with us. It's clear we've gotten off to a rough start here. I'm willing to take a step back and start again if you are, sir."

The sharpness of the general's reply caught the entire room off guard. "You have no authority to hold me. The longer you keep me here, the more dangerous it gets for everyone. Respectfully, sir, the time has passed for stepping back. Now step aside, and I'll return to my men."

Unbelievably, the man who had struggled just to walk a few hours before now moved hurriedly out of the office, pushing Dale aside and walking so quickly toward the front door of the City Hall building that several seconds elapsed before anyone tried to stop him. Finally, Luke said, "William . . ." but his son was already after the general, catching him just in front of the walk-up window where citizens in the old world would come to handle official business, and Miss Margie would scream curses at Talinda, the diminutive but pretty city clerk. With something close to zero effort, William held the wispy general by the collar. A feeble attempt to resist produced a small tug against the young islander's inveterate strength, but in an instant, the general knew his great escape had ended.

Back in Big Chief's office, the general's combativeness eased.

"Let's try again," Luke said. "Who are you?"

"My name is Major General Clarence Gill. On the day the big war started, I was the commanding officer at Fort Rucker and the Army's Aviation Center of Excellence."

"What's a Fort Rucker?" William asked.

Thomas was powerless to resist an ill-timed chuckle.

The general paused a moment. "Oh . . . yes, of course," he said. "You grew up after everything ended."

"Yes, sir," William answered, continuing to show respect for a man he had manhandled just a few minutes earlier.

"Army bases were called forts back then. I was the senior officer at Fort Rucker."

Dale was no longer just standing in the doorway. He had fully inserted himself into the proceedings by then and made no effort to hide his enthusiasm about everything the general had to say.

"We haven't heard a lot from the rest of the world," Dale interjected. "But folks come through from time to time and tell us what they've heard. Mostly, they say everything's gone. Did your base survive?"

"No, I don't guess I would say that it did," General Gill replied with a distant note of regret in his voice. "Fort Benning was just under a hundred miles from us, and it was totally erased from the Earth. I don't think archeologists from the future will be able to dig up enough to know it was ever even there. We got hit hard at Rucker, but nothing like Benning. Maybe the bomb meant for us went offline a little. I don't know. We lost most of the base, but some of us lived through it. I remember seeing the bright lights and then feeling everything go dark and wild. There's a day or two after missing in my head. I assume it must have been terrible."

Even Luke, whose antennae were still raised in skepticism of a man he was predisposed to not believe, was taken in by the story. He asked, "Did you hear anything from Washington afterward?"

"Not from Washington. No one's going to hear anything from there ever again. The life of a capital is a hell of a lot shorter than the half-life of Uranium."

Luke didn't let up. "Not Washington then... but wherever else they might have taken the President or the rest of the government. Mount Weather or Raven Rock, maybe?"

"What do you know about Mount Weather?" the general asked.

"I'm sure not much," Luke replied. "But did you hear from anyone?"

"Not for some time."

"How long?" Luke pressed emphatically.

General Gill looked away from the young mayor, pausing for an endless few seconds to consider his response. This was a length of time sufficient for Luke and Thomas to see uneasiness reasserting itself in the general's countenance. Whether the uneasiness was evidence of subterfuge or just the lingering of a hard memory was difficult to assess.

"Many years," the general relented. "They all start to run together after a while."

Luke had so many questions peppering his brain that he had trouble picking out which one to ask next. "How many soldiers are at the bridge?"

The general replied instantly, "One thousand and twenty-four. Those men are mostly from the 198th Infantry Brigade."

"Infantry?" Thomas asked incredulously. "You flew here."

General Gill replied, "I didn't say *I* was from the infantry. I've been a pilot since just after the academy. The 198th is a training brigade from Fort Benning. At any one time, there would be between 1,500 and 5,000 young soldiers in the 198th, most fresh out of boot camp and just starting to learn real soldiering. Around 800 were on training maneuvers away from Benning when the bombs fell. They showed up on my doorstep beaten all to hell a few days later, and they've been with me ever since. The other 224 are either from Rucker or stragglers that showed up over time."

Before he could be drawn further into the story, Luke said forcefully, "Tell me why you are here—here specifically. Of all the places, why did you come to Cedar Key?"

The general folded his arms and sighed imperially. "I've been trying to tell you that since I got here."

5

THE VIRGINIANS

By noon, the last of the burning bridge had collapsed into the channel, and the smoke had dissipated enough that Big Chief's watch standers on the widow's walk could finally see the full army on the mainland. The militia on the ground were starting to see bits and pieces as well, and a feeling of dread spread through them.

Hayes anchored the *Cogency* in the middle of the channel. He could clearly see the whole of the army amassed there, and he himself could be clearly seen. Ryland Beecham captained a small skiff in a slow patrol of the channel as the wind allowed, and Gibbs Yardy, a captain the same age as Luke, led a second patrol consisting of a small crew of men on a birddog boat retrofitted with long wooden oars to augment its sails. In the old world, Gibbs had married into the Southern Star wholesale clam dynasty, rising quickly into a leadership role but enjoying the prestige of the position for less than a year before the smokestacks fell, and along with them the business of clams. Further back, the rest of the fleet took what shelter they could behind a small mangrove island closer to the shore on the island side of the Number Four Channel.

On the mainland, Major Joshua Lawrence paced along the shore, scanning the channel to keep track of the boats gathered across from his position. Now and then, he would catch a flash of movement in his field of vision and raise his binoculars up to investigate more closely. He was a generally placid man, cool under pressure and lacking the kind of temper that was so often the undoing of otherwise competent leaders. Something about the present circumstance put him uncharacteristically on edge. By his estimation, the numbers were on his side, and handily so. Still, Major Lawrence had come to a similar conclusion as Luke Buck—they might and probably would win a shoot-out, but his men were dangerously concentrated by the terrain and would almost certainly take heavy losses in the encounter. If the general did not return soon, the major would have to take some kind of decisive action.

The men were mostly oblivious to it, but Major Lawrence had seen a shift in the general since the ordeal in Virginia a few months back. The stragglers from the 198th Battalion were mostly just kids when General Gill took them in at what remained of Fort Rucker. No amount of bad business could threaten their allegiance to a man who had cared for them all these years and, more importantly, had given their lives a sense of purpose that made the monotony of the end times something akin to bearable. The general was naturally given to speaking in elevated terms, about even the most mundane routines of Army life. He spoke always about the mission, even when, for years at a time, the mission was little more than making it to another day. Since blood had been spilled in the Shenandoah Valley, however, an insatiable energy had overtaken the aging leader.

When that brief first skirmish ended between the 198th and the Shenandoah Home Guard, the general had retired for the evening to his tent, content to let the sad force retreat in the night to lick its considerable wounds. It never occurred to him that the fifty or so poorly-armed townspeople would still be blocking the road into Harrisonburg at first light. And yet, there they were—ragged, stupid, and magnificent. It's possible they had not been able to fully comprehend their disadvantage in the low light of the previous evening, but now, as morning made clear the hopelessness of their stand, still they stood in the road. The general was moved to great emotion by the brave Virginians, and on another day, he might have at least attempted diplomacy, but on the heels of the news he had received eighty miles away at Mount Weather, and the harassment his troops endured on the road in the previous days, he would choose · overwhelming force.

Mount Weather in northern Virginia was an almost 800-mile march for the general and his men, and they had made it under the thinnest of pretenses, a ten-second garbled radio broadcast from the Federal Emergency Management Agency's National Radio System. This system used a high-frequency band to connect government agencies and the U.S. military to the individual states. Notably, it was the frequency that allowed the President to access the Emergency Alert System utilized for national emergencies. The general kept a receiver for this system in his office at Fort Rucker and had used every ounce of resources and ingenuity he and his men could muster to keep the radio operational through the many long years since the world exploded.

For a few minutes each day, for more than nine thousand days without fail, the general had switched on the receiver and listened for a broadcast he was sure would never come. On a Tuesday in late September, when at last he heard a break in the usual hum of static, he was hit with a rush of uncertainty about whether he had heard it at all. After so many years of a routine that had never produced even the slightest of variation, he felt unsure first of his ears and then of his mind. As the day passed, however, he grew convinced that some kind of deliberate broadcast had been made. Thus convinced, his next emotion, washing over him in a heavy wave, was profound guilt. For two decades, he had focused on the fortification and modest rebuilding of Fort Rucker, as well as the care of the men in his charge. The thunderclap of the brief, incoherent broadcast suggested that something of the government remained, and he had done nothing to find or protect it. As a career military man, he could not shake the shame of his prolonged inaction. More than anything else, it was this shame that sent his army on the month-and-a-half march across Georgia, North Carolina, and the great width of Virginia to its northern reaches.

Mount Weather first came to the general public's attention in 1979 when a TWA flight crashed into the mountain, killing 98 passengers and crew. In press coverage of the crash, news agencies reported on the crash site's close proximity to a government facility on the mountain, which was shrouded in mystery and innuendo. Atop the mountain sat the relatively innocuous center of operations for FEMA, and the control station for the National Radio System. The public was titillated to learn that more than 300 feet below the surface, carved into the Precambrian basalt rock of the mountain, was a 600,000 SF self-sustaining facility that played a large role in the continuity of government plan for the United States in the event of an enemy attack that threatened Washington, D.C., fifty-one miles to the east. After the September 11, 2001, attacks, most of the congressional leadership was evacuated to the Mount Weather facility by helicopter.

The general had every expectation that the facility would have been heavily targeted by the enemy, but the few seconds of unique sound broadcast through his radio receiver were enough, after so long a period of silence, to awaken the great myth and glory of a nation in the despairing mind of its lifelong servant. The sounds, if they had indeed come from the mountain, animated the possibility, however remote, that America, like Lazarus, had come from the dead.

The resurrection proved temporal, shitty, and brief. When at last they reached the place where Mount Weather was supposed to be, the general's nascent faith was tested by the endless chasm he encountered there; his spirit waned as lifelessness surrounded his army and thickened like a fog. He lingered in the secular disquiet of that place, taking it in, feeling the weight of defeat. Here, a fortress had been built to withstand the full measure of human destructiveness, and here it had crumbled. The physical loss was tolerable. Some number of important people—congressmen, generals, scientists, perhaps a President—had burned to death here, and that was as measurable, dissectible, and reconcilable as a jar of gumballs or a frog or the number of square feet in an acre of land. To the general, what remained incalculable, what was impossible to believe, was that America had proven no more exceptional than the splitting of a single atom. Somewhere, maybe, its amber grain still rolled in waves, and fruits were growing on the plain. He had seen no alabaster cities gleam, but in truth, he told himself as the old ideas pushed back against the dark math before him, they might yet. There were other fortresses and more men like him, and even if they had also fallen, he remained. His army endured. He had heard the signal from the radio receiver. He had heard it. He was sure now that it had come, sure as the shining seas, spacious skies, and mountain majesties. The urgency of the mission was amplified now in the general's mind by the emptiness at Mount Weather. Its scope and purpose had materialized in the flat black of the giant hole. It no longer mattered from whence the signal had come or what it might portend. The great purpose of his life was suddenly before him. So long as he had men to command, America lived.

He and his army were the signal now.

The march to Mount Weather had bypassed the town of Harrisonburg on the way up, opting for a route to the south along US-Highway 340, but sections of washed-out road and several shots fired at them from a tree line outside the town of Front Royal persuaded the general to alter his return route. On the way back, they followed the US Highway 11 corridor, running between and more or less parallel to Interstate-81 and the serpentine North Fork of the Shenandoah River, where fresh water was free and easy to be had. This route was more scenic, but not without danger. As they passed near or through the towns of Locust Grove, Edinburg, and New Market, they took sporadic fire, always from a tree line or other concealment such that there was little to fire back upon. Three soldiers received superficial wounds, and a fourth lost two fingers on his left hand. Despite the engagements, the general pushed on, invigorated by some new internal force that led him to push the men an average of five more miles per day heading back to Fort Rucker than they had made marching away from it. This new route ran through the heart of Harrisonburg and toward the altercation with the Shenandoah Home Guard, holding a line along Market Street and a defensive position around the circa 1897 Rockingham County historic courthouse, resplendent and quintessentially Southern with its molded cornice and heavy stone balustrade in the Romanesque Revival style.

It had somehow escaped the attention of the general and his closest subordinate, Major Lawrence, that morning was breaking on Thanksgiving Day as the outline of the courthouse became visible in the growing light, and the coming engagement took shape ahead of them on the road. The prolonged marching and the diminishing morale of the troops would likely have overpowered any possible sentiment for the old holiday or mercy for the bloodied Virginians that continued to block their path. Still, something was lost in the forgetting, making the coming violence even more regrettable. The general gave the order, and a block of several hundred troops marched forward toward the courthouse and the Virginians' line.

Georgie Pilsner stood shoulder to shoulder with his Harrisonburg neighbors, those few that had survived the day of the bombs and the hard years that followed, and watched the endless line of men advance toward them. He had not undertaken the events of that morning with a death wish, but neither had he sufficient investment in the world of the living to trade his home or his honor for some allotment of additional days.

They had all decided in the night, of one accord, to stand.

When the general had finished talking, Luke Buck shook his head in disbelief. He opened his mouth to say something in return, but no words came.

Dale Warble broke the silence. "Wow!" he exclaimed, like a child seeing a magic trick close-up.

"That's one way to describe it," Thomas replied flatly.

William looked toward his father, who hesitated still.

Luke had a hundred additional questions about how the U.S. Army, silent for a quarter century, had sprang miraculously back into existence, but this was now easily the least preposterous part of the story. General Gill had looked the young mayor in the face, with every hallmark of sincerity, and explained how the 198th Battalion had marched all the way from Alabama to Cedar Key to meet a U.S. Navy aircraft carrier.

"An aircraft carrier," Luke replied at last. "So we've got a Navy now, too?"

His tone was smothered in incredulity, but the general, anticipating such a response, was unfazed.

"Yes. As far as I know, it's the only ship that survived. It's an older Nimitz-class that's powered by its own nuclear reactor. The reactor is several years past its estimated service life, but they've kept it going somehow."

It was all science fiction to an island where meals were cooked on open flames, and boats could only move by wind or paddle. Lara Budd and three other healthy island women had died in childbirth since the smokestacks fell; a fever or diarrhea could be as fearsome now as the Black Plague; a candle was an almost unimaginable luxury, and time was mostly told by the sun or moon, but the general talked as casually about a nuclear reactor as he would a pine tree. Luke stared blankly at the old man, stone-faced.

With the momentum of the exchange slowing and the moment sitting heavy in the air, Luke finally asked, "Where has this supposed ship been all this time? What took them so long to contact you?"

"I couldn't tell you," the general replied smoothly. "For a long time, my men and I were isolated from the rest of the world, like you are here, and I was sure as anyone the war had been lost."

Luke was struggling to contain his building anger. "Look around, General, we sure as shit didn't win."

"Maybe not. But maybe we lost a little less than they did. I don't know. For twenty-five years, I heard the same nothing as you. A few months ago, I started getting short messages from the National Radio System . . . just garbled sounds at first, but eventually actual messages. I don't know why they started coming or why it took so long for them to come at all. There's a whole hell of a lot that I don't know yet. But what I do know is that I received an order to come here and meet the carrier, and whatever it takes, that's exactly what my men and I are going to do."

Luke pushed back. "Let's assume for a minute that any of that is true. You still haven't told me why you came *here*. Cedar Key is as about as far from any kind of war as you can get."

"This is where I was ordered to come. They didn't say why, and I didn't ask. We just started marching."

"You've got some kind of faith in a radio broadcast," Luke replied.

"Following orders is a habit. I may be a general, but I'm still a soldier in the chain of command."

Luke would not let him sidestep what he felt was a central issue of the story's credibility. "But surely you've thought about it. That's a long way to march without thinking about anything."

"Your shipping channel," said the general. "I'm no expert on Florida, but my wife and I used to vacation in the panhandle. And I've got a map, and I know where the big bases are. A straight line from Rucker to the Gulf would have landed us in the heart of military country. Pensacola would likely have had its harbor destroyed by the bombs that came for its Naval Air Station, maybe enough that deep-water ships would have trouble docking there. There's no telling how many bombs fell on Eglin and Tyndal Air Force bases a little farther east, but every possible port from Destin to Saint George Island would have taken heavy fire."

"Then the Big Bend," Dale chimed in, leaving no doubt about whether or not he believed the general's story.

"Exactly," the general continued. "More than a hundred and fifty miles of marshy, shallow shoreline running east and south until—"

"Cedar Key," Dale interrupted,

"Yes," the general said with an assured nod. "Your shipping channel looks plenty wide to hold a ship."

"A Navy ship in Cedar Key," Thomas mused. "Can you imagine?"

A moment of connection sprang up between a father and his son, as Luke smirked, even in the midst of all the tension, because he knew the history enthusiasts were both thinking of the same story. In the late 1800s, Cedar Key endured the tyrannical reign of a mayor named William "Billy" Cotrell, who terrorized the island with cruelty, intimidation, and even murder to serve his own misanthropic goals. His brutality became so unbearable that an elderly widow named Rose Bell wrote to then-President Benjamin Harrison, pleading for his help. The President dispatched an agent to investigate. The reports that were sent back to Washington convinced the President to send a U.S. Navy warship carrying a complement of marines to depose the despotic mayor by military force, the only such instance in United States history. The Civil War was then only two decades in the past and still an open wound for Southerners, so the islanders were skeptical of a federal warship steaming into their shipping channel. The prospect of an aircraft carrier in Cedar Key conjured no less skepticism now.

Luke's mind raced to process all the information coming at him. He felt in his belly that something was off with the general, but there was also a quality of sincerity in the way he so casually relayed what would be, if true, world-altering information. Already, the new mayor was weighing the repercussions of several possible decisions he might be about to make.

To gauge the general's reaction, Luke mused aloud, "If I let you and your army onto the island, and you're as full of shit as you sound, I'm not sure there would be much we could do to keep you from pushing us all into the Gulf and taking what we have built and protected here for all these years. I'll level with you, general. There are just over four hundred of us, maybe two hundred and fifty able to fight worth a damn, and another hundred or so that'd go down trying. As long as you're on the other side of the channel, we still have some chance to defend the island. Once you're over here, we're out of options."

The general's reaction was unambiguous. "If I don't return soon to let my second in command know you are welcoming us onto the island, to do the official business of the nation, he will spare nothing to take it from you and force you out of our way. I apologize for the bluntness, Mr. Mayor, but the stakes are too high to tolerate any further delay."

There were no more idle threats to be made. General Gill had shown his cards to everyone in the room. For the moment, Luke swallowed the overwhelming impulse to put his hands around the old man's neck and squeeze the charlatan's life from him. He had heard enough.

"William . . ." Luke called to his son.

"Yeah, Dad?"

"Listen closely. Go grab a handful of fellas that aren't down at the channel and head over to the workshop under my house. Gather up saws, hammers, and crowbars if you can find them. Jamie Mitchell might still have a working blowtorch. Bring that, too, if he does."

"Yes, sir," William replied. "Where are we heading once we get it all together?"

Luke steeled his nerve for the order he was about to give, wishing briefly that Mr. Hayes was there to tell him that he was making the right choice, but knowing the moment demanded action.

"Get to the city park as quick as you can and cut the rotors off that helicopter."

The chief's office became an instant flashpoint of movement and sound. Dale Warble's confused wail found almost melodic synchronicity with the general's fury as both men shouted protests at the young mayor. Thomas, dumbstruck and proud, instinctively positioned himself between his son and the general as William headed past them.

"Wait," William yelled above the ruckus as he paused at the door. "What's a rotor?"

"The spinny part at the top . . . the metal blades that make it fly," Luke answered, shaking his head.

"Oh yeah. That makes sense," replied the heedless younger Buck, who darted from the room and set out for the joyful work of destruction.

6

GEORGIE PILSNER

Before there was Hayes and Rolf, there was Georgie Pilsner, Thomas' best friend from high school. For a time in their early twenties, Thomas and Georgie lived across the street from one another in dueling church student centers adjacent to the University of Florida. Thomas, a reformed Pentecostal masquerading as a Presbyterian in exchange for a tiny apartment in the back of the church, would lean out his window and yell lighthearted obscenities at his friend, and Georgie, an occasional Methodist, would respond in kind. They were living for free and wanting for little in the lap of American abundance, spending student loan money they never intended to repay on vintage guitars, nice dinners, and Pearl Jam CDs. There was every reason to believe it would all go on forever.

On the morning the smokestacks fell, Georgie, his wife, and their four children were sleeping peacefully in their home near Harrisonburg, Virginia. The furnace had stopped working sometime in the night, and just as the sun began to filter across their corner of the Shenandoah Valley, the cold outside slipped through the walls of the house and under the covers of Georgie's bed. His wife, Hannah, continued to dream in the cocoon of covers she had pilfered from him in the night, but Georgie's exposed calves, cartoonishly powerful like a pair of Popeye arms mounted on the wrong part of his body, were twitching against the chill air. He fought against the injustice of waking for as long as he could, but the cold eventually won out.

Georgie was a thoughtful husband. When he realized the house was freezing, he resisted the urge to burrow next to the warmth of his wife, choosing instead to quietly leave the Eden of their bed and head downstairs into the basement to check on the furnace. For a man who made his living as a professor of literature, Georgie was surprisingly handy. There were a fair number of possible furnace problems he could repair himself, saving the expense and delay of calling in a tradesman. When he unscrewed the two screws that held the front cover of the furnace and removed the thin metal panel, he saw immediately that the pilot light—a small, continuous flame that ignites the main burners when the thermostat tells the furnace to produce heat—was no longer lit.

Georgie knew the gas bill had been paid, and he didn't smell a leak. His first thought was a clogged pitot orifice preventing the pilot light from receiving the small amount of gas required to stay lit. This was a common ailment of aging furnaces, and Georgie had faced it enough times that he kept a thin piece of wire looped around a nail on the basement wall as a clearing tool. He poked the wire in and out of the orifice, finding and clearing a small bit of debris almost instantly. When a single match was enough to call the delicate blue flame of the pilot light back into existence, Georgie felt a warmth not only from the main burners igniting but from the satisfaction of a job well done. He indulged in a self-satisfied smile because he knew his family would wake a few hours later to a comfortable home.

When Georgie's left foot hit the second step of the stairs leading from the basement up to the main house, a familiar creak rang out, a haunting little staccato note that would mark the last clear memory of the day he lost everything that mattered to him in the world.

The National Security Agency's Sugar Grove Station is located roughly thirty miles from the Pilsner home, just across the border in West Virginia. This station is situated in a 13,000-square-mile rectangle of land designated as the U.S. National Radio Quiet Zone, where all radio transmissions are restricted by federal law to facilitate scientific research and the gathering of military intelligence through surveillance. In the old world, the Sugar Grove Station monitored all incoming radio transmissions for the eastern United States. In a war where a nuclear weapon had been used on the civilian power plant across the bay from Cedar Key in Crystal River, the Sugar Grove Station was absolutely on the target list.

If the 100-kiloton bomb meant for Sugar Grove had found its target, the Pilsners would have had a fighting chance for survival. Shenandoah Mountain, at the tail end of the Alleghany Mountain range that formed the hardened border between the two Virginias and outlined the western edge of the fabled Shenandoah Valley, would have shielded much of the blast and fallout from the residents of Harrisonburg. There would be no mechanism for determining which of the myriad circumstances had caused the deviation in the bomb's flight path on that frozen February morning. No explanation could have softened the blow Georgie Pilsner would receive when he regained consciousness the following day and began the slow work of clawing his way out of the hole where his basement had been.

There were no bodies to bury, no photographs, no trivial keepsakes remaining to prove that the Pilsner family, save for the battered patriarch, had ever existed at all. Vanished, except in the vagaries of his memory—compromised as it was by the impact his head and body had sustained when the house above him was swept away by a shockwave straight out of a Joe Haldeman novel—was his indomitable wife Hannah, their poised oldest child Quinn, Oswald the endlessly inquisitive son, Guinevere the beautiful and kind, and Francis the irrepressible youngest.

No man could be expected to endure such a loss and then be judged harshly for deciding to follow those he loved into the darkness, if only for the thin hope of finding them there to offer the protection he had been unable to provide in life. Certainly, such a siren call had reached out to Georgie Pilsner time and again since the creak on the second stair in the basement. His refusal to answer was a heroism, a final act of service to those he cherished, a preservation of their existence in a lonely but determined mind.

When the initial die-off ended, Harrisonburg leaned on its Central Appalachian heritage, finding most of what it needed in the rich abundance of the Valley. In the old world, there was often consternation between the poorer mountain counties and the general affluence of Harrisonburg, but removed from technology and connection to larger metropolitan areas, it didn't take long for all of Appalachia to blend together again. By profession, Georgie Pilsner had made his living with words, but by daily ritual, he was a man connected to the earth and the old ways of living. His wife had been a doula and a midwife and cheerfully passed to her family all the granola hippie skills that came with that culture.

The Pilsners grew their own vegetables in a quarter-acre backyard they called an urban farm. Two smaller side yards had been lined with fruit trees, most of which were swept away with the rest of the house, save for a determined Bradford Pear whose resplendent white blooms smelled like nothing so much as semen. Springtime in Appalachia is a visually stunning and olfactorily putrid time, as millions of Bradford Pears, like a nation state of stiffened teenage boys' socks, sing their pheromonal song. Harrisonburg was less inundated with the smell than other parts of the Valley, but it was there if a nose knew where to look. Like so many of Earth's beautiful things, the Bradford Pear is interlaced with difficulty and hardship. The fast-growing invasive species outcompetes local flora, dropping sad, messy fruits that provide little nutrition for native animals. As it matures, its weak branches split into V-shaped crotches that break in the slightest of winds, causing problems even in death. Over time, Georgie grew to love the annoying little tree, the weakest and least beneficial from the Pilsner orchard, that survived the fall of Harrisonburg out of pure, semen-drenched spite.

In the first weeks after waking in the hole, Georgie mostly just walked about, searching aimlessly for a family he knew he would not find. He was seldom alone. Everywhere there were walkers, shuffling bewildered from place to place, looking for nothing in particular but unsure what else to do. Occasionally, he would see someone he knew, and they would ask, out of politeness or habit, about his family. Early on, he did his best to reply, but the pain of doing so became unbearable, and he began to avoid people altogether.

He found what food he could from the rubble of stores and half-destroyed houses. Late one dark evening, while walking down the middle of what had been a main thoroughfare in town, Georgie tripped over something that sent him tumbling onto the asphalt. After collecting himself from the hard fall, he completed a quick self-assessment to confirm he had no serious injuries, then discovered the obstacle to be a large plastic tackle box, loaded with hooks, line, sinkers, artificial worms, spinner baits, and lures of various types and designs. It was just sitting there on the yellow center line, in strangely perfect condition. He had no rod or reel, but he took the tackle box anyway and spent that night sleeping under a tree in a vacant lot where a house used to be, dreaming of a fried catfish sandwich.

The years began to roll by. There was difficulty, always, but also a slow renewal of humanity throughout the Valley. Electricity had only become ubiquitous in the region in the 1970s, so the transition to the old ways of living was a little easier there than in other parts of the country. The catfish sandwiches eventually came for Georgie. When he cooked the first fish he ever caught with his top-shelf tackle and homemade pole, he said out loud to himself, as though he were ordering at a restaurant, "I'll have one of your finest catfish sandwiches, please . . . hold the bread." It would be a few seasons more before bread was a thing that could be easily had, after crops began to supplant the places where yards and ballfields and meadows had been.

Georgie built a makeshift roof over the hole that had been his basement and, over time, was able to scrounge materials for walls and a floor. When he and Hannah were newly married, they had rented a low-ceilinged stone cottage in Jacksonville, close to the college where Hannah was completing her studies. When Thomas Buck first visited his best buddy and bride at their new home, he joked that his 5-foot-5-inch friend Georgie had found the perfect Hobbit house. Georgie laughed now at the memory of a joke that had annoyed him all those years ago, and looked about his underground abode, feeling some measure of pride in his work and daydreaming about life in the shire.

Harrisonburg after the fall was no Eriador, but the lonely land began to heal over time. After a long period of relative solitude, over which he mourned his lost family, punishing himself for not spending another last few minutes in bed with his beautiful wife that awful morning—missing his chance to be taken alongside her by the blast— Georgie made an effort to reassimilate into public life. He found that surviving friends were still his friends, and he was happily readmitted to the town's social life. All of his guitars, even his prized Emmylou Harris model Gibson L-200, had been swept away with the house above the basement, but it didn't take long for him to find an old Yamaha student model acoustic sitting unused at a friend's house. It was given to him in exchange for a promise to play it at get-togethers like the old days. When the strings of his first G-chord pressed into fingers whose playing calluses were long faded, Georgie felt a warm nostalgia alongside the stinging pain, remembering when he was a new player and the world stretched long and wonderful ahead of him.

When a band of outlaws from neighboring Waynesboro laid siege to downtown Harrisonburg in the seventh year after the fall, killing two and making off with critical supplies, men and women of Harrisonburg formed the Shenandoah Home Guard and began the work of training for the common defense of their homes. Georgie Pilsner was an early volunteer, finding that he took to soldiering, such that it was, as easily as he would an iambic pentameter or a minor pentatonic scale. He was an especially skillful shot with a rifle, though over time, even with only limited target practice, rifle ammunition dried up. An older gentleman in town was a shotgun enthusiast and, as a hobby, had created a shotgun shell-reloading operation in his garage on the eastern edge of town. His stockpile of supplies and equipment had somehow escaped the worst on the day the bombs fell, so he was able to provide an abundance of shells to the Home Guard.

After an initial frenzy following the attack and formation of the Guard, where enthusiasm and esprit de corps peaked in Harrisonburg as nearly everyone worked together to defend their hometown, life began to slow again, as it so often did in the new world, into a punishing, monotonous crawl. The Guard still met regularly, but as the years piled up with no meaningful additional attacks, the heart went out of the endeavor. Georgie Pilsner had long ago been elected leader of the Guard by the time General Gill and his men marched into town, and had, for more than a decade, singlehandedly kept the force together through his mindful leadership.

In the waning twilight on the day before Thanksgiving, Georgie urged restraint until the intentions of the opposing army could be assessed. He called out to the advancing columns, asking them to halt and state their business. Through binoculars, he could see the exaggerated details of the general's face. He looked impossibly old. The deep ridges of his forehead, spotted skin, and turkey waddle neck were out of place with his crisp military bearing and impeccable uniform. Georgie lingered on the image of the unusual old man for a few moments more before lowering the binoculars and shouting again for the army to halt. When no reply came a second time, John Wilton, a hotheaded former chiropractor, discharged his shotgun in the direction of the 198th Battalion. He shouted that it had been an accident, but few among his peers believed him. It didn't matter. What followed was a devastating hail of return fire that sent the members of the Home Guard scrambling for cover behind the courthouse. They fought back as best they could, but their efforts were futile. Two were killed instantly, and three others were grievously wounded. Only the sanctuary of nightfall had saved them from being overrun.

The long night in the courthouse was weighted down by the two deaths and scored by the sounds of the wounded as they suffered through what basic care could be provided to them. There was a heated discussion about whether or not the men encamped on the other side of Market Street were the legitimate American Army, and a wild list of theories about what it all might mean, but no serious consideration was ever given to capitulation. An army had brought violence to Virginia for the first time since the Battle of Cumberland Church in the waning days of the War, as General Lee effected a tactical retreat to Appomattox after the fall of Richmond, the state's capital, four days prior. Then, as now, Southern intolerance for an occupying federal force was unassailable, though the defenders' physical position did not enjoy the same impregnability. There were some among the Guard with inclinations toward reasonableness, but none with bravery sufficient to overcome the hot passions of the assembly. The Shenandoah Home Guard, suddenly a post-modern conjuring of the Army of Northern Virginia, heeding the foolhardy admonitions of the Confederate ghosts among them in the old courthouse, was as good as dead the moment they resolved to stand at first light.

In the final analysis, the judgment of who fired first the following morning was irrelevant. Georgie Pilsner was sure the first shots had come from the rifles of the opposing army, but General Gill would write in his diary that evening about the defensive nature of their engagement with the Virginians, conveniently omitting the incredible brutality that followed once the locals were put down. He would not record the sacking of Harrisonburg after the brief battle, or the near-total pillaging of almost every home, human, and building within a mile radius of the main road. His record noted a small increase in his store of supplies as he and his men continued their march back to Fort Rucker, but left out the savage means by which this increase had occurred.

In the final moments before the firing began, Georgie Pilsner held a shotgun to his shoulder, mindful of the journey each breath into and out of his chest was traveling, and made peace with the end. Everything happened so quickly thereafter that no one saw the moment or circumstance of Georgie's fall. Thundering sound muddled the minds of the guardsmen on the line, and they began firing their shotguns long before the advancing soldiers were in range. Georgie held out longer than most, but when finally he pulled the trigger of the over-under 12-gauge, a flash of light and a percussive force removed the obdurate literary soldier from the fight. An overloaded shell had expended its energy into the aged, pitted barrel of Georgie's shotgun, exploding inches away from him and sending a length of hot metal hard into the side of his face. It seared a six-inch crevice into exposed jawbone and crumpled him into an undignified heap on the narrow dirt path between the courthouse and the cemetery.

There he lay for several hours, indistinguishable from the dead. When life returned to him, indistinct and painful, Georgie beheld the destruction of Harrisonburg in brief moments of clarity as the fog in his head waxed and waned over the coming days. The exploding shotgun had been an improbable stroke of luck that kept him from the rain of .308 and 5.56 rounds that killed every other member of the Guard, though he would never view it as such. Twice now, Georgie had been denied passage to see his wife and children; the thin pillars of life continued to hold against his will, an affirmation of the closely-held self-recriminations that eat at the hearts of men.

For reasons lofty or trivial or something in between, Georgie's punishment in the new world continued.

7

— · —

Amen Corner

After the new mayor's order to destroy the helicopter in the park, Dale Warble could only be described as radicalized by the ordeal. He raced out of the chief's office, resolving to stop William before the order could be carried out, but when he caught up with the hulking younger man, his good sense kicked in, and he lost his nerve. His insides continued to boil. At long last, a reason for hope had come to the island, and he had witnessed firsthand the new mayor's determination to turn it away.

Dale was 38 years old on the day the old world died. Until those last tense months leading up to the end, his golf cart rental company had been a cash cow that afforded him a comfortable lifestyle and a measure of prestige on the island. When he began to go prematurely bald in his mid-20s, Dale took to wearing a backward baseball cap everywhere he went. It was a perfectly reasonable fashion choice for a younger person and drew no particular notice. He became so accustomed to donning a cap on his way out the door each day that the ritual ingrained itself into his life such that he wouldn't dream of leaving the house without it. As Dale steamed toward the end of his thirties, the backward hat took on a quality of eccentricity that would raise an occasional eyebrow but not a scandal. Now, at 63, it was indefensible, a mesh gilding of a wrinkled, lily-white head that was half again too big for its body. To his credit, Dale leaned into the crackpot aesthetic as he aged and was generally liked by most on the island.

Likeability is not a hard requirement for small-town rumoring, but it helps. Dale lacked the spirit and physical wherewithal for direct confrontation, but he was exceedingly capable of pushing back against the new mayor by talking behind his back to anyone who would listen. The first person Dale ran into on the street was Benji Iverson, the former owner of the coffee shop on 2nd Street that was lost to the great fire in the first year after the smokestacks fell.

"Benji, Benji!" he yelled as he waved both hands above his head, crazed as though overcome by the Holy Spirit.

"You okay, bud? What's going on?"

The righteousness in Dale's belly was overwhelming his customary coolness.

"Benji . . . that's the American Army down at the channel. I heard the whole story. I mean, the actual American Army and they're here to meet the Navy and the mayor is picking a fight with them."

Benji replied, "What Navy? You sure about that, Dale? Hayes was the one who gave the order for invaders at the bridge. I know Luke's new at this, but Hayes wouldn't have given the order if he didn't believe it."

Dale shook his head like a man being told the moon was made of cheese. "I was there when they questioned the general. I was in the room, Benji! There's still a chance we can win this war, but Luke is trying to stop it."

"What war?" Benji asked, unable to mask the doubt in his voice. "Whatever war there was has been over a long time, bud."

Dale didn't waste the additional few seconds required to speak again before pushing past Benji and heading toward the house of Jonie

Bartholomew, a current member of the town council. She was elected after the long-serving and dubiously-coifed Slim Worthman closed his eyes during a council meeting and quietly died there in his seat next to old Mayor Hayes. Jonie had been a lawyer in the old world. She was persnickety, competent, and dogmatic about policy issues that mattered to her. Even now, at 81, a youthful hue sat comfortably on her delicate face, framed by flowing silver hair that caught the sunlight, giving her an otherworldly quality.

Dale found the councilwoman in her side yard garden, planting collards and cherry tomatoes. "Joni!" Dale yelled as he shuffled up the hill toward her.

"Hey neighbor," Jonie replied, continuing her work.

"You have a minute to chat?" Dale asked.

"Sure, as long as you don't mind if I keep planting while we do. When I'm nervous, I like to keep my hands busy. I should be down at the channel, but I'm moving too slow today to be any help."

"That's why I'm here," Dale replied, excitedly. "It's not what it looks like. I don't know why Hayes and Luke are saying we're being invaded. I was in the room, Joni . . . they've got it wrong, but they won't listen. I was there!"

"You were where? What room? You're gonna have to slow down a little. You're not making any sense."

Dale did his best to collect himself and begin again. He told the story of the encounter in Big Chief's office, casting Luke as the antagonist and the general as the great embodiment of America itself. Joni had dealt with Dale many times over the years, both as a neighbor and on council business, so she knew to temper her response to his story.

"I'm not doubting you," Joni said, diplomatically, before laying out the reasons for her obvious doubt. "It was Hayes who gave the Condition One order, right?

"Well, yes, but . . ."

"That old coot is a pain in the ass, but he's not reckless. I'm inclined to trust his judgment."

"This isn't about Hayes," Dale said with annoyance in his voice. "Luke just sent his kid to cut the rotors off the general's helicopter, and if we don't let the Army onto the island to meet the Navy, we're gonna have to fight them."

"What?" Jonie replied with a gentle, rebuking smile.

"What part don't you get?" Dale asked in a huff.

He had worked himself into a froth now, and he knew he was losing the councilwoman. Joni may have been skeptical of his account, but it was not in her nature to ignore a serious issue, however it was being framed to her. She took off her gardening gloves and shook the dirt from her clothes, leaving her tools on the ground and turning to head for Big Chief's office.

"I'll look into this, I promise," she said.

Dale nodded awkwardly, then set out to find more people to tell.

Back in the safety of his underground home, Georgie Pilsner sat in the quiet stillness of the overnight hours, staring across a makeshift table at the gun. His friend and fellow Guardsman, Leo Harper, never left home without the Colt Model 1908 under his jacket, in a shoulder holster. The gun and the holster had been worn by his great-grandfather, an Army colonel, throughout the Second World War. Lower-ranking officers generally carried the larger Model 1911 .45-caliber sidearm conspicuously in a hip holster, but it became a status symbol among higher ranks to conceal the smaller, hammerless Model 1908 under their uniforms. The weapon was the only meaningful heirloom in the Harper family, passing down through male heirs until it reached Leo. When Georgie first regained consciousness among the bodies of his fallen fellow guardsmen, Leo was closest to him, twisted into an undignified arc with an arm bent upwards, exposing his great-grandfather's pistol. Georgie did not remember taking the gun from his friend's body, but as he regarded it now on the table, he felt sure he had done so in a spirit of reverence.

The Harper family had a maternal tie to Southern military royalty. Leo's mother's forebears were Scottish and Anglo-Huguenots who had been in the region since before the Revolutionary War; the most famous of these was Leo's namesake, his 4-greats uncle Leonidas Polk, the renowned Confederate general and Episcopal minister. General Polk had attended the Virginia Theological Seminary in Alexandria, a hundred airline miles to the east of where his distant future nephew would fall alongside Georgie Pilsner.

Now and then, as the small hours dragged on, Georgie would hold the undersized pistol in his hand, feeling its weight and the tactile sensation of the textured wood in its grip. More than once, he lifted the gun quickly to his head, closed his eyes, and gritted his teeth with as much force as he could stand, hoping the labored routine would conjure the will to finally pull the trigger. Each time he failed, the walls of the room moved closer in toward him, and the thought of remaining in the haunted tomb of Harrisonburg grew more intolerable.

At dawn, Georgie's brains were still intact, but his heart and spirit were broken. He packed what supplies he could carry in a rucksack, fitted the holster and the Colt to his left shoulder, slung the student model guitar over the right, and walked away from Virginia for good.

Heading south out of Harrisonburg, Georgie witnessed the second plenary destruction of his hometown. Many of the buildings that had survived the day of the bombs were now torn apart or burned. Beyond the courthouse, in the direction of the army's march back to Alabama, there stretched a path resembling the jagged scar a tornado leaves upon the land. The first few bodies he encountered drew out the requisite emotions a decent person is expected to feel in response to death. By the tenth, faces Georgie knew well began to blur. When finally the bodies became indistinguishable from the rest of the debris, he could stand it no longer. He turned perpendicular to the swath of destruction and kept his head down until he had put some distance between himself and the heart of the lost city.

By the time Georgie took notice of his progress, he had passed the ruins of James Madison University, crossed over Reservoir Street, and found himself following the US-Highway 33 corridor on a south by southeast heading past the city limits. On his left was the southern end of Massanutten Mountain, whose synclines folded into the perfect saddle-shaped ridges that made the ski resort there so popular in the old world. The sight of the mountain sent a quick stab of nostalgia into Georgie's stomach, as he remembered the occasional bartending shifts he would work at the resort in lean financial times. It had been a good way to pay an unexpected bill or quickly gather the cash for whatever new guitar was calling to him. His encyclopedic knowledge of spirits and professorial demeanor made him so popular that the resort generally let him work whenever he wanted.

As he tried to push the images of the walk from his mind, Georgie's thoughts drifted comfortably to the mahogany bar and the way the lounge's low lighting made starbursts in its epoxy resin sheen. His best friend, Thomas Buck, was often described as the charismatic one, but Georgie possessed his own kind of magnetism that drew in a more discerning crowd. He was not afflicted by the cloying need to be adored that had so often been the undoing of his friend, but when he needed to be *on*, at the bar or on a stage with a guitar, he never had trouble finding the switch. Georgie and Thomas were the kind of friends who set the corner posts of a life; in times of acrimony and delight, the bedrock of a lifetime friendship tethers a person to the solid ground of a spinning Earth. When the decision was made to leave Virginia, there was only ever one place Georgie would go—home to Florida and his friend.

Avoiding mountains and the big cities between Harrisonburg and Cedar Key were the only real criteria for the route Georgie would choose. Using a compass and a fold-up road atlas salvaged from an abandoned gas station, he navigated to avoid Charlotte, Atlanta, and Jacksonville, which would almost certainly be fraught with risk. He managed roughly seven miles a day in the beginning, as his legs and resolve settled into the routine. By the end of the first week on the road, he was covering more than ten on most days, and eventually could walk as many as fifteen. On the ninth day, following Highway 26 to stay west of Lynchburg, Georgie saw a small green sign announcing the Appomattox city limits. A few hundred feet ahead sat an ornate stone display holding a bright blue oval sign that read:

Welcome to Historic Appomattox
Where Our Nation Reunited

Georgie rolled his eyes at the sign's dubious claim. Certainly, Robert E. Lee's surrender at the Appomattox Courthouse was the beginning of the end for the Confederacy, but Johnston would not surrender the Army of Tennessee to Sherman for another seventeen days, Kirby Smith's Department of the Trans-Mississippi would hold out until May, and the CSS Shenandoah, an armor-framed warship, continued attacking Union merchant ships into the summer of 1865. Even after the last shot of the war was fired, variously claimed to be in Palmito Ranch, Texas, or Waynesville, North Carolina, or even in the Bering Strait off the coast of Alaska, few on either side of the conflict would feel as though the nation had been reunited. Even generations after Reconstruction, the word Appomattox would elicit a range of emotions, none of which, to Southerners, had anything to do with unity.

Whenever Georgie thought about that February day when the world destroyed itself, it seemed unfathomable that any form of human conflict could ever rise to such a level, and yet, as he walked now through the heart of Appomattox, the weight of his own nation's fraternal bloodletting sat strangely heavy on his heart. Men, it seemed, were born to fight and die; it was always only a matter of time until the technology of war caught up with the depravity in their hearts.

Thereafter, Virginia passed uneventfully. A long stretch of backroads took him through a rural corridor between Raleigh-Durham and Greensboro, North Carolina. On the extreme outskirts of Charlotte, once the financial capital of the South, he had to shoot the biggest of a four-man crew in the belly to escape a mugging. He had been prepared to shoot them all if necessary, a thought that sat uneasily on his mind for the duration of his journey, but the remaining men shrank quickly away from Leo Harper's pistol, and Georgie was able to keep moving south.

A southern jog around South Carolina's capital city of Columbia angled him toward the town of Augusta, Georgia. Here, he made a diversion purely for curiosity's sake or, as he would reason to himself later as a rationalization for the additional risks he had undertaken, for a study in the class structure of America. Augusta was, of course, the beating heart of the golf world, where the historic Masters tournament would take place each year in April, along with the blooming of the azaleas. The Augusta National Golf Club was the paragon of exclusivity; only the richest and most powerful people in the world had any chance of ever becoming a member there. In fact, extreme wealth was not sufficient in itself to gain membership. There was an unspoken but enforced class threshold required for consideration. The nouveau riche or unconnected need not apply. Indeed, no one need apply, as there was no formal application process by which an outsider could earn their way down Magnolia Lane and into a private locker at the club.

When Georgie found the Magnolia trees stripped bare along the club's iconic entrance, he felt a weird sense of loss. The famous clubhouse whose shape was the basis of the trophy presented—along with the fabled Green Jacket—to the winner each year, had been pulled apart a board at a time. The fairways and greens were overgrown and neglected, but the towering pine trees and shape of the holes were still recognizable as the ones he had watched on television every year since he was a child. He lingered the better part of a day on the course that Bobby Jones, Alister Mackenzie, and Clifford Roberts had built in the first few years of the 1930s as an American homage to the Old Course at Saint Andrews in Scotland, the birthplace of the game.

Cordoned off as it had always been from the trivialities of the world, the felled high cathedral of American golf felt in the moment like a heavier loss to Georgie than the fall of Washington. He had not known that the powerful members of the club, sensing the building unrest in the world in those months leading up to the flash, had spent more than a hundred million dollars hardening Augusta National's defenses, creating an elaborate, foolproof plan to protect it from a world in turmoil. To the wide-eyed traveler strolling its ruins, the club would seem to have fallen in populist solidarity with the rest of the world. In truth, supported by its endless wealth and careful contingency planning, Augusta National was able to defend its perimeter and continue to operate with some semblance of normalcy for a full month after the bombs fell until, at last, the displaced masses overran Magnolia Lane and chewed away its opulence over the span of a single weekend. There was a time, however, as Paris, London, and Moscow burned alongside D.C., when the masters of men chased a little white ball through an artificial paradise that was holding out, preposterously, against inevitable collapse, believing until the moment the gates came down that the rest of the world would yield forever. It was a shame that Georgie was denied this information; he of all people left on Earth would appreciate the absurd story, an archetypal American allegory if ever there was such a thing.

Pine Warblers and Carolina Wrens sang through the trees, haunting and bright, as Georgie stopped for lunch near Amen Corner. He ate jackrabbit jerky and home-canned field peas on the little stone bridge over Ray's Creek near the 12th hole, and felt, for a while in the cold afternoon sun, like a king.

8

—·—

OLD FOLKS AT HOME

The ebb tide was racing toward the low, exposing a wide mud flat between the channel and the shore. Hayes David stood at the helm of his navy's flagship, stoic as Marcus Aurelius on the frozen Danube. He was an old man now, with an ear and a little toe shot off in two new-world wars, but despite a limp and his asymmetric face, seventy-two years of life adorned him more like rugged armor than age. The Gulf yields to no man, but whenever Hayes captained a boat upon it, his father's spirit was never far away, interceding on his son's behalf with the ancient waters and the wind. Calm authority is the uniform of a good captain, and Hayes' was adorned with a lifetime of medals hard-earned on the water. As the tide continued to slip away, two smaller boats patrolled behind him, but it was Hayes' position in the center of the channel that commanded the attention of the army on the mainland. In the face of an enemy more fearsome than the island had ever encountered, the old captain stood firm.

Major Joshua Lawrence busied himself with the work of keeping his men on alert while he waited for a helicopter to reappear above the tree line. An hour earlier, he sent a dozen men to scout the mainland for supplies or another way onto the island. Two of these scouts discovered the Beecham homestead on the sprawling 40-acre peninsula a quarter mile from the army's encampment. Ryland Beecham had grown up there with his brother, Lex, and mother, Leanna, a free-spirited adventurer who did not return from a sojourn down the Nile River she had been on when the smokestacks fell. After several months of hoping for something he knew in his gut was impossible, Ryland accepted the loss and moved back home to his mother's house.

Leanna's peninsula became a kind of hunting camp from which Ryland and his best buddy Luke Buck would set out into the scrublands in search of game. The peninsula was where Luke first wooed his wife, Kinsey. An overnight by a fire on its southern shore had drawn the young lovers into the deep embrace of a lifetime connection. When a dozen islanders launched a retaliatory strike against the murderous Little Don Meade in Sumner, the peninsula was the forward operating base of the mission. Before the friends and neighbors embarked on their dark business that day, they shared a tailgate feast of pickled eggs and okra from Leanna's storehouse, a makeshift communion in remembrance of lost friends and a lost world. A channel of water and a stretch of muddy grass separated it from the island proper, but Leanna's peninsula was a beloved and vital part of Cedar Key.

When Ryland saw the soldier dragging his mother's kayak through the mud toward the channel, he knew immediately that the army had found his home. He sailed his boat as quickly as the wind would allow toward Hayes and the *Cogency* as Gibbs Yardy followed suit. It took some time for the soldier to trudge through the knee-deep low-tide mud, but he eventually climbed into the kayak as he slid it into the shallow water of the channel. With considerable difficulty, he began paddling toward the three boats, waving a makeshift white flag above his head.

Crossing the Florida line south of Fargo, Georgia, along the old Highway 441 corridor, Georgie Pilsner was overcome with nostalgia. Thirty years as a Florida ex-pat in Virginia had cleaved him from the culture of his childhood, but as he breathed in the wet, heavy air of the swamp after so many years away, he felt like Odysseus, basking in the nostros of returning home. The Pilsners had left the Sunshine State to be nearer Hannah's family, and for work and school opportunities closer to the nation's capital, but Georgie had also privately been elated to leave the smothering heat for a cooler climate.

For most of his life, the pursuit of intellectual interests had won out over the physical maintenance of his body; combined with a treasonous hairline and his penchant for wearing a moonshiner's beard that hid a classically handsome face, his countenance made him always look older and softer than he was. For a man who looked thirty when he was fifteen, and fifty when he was thirty, at seventy-one, he somehow still only looked fifty, and his body had been transformed by struggle into a hardened shield. Beneath a beard longer and more unkempt than ever, his jawline had squared and his neck thickened with the muscles of daily physical labor. His once preposterous calf muscles were now paired with powerful thighs, a flat belly, and a broad, defined chest. The erstwhile bookish professor had been reborn as totally as Saul on the road to Damascus. The new world had made him magnificent—Odin with both eyes, a silverback gorilla with a master's degree in creative writing.

Georgie continued south and west. Some part of him wanted to turn east toward Jacksonville, where he had lived much of his adult life, but he knew its navy bases and the shipping port would have been irresistible targets for the enemy in the big war. Also, whenever he met travelers passing through Harrisonburg over the past twenty-five years, Georgie had always asked them what they knew about his former hometown. Everyone who had actually been to Jacksonville reported its total destruction, and Georgie was pragmatic enough to know they were telling the truth.

After two and a half uneventful days of walking, and a purposeful turn away from Lake City, Georgie slept on the banks of the Suwannee River in the tiny town of White Springs, a few miles upriver from the Big Shoals, the only class three whitewater rapids in the state. A day later, he was camped outside of Live Oak, and two more after that, he was crossing the serpentine Suwannee yet again just outside the city limits of Mayo. He spent the next day and a half hoping he was following the rural Highway 51, but increasingly unsure if he was where he thought he was on the map. Even in areas that had been largely unaffected by the falling bombs, street signs seemed to grow scarcer each year. Twice in south Georgia, he had walked miles in the wrong direction before finding some natural landmark that guided him back toward his intended route.

Just before sunset, at last, the major landmark of US-Highway 19 appeared before him. Before Interstate 75 drained the lifeblood from it, US-19 had been the major north/south route through the state. It was still a moderately traveled thoroughfare leading up to the flash, but many of the roadside towns, stores, and attractions from its heyday had faded over time. Georgie knew that from there on out, all he had to do was follow US-19 until it hit State Road 24, then take a single right turn and it was straight on until he hit the Gulf in Cedar Key. That had been the plan, anyway. The lack of signage and a fading memory of the area after so long away from it made the roads to the Gulf front towns of Suwannee, Horseshoe Beach, and Cedar Key blend together. They were each two-lane, poorly paved stretches of more than twenty miles through slash pine and floodplains, with few side roads or other landmarks for navigation.

Georgie correctly determined that he was, in fact, at the intersection of State Road 51 and US-19 when he began his walk south. He would stay on the lookout for three bigger roads on his right, the third of which would lead to Cedar Key. His big mistake came when he mistook a smaller country road for Highway 351 to Horseshoe Beach, so that by the time he reached Highway 349 to Suwannee, his count convinced him that he was turning west onto State Road 24 and was only twenty-one miles from his friend.

As he headed toward the Gulf, he walked with renewed energy. Nothing looked like what he remembered, but that was true of so much of the world now that it was easy to convince himself the Number Four Bridge was just around the next bend in the road. When darkness began to fall, Georgie was still three miles from the Gulf, so he decided to make camp and start fresh in the morning. He slept in a sleeping bag under the stars of a dazzling winter sky and dreamed happy dreams for the first time in as long as he could remember. He awoke with the dawn and was walking by the time sunlight filtered onto the road. There was an outlandish spring in his step and a brightness in his eyes long darkened by the world. He sang an Indigo Girls song and felt as close to fine as he thought possible while the few remaining miles zipped by.

When he saw the first buildings ahead, Georgie knew he had taken a wrong turn.

The town of Suwannee is situated on the north bank of the Suwannee River, two and a half miles upriver from its confluence with the Gulf of Mexico. Here, the river is wide and languid, and as it nears the Gulf, it begins to resemble an octopus reaching its multiple freshwater arms into the salty bay through a series of splits and winding creeks. The town is sometimes described as a redneck Venice, because nearly every parcel of land within the city limits is situated on one of a series of manmade canals that all connect to the river and the Gulf. The existence of the canals marks the end of the comparisons. Suwannee is a lower-middle class Shangri-la, containing a mix of aging condos, singlewide mobile homes elevated high on concrete blocks to escape the frequent flooding of the river, ramshackle cottages that sit on the ground and are built to simply hose out after every flood, and countless campers, converted school busses, sheds, and tents, all with a dock on the canal and boats that run the gamut from skiffs to old houseboats to commercial fishing trawlers. Even before the flash, Suwannee was an outlaw river town where folks took care of themselves and meted out what justice was needed without a thought of involving authorities that would be hesitant to come if called. In the new world, its wild west aesthetic only amplified.

When Georgie reached the corner of Highway 349 and Bay Street, he was met by guards stationed at a barricade made from old cars and barbed wire salvaged from cattle pastures outside of town. After weeks haggard by the road, the already menacing-looking traveler put the guards naturally on edge.

"Halt there, please," one of the two middle-aged guards called out.

"Yes, sir," Georgie called back, raising his arms above his head.

"Are you armed?" the second guard asked.

"I am," Georgie replied. "But I'm friendly."

"All the same, we're gonna need you to lay your weapons on the ground. We'll collect them, then you'll be clear to come in if you have some business here. When you leave, you'll get the weapons back."

"Suppose I give up my gun . . . then what's to stop you from robbing or killing me?"

"Nothing, really. Except you don't seem like you got much worth taking, and we're not animals that go around killing folks for fun."

Georgie could sense no deception in the guard's tone, but it would still be a risk to hand over Leo's gun. "Why should I trust you?"

"No reason, I reckon, except we could have shot you long before you made it this close to us."

"That makes sense," Georgie relented, before lowering his arms, taking off the shoulder holster and pistol, and laying them on the ground. "If it's alright with you, I'd like to keep the guitar."

"That's fine," a guard said with a wide, gummy smile. "But if you try to hit one of us over the head with it, we're gonna feel pretty cross about it."

Georgie was caught off guard by the moment of levity and laughed so heartily that the guards joined in, and the tension quickly drifted away from the exchange. When he explained that he had no real business in Suwannee and that he had indeed arrived there by mistake on his way to Cedar Key to meet his friend, one of the guards led him away from the barricade toward a marina on the bank of the river.

"Senior Chief is from Cedar Key. He'll wanna talk to you."

"Senior Chief? Like the petty officer? You fellas from the Navy?" Georgie asked.

"Coast Guard. A bunch of us came here a little while after our base down south was destroyed. We had some trouble settling in, but we've been here ever since."

Georgie said, "I wonder if the Senior Chief knows any of my friends on the island."

The guard chuckled. "Oh, I think you'll be surprised how well he knows them."

When they had walked almost a half mile, the big metal drydock building of the Suwannee Marina came into view. To its side, in the deep-water cut running off the main channel to the river, was a sight that took Georgie's breath away. The 87-foot Coast Guard Cutter Sawfish, with its twin 50-caliber machine guns mounted on the bow, floated in the tea-colored water, projecting power and awe. The Sawfish was impressive in its heyday, but terrifying now in a world so far regressed from the age of wonder.

"Whoa," Georgie said, wide-eyed with what could only be described as amazement.

"I still feel that way about her, too," the guard replied.

"Are those sails?" Georgie asked.

"Yes, sir," came a laughing reply. "We ran out of diesel about twenty-five years ago. She's a little big to paddle."

"Whoa," Georgie said again, at a loss for words for one of the few times in his life. "So there's still a Coast Guard?"

"Well, best not get carried away. As far as we know, we're what's left, and all we're guarding is this town and a couple mile stretch of river in front of it."

"Still," replied Georgie. "I'm glad to know you're here."

As they crossed the gangplank from the dock to the Sawfish, the senior chief came out of the pilot house to meet them.

"We've got a visitor, Senior Chief."

"From where?"

"Virginia," Georgie replied. "But I'm from Florida originally."

The guard said, "He got lost on his way to Cedar Key and ended up here."

"You must have been coming down 19 and took a wrong turn," the senior chief replied.

"How'd you know?" Georgie asked.

"I grew up around here and used to ride up and down 19 all the time."

Georgie replied, "Your man says you grew up in Cedar Key. You might know some of my friends there . . . maybe not my buddy Thomas, but his best friend on the island was the mayor last time I was here. Hayes David? His dad is Mark David. They're clam farmers."

The senior chief could only smile and chuckle to himself.

"I do know them, yes," he replied. "I know them quite well."

"What a small world," Georgie said. "I mean, it's gotten a lot bigger since everything went to hell. It took me two and a half months to walk here."

"What's bringing you back to the Gulf Coast?" asked the senior chief.

Georgie's face betrayed him. A wave of emotions leaped to the forefront of his heart as he thought about how to formulate a response.

"I lost my family on the day it all started. All of them. I don't know why I wasn't taken alongside them, but God somehow saw fit to leave me behind. I did what I could to keep on with things, and I'd been at it for a long while until my town was overrun by an army and almost everyone I knew was killed."

"An army? What kind of army?"

"It looked a whole lot like our Army, except everybody was older than they should have been. They had a guy dressed like a general leading them who looked like the Crypt Keeper. He had silver stars on his shoulders and everything. And they all had rifles."

"How many were there?" asked the senior chief.

"I don't know. Hundreds at least."

The senior chief seemed puzzled by the story. He said, "I sure haven't heard anything about an Army . . . or a Navy or Air Force or Marines either for that matter."

"Until the day they marched into Harrisonburg, neither had I," Georgie replied. "And of all the travelers that passed through town over all those years, not one had even heard a rumor about an army . . . until a few months ago when one showed up and killed almost everyone I knew."

"I'm sorry," the senior chief replied with genuine concern in his voice.

"No, no," Georgie said, embarrassed. "I didn't mean to burden you with all that. What I meant was that I just didn't have anything left in Virginia. My best friend lived in Cedar Key, and I thought I'd head his way. I always loved spending time there, and I figured the island might have missed out on the worst of it."

The senior chief paused, pushing against a sudden arrival of complicated feelings about Cedar Key and his own role in the island's struggles. Thankfully, a lifetime of military command had equipped him with a stoic look that gave him cover as he replied, "They're doing alright. It's taken some time, but Suwannee and Cedar Key worked their way into peace after some early trouble. On good days, I'd even venture to say we're friends."

"That's great," Georgie replied. "I'd like to rest a day or two before I start back out walking, if that's okay with you, but I can take a message or deliver something for you if you want. I figure with the backtracking, I can make it to the island in 4 or 5 days."

Suddenly, a commotion blew up outside the pilot house of the Sawfish. Something was happening that had folks yelling and moving.

"Please excuse me," Senior Chief said as he rushed past Georgie and onto the deck. Georgie followed after him.

A man called from the dock, "Fire above the tree line, Senior Chief."

"Where's it coming from?"

"South of us somewhere . . . hard to say."

The senior chief called to one of the men near the bow of the Sawfish. "Petty Officer Smith, get the binoculars and a compass and climb the mast. See if you can see anything."

The younger man retrieved the items from the pilot house and began a slow climb up the center sailing mast. When he reached the top, he scanned the horizon, finding the fire quickly. From the fifty-foot height, the curvature of the Earth would only allow him to see a little over nine miles away, which, it turned out, was about four miles too short to see the base of the fire to better pinpoint its location.

"Anything?" the senior chief called up.

"Just a sec, let me get a heading. The fire has to be huge for this much smoke."

The petty officer gripped the mast tightly with is legs as he used both hands to move the compass about.

"Looks like . . . uh . . . heading of 146 degrees, Senior Chief."

"That's nearly directly southeast. How far you think it is?"

"Ten or fifteen miles, maybe."

"Goddamnit," the senior chief replied. "You sure?"

"Pretty sure. That's gotta be close to Cedar Key. Wait . . . you don't think it's . . ."

"The signal!" Senior Chief yelled. "Get down from there and muster the crew. Get the Sawfish and three of our bigger boats ready to go. Condition One. Now!"

"What's going on?" Georgie asked worriedly. "Is something happening in Cedar Key?"

"You're about to find out. Did you leave any weapons with the guards when you got to town?"

"I did. A gun."

"Good," the senior chief replied. "Go get it and get back here as quickly as you can. We're sailing for Cedar Key within the half hour."

All around the marina and adjacent canals, movement energized the morning. Georgie covered the mile round trip to the barricade and back in a hard jog, making it onto the Sawfish just before its crew began to shove it away from the dock. The four-boat formation held seventeen men and two women, haphazardly uniformed but operating with the obvious military precision of a group that had been together for a long time. Georgie felt a rush of exhilaration to be on board an actual military vessel, pressed into its service, and heading to help a place he loved.

The senior chief looked across the deck of the Sawfish with pride, as the crew he had led for a quarter century sailed the boat with Swiss precision. He looked toward his newest crew member and said, "I'm sorry, friend, I don't think I caught your name."

"G.M. Pilsner," he replied as his profligate beard blew wild about his smiling, square face. "But my friends call me Georgie."

"The honor is mine," the senior chief said, extending his hand. "I'm Isaac Skipjack."

9

MARK DAVID

No man is entirely himself, separate from his fathers. A boy raised alongside the man who helped make him is unlikely to escape the proclivities of several generations of men who look a little like him in old photographs. In small towns, Southern ones especially, a boy's father is as much an identification as his driver's license.

"That's Mark David's boy," somebody would say when Hayes was still finding his way as a gangly young kid at the helm of his first mullet boat. "He'll be alright."

In the same way that Thomas learned to tell stories and seek foolhardy adventure from his father before he died, Hayes learned the intricacies of the Gulf and attention to detail from his. Both friends, though, in ways fundamentally different and utterly similar, had learned to love by watching their dads. When Thomas first arrived in Cedar Key, fatherless and adrift, Mark David got a kick out of watching him get his ass kicked by the Gulf as he bumbled his way into clam farming. What began as amusement grew over time into a kind of paternal affection for his son's eccentric friend until, eventually and without it ever having to be said out loud, another son was learning from him.

It was the second time he had taken in a dead-dad straggler.

In the spring of 1998, clams began disappearing from leases in Cedar Key. It was the early years of the clam industry, in the immediate aftermath of the state's ill-conceived constitutional amendment to ban commercial net fishing in the coastal waters of Florida. Men whose families had earned a living on small mullet boats for multiple generations were suddenly displaced from the only work they had ever known. A single persuasively worded paragraph on a ballot decimated the working waterfront in Cedar Key. Proud watermen that had only ever known the solitary self-sufficiency of a life on the water were sent, spirits broken, to jobs in factories or mowing yards or to the false solace of the bottle or the gun. A government-sponsored program to retrain displaced net fishermen as the state's first commercial clam farmers provided a ray of hope, but an entire industry had to be created from the ground up, and the going was slow. In subsequent decades, the business of clams would grow to provide good livings for many and prosperity for some, but in the spring of 1998, the new Cedar Key clam farmers were just beginning to scratch out a living, and only barely. Stolen clams, even in small numbers, could be the tipping point between survival and being pushed off the island.

FWC and other law enforcement agencies made no headway in catching the thief. Local farmers began to take shifts patrolling the leases throughout the night. Several weeks passed with no success. Clams continued to disappear. A boiling of the blood overwhelmed the island. Finally, on one such patrol, Mark David and his best friend Allen Mikes happened upon a boat in the darkness on the Gulf Jackson leases off the northwestern coast of the island. In the boat, sitting atop a hundred bags of stolen clams, sat a scraggly, unrecognizable figure, caught in the beam of Mark David's spotlight, frozen in place and fixed in time forever. Allen Mikes, crazed with righteous anger fueled by months of lean dinners and sleepless nights, leaped across the gunwales of his boat and onto the faceless man, washed out by the blinding light and the place he was holding for the lost lives and livelihoods that disappeared with the nets.

The man withered under the blows from Allen Mikes. He had not been able to mount even a feeble defense, or had simply chosen not to out of shame. He seemed content to die there atop the clams, and Allen Mikes was determined to oblige this contentment until Mark David intervened, reasoning that it wasn't only their place to make such a decision. With yelling and bad feelings between the two friends, the blows eventually stopped, and the boat with the stolen clams and the battered thief was towed back to the boat ramp and a waiting crowd of angry clam farmers.

The thief was Buddy Skipjack, a displaced mullet fisherman and a man generally liked by his fellow captains and most folks in town. Even once this fact became known to the mob at the boat ramp, there would have been no outcome for Buddy but brutality if Vernon, the Chief of Police, had not intervened to arrest him and take him to the Levy County jail, thirty-four miles away in Bronson. Relieved to be away from the men at the dock, Buddy Skipjack found renewed energy in the back seat of Vernon's police truck. On the way to the jail, he chatted amicably with the chief, who was, above all else, a gracious man with a streak of kindness that didn't always square with the harshness of his profession. Buddy managed his shame with something akin to resolve, and Vernon was decent enough to skip the lecture about his crimes.

Four miles away from the jail, with a smile on his face, Buddy grabbed at his chest and whimpered something soft and low.

"What's that?" the chief asked from the front.

Buddy did not answer. He looked through the back window at the passing pine trees, marveled at the way they blurred together into something beautiful and strange, then slumped over, dead against the glass.

Chief Vernon was oblivious to Buddy's departure for the hereafter until he reached the jail, opened the back door of his truck, and watched the lifeless body fall out face-first on the asphalt parking lot.

"Well, shit," the chief thought to himself. "This ain't good."

Buddy's death created a whirlwind of controversy on the island. The coroner's report listed heart attack as the cause of death, and did not cite the beating as a contributing factor. Few who saw his battered body at the open-casket funeral believed it, least of all an already motherless 17-year-old son now left to shoulder a dead father's tainted legacy. A wall of silence from the clam farmers, and even Chief Vernon, cultivated the mystery surrounding Buddy's death until it became a kind of cautionary tale told only in hushed tones and innuendo. Eventually, the story slipped into the realm of folklore, and most folks returned to the routines of everyday life. Life would never be normal again for Isaac Skipjack, the surviving son, left to survive alone in the world. This distasteful chapter in island history could have ended there, with Isaac slipping away like so many other lost boys of the South, if the loving heart of a good man had not intervened.

Mark David was a man as good as any and better than most.

He had grown up on the island and left it only to serve as a Boatswain Mate in the Coast Guard before returning to take up his father's work on mullet and blue crab boats, and to run the David family fish house that bought and sold the catch of other Cedar Key watermen. When the government came for the nets, the David family took up the new business of clam farming and grew it over time into a prosperous living. The early phase of this success was just beginning on the morning Mark David saw Isaac Skipjack sitting on a bench near the boat ramp, skipping school and staring quietly into the Gulf.

If Mark David had been a lesser man, if he had dropped his birddog boat in the water and headed off for the day's work on the clam leases alone, the lives of so many people on the island would have gone so differently. In a thousand replays of that morning, however, no alternate sequence of events could ever have transpired. He was always going to challenge the truant teenager on the bench, and Isaac was always going to bristle in response.

"You okay, son?" Mark asked.

Isaac coldly thanked the elder waterman for asking, then reminded him sharply that he wasn't anybody's son anymore. There was no escaping the heavy gut punch of the boy's confrontational grief. Mark David gripped the throttle of his birddog firmly, trying in vain to will it forward, to leave the trouble of the boy in his wake. His mind thought it might be willing, but his hand and his heart would simply not comply. By then, he could no longer see Isaac Skipjack at all, but rather his own son Hayes, and he could bear the image of the boy on the bench no longer. An ultimatum was given under threat of calling Chief Vernon to haul Isaac back to school, and before either man had time to think it through, Isaac was on the boat, motoring toward a day of work planting clams together. Thereafter, they were seldom apart.

Like so many of the great relationships in a life, timing was a key factor in Isaac finding a place firmly under the wing of the elder waterman. A regional supermarket chain with locations across Florida had just signed a contract with the David family to supply clams to its stores. It was a mad dash to spin up capacity to meet the supermarket's demand. Isaac was a hard worker and a fast study. By the end of a single week working alongside Mark David, he had established himself as a valuable crew member. Before long, it was just understood that if Mark was on the boat, Isaac would be with him. The two men formed an entire crew when most other boats were run with three. Isaac became a frequent dinner guest at the David house, and by the end of his first summer working on the boat, he had a regular place at the table and was in trouble if he ever skipped a meal.

For Christmas that year, Isaac was gifted one of the company pickup trucks as his first vehicle. Twenty-three-year-old Hayes David, recently elected as the youngest mayor in Florida history, took time away from his duties at the city to teach Isaac to drive along the backroads in Sumner and Rosewood. Isaac received his first-ever nickname when Hayes morphed Skipjack into *Skipper*. Because the new name evoked the image of a confident boat captain, a thing Isaac was becoming more every day, a little shot of dopamine would hit his brain anytime someone in the David family addressed him as such. By all accounts, Isaac had found a family and a father where neither had existed before. In a just and reasonable world, it would have gone on like it was forever. Isaac loved and was loved by the Davids. He had improbably sidestepped a near-certain fate, sentenced to him the day his father died in the back of the police truck. There was no good reason, save for God distracted by business elsewhere in the universe—maybe another trifling wager with the devil, double-or-nothing, after Job's faith held ludicrously firm—for it all to have ended the way it did.

At the hardware store, on a Tuesday afternoon as ordinary as a pair of socks, near the PVC pipe on the rack in the fenced side yard, the world revealed its wicked heart. Isaac was there to pick up a load of pipe that would be cut into stakes that held bags of planted clams on the bottom of the Gulf. As he did the mental math to determine how many of the twenty-foot-long pipes he would need to make enough 10-inch stakes for the three hundred bags he and Mark David would be planting later that day, he overheard two older islanders near the baseboard rack joking about his dead father. Of course, they did not know that Isaac was nearby, or they would have never, out of gentility or cowardice, said what they said out loud.

"I hate a thief more than anything," said a small, round man in a high-pitched voice.

"Me too," replied the other, a bigger man with thin lips and eyes set too close together. "Ol' Buddy always seemed alright to me, but when they caught him stealing clams, he got what he had coming."

Both men laughed as casually as if they were joking about a squashed bug.

"Well, he sure won't be stealing anything else," came an effeminate reply. "Mark David made sure of that."

There was insufficient time for Isaac to fully process what he had heard, but the cruelty of the men's laughter hit him like an electric shock. He ran full speed into the man who had evoked the name of Mark David, crashing him hard onto the gravel ground. Isaac swung wildly at the downed man, landing several haymakers to his head and abdomen, and would probably have beaten him to death there if the big man hadn't intervened. His efforts to pull Isaac off his bloodied friend were futile. Isaac only stopped swinging when a hard left hook caught him squarely in the jaw, scrambling his brains and sending him stumbling out of the hardware store toward his truck. As he drove away, his mind replayed what he had heard, over and over again.

A boy with a different upbringing might have taken time to cool off and reason through the feelings that were overwhelming Isaac as he drove angrily around the island. This was not the first time he had overheard people talking about his father. In small towns everywhere, gossip is the gold standard of social currency; everybody from meth heads to Me-Maws in the front pew at church turn spendthrift when they've got a good story burning holes in their pockets. Isaac had always tuned out the whispers, believing, as all sons must, that his father was a good and innocent man.

The episode at the hardware store came at the most damaging of times, on a day when his father's memory was everywhere he went. He felt him first during a visit to the dentist earlier that morning, a final check-up in a months-long process to replace a missing front tooth with an implant. When he asked the dentist how much it had cost, since he knew his father had paid it all upfront, the dentist sidestepped the question. It was the first time he had seen Isaac since his father's death, and he used the opportunity to assure him how much Buddy had loved his son. He wouldn't say the actual amount, but assured Isaac that it represented real effort on his father's part, especially in the lean times on the island following the net ban. When he stopped for lunch at the Big-T restaurant in Chiefland, Isaac sat where he and his father had always sat, remembering the old days when each booth had its own miniature jukebox, and they would sing old country songs together while they waited for their food.

Now, as the blood continued to run from his mouth and the adrenaline began to fade away, a sharp, specific pain in his new front tooth changed the course of his life forever. He knew then, as the new tooth pulsed and stung, that his father had stolen the clams. Worse, he knew why, and he was unable to withstand the emotional overload that followed.

It might not have even mattered to Isaac that Allen Mikes had been the one who administered Buddy's beating, or indeed that Mark's intervention had saved his father from dying atop the clams in the boat. To a son having just had so profound a realization about a lost father, nothing but self-sabotaging rage would suffice. In such a state, Isaac made the unavoidable conclusion that Mark David's kindness all this time was the result of a guilty heart. When he confronted him with what he had overheard at the hardware store, the older man hesitated, and that was all it took to send Isaac running away from the island.

When Hayes and his father found Isaac's truck abandoned on the island side of the Number Four Bridge, Mark David closed his eyes and stood quietly for a long time because he knew his boy was gone for good.

Over the decades that followed, both men would carry the hurt for one another like a faithful vigil. Mark David had no choice but to continue on with being Mark David, and Isaac joined the Coast Guard, becoming a Boatswain Mate, ironically, like the surrogate father he left behind on the island.

On the day the bombs fell, and the old world ended, Isaac was a Senior Chief Petty Officer who found himself suddenly responsible for two dozen young Coasties as they raced away from the destruction of their base in Fort Myers aboard the 87-foot Coast Guard Cutter Sawfish. After a solid year of struggle, the desperation of being responsible for a crew of people he was failing to protect, or even properly feed, turned his thoughts to the one place he knew would have the resources they needed to survive.

With the Sawfish and a flotilla of smaller boats fitted with crude sails, Isaac Skipjack set a course for Cedar Key. There he found the old ghosts right where he left them, and sailed headlong into a two-day war that would stretch from Cedar Key to Suwannee and end with his self-imposed exile in the outlaw river town.

10

WE AIN'T FORGOT

The muddy kayak pulled alongside the Cogency, and Hayes helped the soldier with the white flag climb aboard.

"I wasn't sure you were gonna make it through the mud," Hayes said in a friendly tone.

"No, sir, I didn't either. I've never seen mud like that."

"There ain't no other mud like that," Ryland said gruffly.

The old mayor was taking an amicable approach, but Ryland was on edge. The sight of his mother's kayak turned the normally tranquil younger captain choleric with anger.

"You took that from my mama's house," Ryland said coldly.

"I'm sorry," the soldier replied genuinely. "I didn't mess nothing up. The major sent some of us out scouting to find a way to get here to talk to you."

Hayes interjected, "That's just fine, son. Everything's okay here . . . right, Ryland?"

His normal temperament reasserted itself, and Ryland replied, "Right, Mr. Hayes. We're okay."

The soldier's apprehension seemed to let up a little.

"Where you from?" Hayes asked.

"Arkansas, sir."

"Whereabouts?"

"You probably wouldn't know it. Up in the northeast corner, an hour west of Memphis, Tennessee."

Hayes ventured, "Wouldn't be Jonesboro, would it?"

The soldier's eyes lit up, and he answered excitedly, "Yes, sir . . . I grew up there. How in the hell do you know about Jonesboro?"

"My best buddy Thomas' family, on his dad's side, is from there. I don't know a whole lot about it. I just remember a story he told me about his daddy jumping off the bridge over the Mississippi River, there between Arkansas and Tennessee."

"Did he survive?"

Hayes laughed. "Broke both his ankles and busted an eardrum, but they say he was laughing like a crazy person when they fished him out of the river."

Just then, all four men in the three boats began to feel the weight of the moment as it lingered. Given the existence of an army on one side of the channel and a makeshift navy floating in it, the chit-chat began to feel perverse.

"We best get to it," Hayes said.

"Yes, sir, I guess we should," the soldier replied. "Major Lawrence wants to know the status of General Gill. Has he been detained? Do you intend to cooperate with us?"

"Well, that depends on what you're asking," Hayes replied. "You boys rolled in here threatening us, and now you're asking for cooperation?"

"I can't really speak to any of that, sir. I was sent here to ask you those questions."

The soldier likely did not see it on his face, but the old mayor's strategic magnanimity was being quickly overrun by the anger simmering just beneath his skin.

"Tell your major that our mayor is talking things over with your general now. When they're finished, however that talk goes, good or bad, we'll return the old man to you. You have my word on it. But you can also tell him that if you boys think you're gonna roll over us on this island, he'd better pack a lunch cause it won't happen without a fight."

The soldier made the ill-fated decision to posture. "Respectfully, sir, you can't possibly think you can stop us, right? We're trying to work this out peacefully, but if you don't have the general back to us by dark, we'll come get him."

The old mayor smiled. "They teach you boys to swim up in Arkansas?"

"Of course," the soldier replied.

"Good deal," Hayes said, as he grabbed the younger man by the collar of his uniform and shoved him overboard as gently and easily as rocking a baby in a cradle. "That kayak belongs to Ryland's mama. We're gonna hang on to it. Swim on over to your major and tell him I guarantee the general's safety. We'll return him when we're done talking with him, and not before."

The shock of the cold water washed the piss and vinegar out of the soldier, who turned without additional protest and swam for the muddy shore.

"Holy shit," Gibbs Yardy said.

Ryland Beecham nodded in agreement.

Hayes David, resolute as the President's desk, shrugged his aging shoulders. "Well . . . something's bound to happen now."

The Sawfish cleared the river and sailed into the Suwannee Sound. Isaac Skipjack looked across the glassy, flat water, breathed in the crisp morning air, and sighed contemplatively. Georgie Pilsner stood beside him, taking it all in. After so long on the road, his sudden change of scenery and circumstance had the old professor feeling like Odysseus once again. He had lost his crew in a hopeless stand at a Virginia courthouse, resisted the sirens calling through the barrel of his friend Leo's gun, defeated monsters on the outskirts of Charlotte, ate a meal in the fallen Underworld of Augusta, and was presently completing the final leg of his journey home.

"How did you know the fire was a signal?" Georgie asked the senior chief as they sailed quickly and quietly through the calm water.

Isaac replied, "I don't know for certain that it was, but based on the location the smoke was coming from, I think it's likely. They have the bridge at the Number Four Channel set up to light on fire easily if they need to stop a large force from crossing it. If we see it we know they need help. We keep a bonfire pile set up at the edge of our town as well, in case we ever need to signal for help from the islanders."

"Have either of you ever had to use it before?"

"This is the first time," Isaac replied.

Georgie was confused. "How could they get a concrete bridge to burn?"

Isaac chuckled. "You've been away a long time. It's a new wooden bridge built just a couple of years ago. They blew up the old one soon after all the bombs fell. I think they realized pretty quick that their best chance for survival was to hunker down on the island and keep the rest of the world away."

"Did it work?"

Isaac's calculated exterior buckled at the question, and a flash of distress washed over his face. "Mostly, yes. About a year into it, my crew and I showed up with the Sawfish and a bunch of smaller boats. I'm not sure how I thought it was going to go, but everything went to shit fast, and we ended up slugging it out up the coast. We killed some of theirs, and they killed some of ours."

"I don't understand," Georgie replied. "I thought you grew up there. You said things were friendly between Suwannee and Cedar Key."

Isaac was annoyed at his own lack of composure for allowing this discussion to develop, but he was in it now and made a snap decision to tell it all. "I did. And we are. A couple decades is a long time for wounds to heal and practicality to win out. It just didn't make sense for us not to trade and work together when we could. My medic fell in love with their nurse, and that went a long way to smoothing things over."

Georgie was incredulous. "But why did you fight in the first place?"

"That's a good question. I've had a long time to think about the answer, and I'm no nearer to it than I was when I started. I left the island on bad terms when I was eighteen years old and never looked back until the world ended, and I didn't have any other choice. The past just spilled over, I guess. Maybe it was always going to, but I've regretted it all this time."

Off the port side of the Sawfish, Hog Island came into view, and just beyond that appeared Shell Mound, a semicircular ridge of shell and earth built by Native Americans thousands of years before the first white man ever laid eyes on the area. More than a billion oyster shells were piled up over generations on an ancient sand dune. Isaac marveled at the formation—a pile of Indian table scraps had survived the fall of civilization, when so many of the great wonders of the world had fluttered away as easily as a dandelion in a breeze. Their approach to Shell Mound also meant they were leaving the Suwannee Sound, and Isaac noted the significance.

"Part of the terms of ending our little war was that the Sawfish would never again sail further south than the Suwannee Sound. We're crossing that line about now."

Georgie replied, "Seriously? In twenty years, this is the first time you've been back to the island?"

Isaac closed his eyes for several long seconds as the memories poured in. When he opened them again, he was ready to tell the story.

"I actually do know your friend Thomas," Isaac began. "I mean, I don't know him, but I know who he is. He spoke at Mark David's funeral. It's the only time I've been on the island since I left for the Coast Guard, and I was too ashamed to tell anyone I was there. I paddled a kayak all the way from Suwannee, through the backwaters, and up the channel that runs alongside the part of the cemetery where they keep all their chickens penned up. I stood back in the trees with the chickens and listened to what I could hear over all the damn clucking. I don't guess I've ever felt smaller in my life."

Georgie thought of putting his arm around the senior chief, but couldn't talk himself into it. There was still a good amount of water to cover, and the emotional levee that had heretofore held everything in had already broken, so Isaac just kept talking. He said the whole story out loud, all of it, from the day on the bench by the boat ramp to the day he left his truck and walked across the Number Four Bridge for the last time. When he got to the second day of the war, when he surrendered himself to the island fleet in exchange for medical help for his friend and medic, Petty

Officer Morgan, Isaac could no longer look Georgie Pilsner in the face. He stared straight ahead, into the cold wind, when he told him that it was Mark David who ordered everyone to stand down. It was Mark David who put the dying man in a fast boat and sped away with him to the island's clinic. It was Mark David, he said with a momentary break in his voice, that had returned to Suwannee several months later with Hayes and the old mullet net to go fishing with his sons a final time before he died.

"When the government came for the nets," Isaac said with difficulty, "Mr. Mark refused to give his up. Many years later, he was interviewed by a film crew about the whole ordeal, and I somehow came across that video. I still think about it all the time. It was nearly thirty years after the net ban, and the old man's heart was still broken. He stared into the camera with tears in his eyes and said to the people who had taken away his livelihood, his life:

We won't ever forget it. We ain't forgot it. We never will.

Your friend Thomas, it seemed, had taken up the open spot left when I ran off. You could tell he loved Mr. Mark like I did. He told the story of his life for everyone in the cemetery—all the details of his military service, his work on the water, and everything he had meant to Hayes and Lida Maria and Miss Bette and the whole island. And then he looked over at the body beside the hole his loved ones had dug for him by hand and said:

Mr. Mark, we won't ever forget you. We ain't forgot you. We never will."

The wind blew somber and cold through a hard half beat of silence, and Isaac continued, "I turned away, kicked a rooster square in the face that was coming at me with his spurs, and ran back to the kayak as fast as I could. I paddled back to the river and never could go home again."

Luke Buck locked the general in the Chief's office, grabbed Benji Iverson off the street to guard the door, then walked with his father toward the city park. When they arrived, a crowd of people had gathered around the Blackhawk helicopter. William Buck was standing atop the machine, working a saw for all he was worth into one of the four rotor blades. He made quick progress through the outer layers of fiberglass-reinforced plastic, but when he reached the internal titanium spar, he may as well have been trying to cut stone with a slice of bread.

"Hold up," Jamie Mitchell called from the ground. "I've just about got this blowtorch going.

Thomas walked around the imposing machine, taking it all in. He had never been that close to a military aircraft before and generally just marveled at its engineering. It took some effort, and he knew he would pay for it the next day, but he was able to pull himself up onto the nose of the helicopter and then up to the top near his grandson. He held onto one of the rotors for support and pointed to the place where all four rotors came together and attached to a single cylindrical mast.

"There," Thomas called down to Jamie Mitchell. "If we cut this piece of metal in half, all four blades will just fall off."

"Whoa," the youngest of the Buck men said, as though his grandfather had just cast a spell. "That's so smart."

The old man turned to begin the slow climb back down when his grandson pointed toward the water.

"Over there!" William yelled. "Out in the channel."

The midday sun reflected its light in brilliant bursts against the painted steel of the Coast Guard Cutter Sawfish.

In an instant, the helicopter was irrelevant. Every person in the park turned in the direction of the city fishing pier and moved toward it as quickly as their variously aged and conditioned bodies would allow. Most arrived at the pier fairly simultaneously with the cutter's maneuver to pull alongside and tie off to it. As Thomas, his son, and grandson sprinted down the long pier to meet the boat, they could see its skipper waving from the helm.

"Is that Mr. Isaac?" Luke asked excitedly.

Thomas strained to get a better look. "I'll be goddamned, but I think it is."

"How long has it been?" Luke asked as the man in question walked toward the gangplank his crew was deploying toward the pier.

"Too long, son. It's been way too long."

Thomas ran to the end of the gangplank, intending to greet the prodigal island son with a warm handshake and thank him for coming to answer the signal, but the next image in his field of view, distorted as it was by a quarter century of age and physical transformation, prevented the diplomacy he had meant to undertake with Isaac Skipjack.

"Georgie!" Thomas yelled. He ran full speed past the skipper and toward his first best friend. An onslaught of formative memories overwhelmed them both—the church songs sang with naked girls swimming in phosphate pits, the road trips in the cheap, unreliable cars of their youth, the apartments in the back of the opposing churches, the guitars they couldn't afford and only one of them could play, the weddings and funerals and the whole lives they had lived together in the old world were all as real and present now as if they were appearing before them on the pier.

"How?" Thomas asked.

Georgie wrapped his taller friend in a strong, aggressive hug and held on for all he was worth.

"It's a long story," Georgie said when he finally let go.

Thomas asked, "Hannah and the girls . . . how are they?"

The look on Georgie's face was a dagger.

"Oh, no . . . brother . . ."

"There's a lot to tell," Georgie said with a stoic face. "We've got time."

At last, Thomas turned to Isaac Skipjack and extended his hand. "Welcome home, Isaac. Thank you for coming."

All of the lost years manifested themselves in the intensity of Isaac's silent handshake.

Luke extended his hand as well. "I'm Luke Buck. I took over as mayor when Mr. Hayes retired a few months back."

"I know who you are, Luke. You were on the boat in the river when I brought my friend to you in the raft."

"Yes, sir," Luke replied. "I remember."

"You were just a kid then. And now you're the mayor. God, it's been a whole lifetime."

I guess so," Luke said solemnly.

"I want to hear about all of it," Isaac said. "But right now, what's the situation? How can we help?"

Luke told a truncated version of the story as quickly as he could, giving the skipper and his crew an overview of the threat they were facing.

"Did you say a general?" Georgie stopped him to ask.

"Yes, sir," Luke replied. "We've got him locked in the chief's office until we can sort out what to do next."

"He wouldn't happen to look like he was a thousand years old, would he?" Georgie asked.

Thomas laughed as he replied, "At least a thousand. This joker grew up in the Roman Empire."

The color drained from Georgie's face.

Thomas could see the immediate agitation in his friend. "What's wrong, buddy?"

"Please take me to him."

11

VOICES IN THE STATIC

Once the general's army had been blooded in Virginia, it was hard to get the taste out of their mouths. For the rest of the march back to Fort Rucker, strict discipline was needed to keep the march up to the pace the general demanded. In nearly every town they passed, and certainly when the army would camp for the night, men would slip away to take what they could from the locals. The general was so singularly focused on making it back to the base as quickly as possible that he overlooked the handful of killings and other brutalities happening at the hands of his men, so long as they didn't slow his army down.

General Gill was not a callous or indecent man. He had lived his life by a code of ethics as admirable as any other, and had served his nation honorably and with distinction right up to the end, and for years after that. The events in Harrisonburg should have been enough, on their own, to alert Major Lawrence and others that something was off with their commanding officer. As the bad deeds piled up on the march home, the change in the general's state of mind should certainly have become apparent, but for all the efficiencies stemming from a solid chain of command, something human is lost in the order. The system is built for the center to hold, not for individuals at the periphery to raise concerns about its overall design.

In such a system, extreme courage is required to do anything other than what everyone else is doing, which is almost always what they're told by those higher up the chain.

There was no one higher up the chain now than the general. Even the lionized, Medal of Honor-winning hero of World War II, Douglas MacArthur, he of the *I shall return* fame, had President Truman to relieve him of command when his marbles got squirrelly and he sought to undermine civilian control of the military. General Gill had no Truman, or any President at all, to rein him in. Major Lawrence knew something was different in the general's energy level and intense focus on the mission, but so far had not even begun to question the mission itself. Indeed, he had no real understanding of what it might even be.

When at last the 198th Battalion made it back to Fort Rucker, the general raced for his office, switched on the radio, and stared intensely at it while a steady hum of static flowed toward him. Occasionally, a blip, or a whine, or a skip in the rhythm of the static would send a jolt through the general's face and hands. When Major Lawrence found him there, hours later, it was in a state approaching rapture.

"Good evening, sir," the major announced as he stepped into the office.

"Joshua, I'm glad you're here."

In their almost thirty years together, it was the first time the general had ever called him by his first name. In front of the men, it was always *Major Lawrence,* but in private, sometimes, the general would use the major's last name like it was his first, in an always-strained attempt at camaraderie. The two soldiers had worked well together for a large portion of their adult lives, but as the major took notice of how off-putting *Joshua* sounded coming from the old man, he was acutely aware that they were not now, and had never been, friends.

"The men are settled in, sir. I gave them liberty for the next two days after the long march."

"Fine, fine, Joshua," the general said without looking away from the radio receiver. After a few moments more, he switched off the machine and turned to his subordinate. "Sit down, Joshua. We have a lot to discuss."

Four days later, the general and his army were marching toward the Sunshine State.

They would have left sooner, but it took time to test jet fuel from the several underground tanks that survived the initial blasts of the great war and fill not only the general's helicopter but a few truckloads of 55-gallon drums of the least degraded fuel available. Since the jet fuel that powers the Blackhawk is kerosene-based, it consists of larger, heavier hydrocarbon molecules when compared to the lighter, more volatile ones in standard gasoline. The complex mixture of ingredients and additives in gasoline causes it to oxidize and break down quickly, in as little as several months. Because jet fuel is basically just kerosene, it can be stored for incredibly long periods, especially in modern military storage tanks. Four older diesel troop carrier trucks on the base also ran just fine on jet fuel, with a little oil mixed in for extra lubrication.

When the destruction of those first few days finally ended, three Black-hawk helicopters and a Beechcraft C-12 Huron fixed-wing aircraft had survived at Fort Rucker, but the general was the only remaining living pilot among the 198th. Looking back on it now, he regretted not training others to at least fly the helicopters, but after his first post-war surveillance flight, wherein he surveyed the total destruction of nearby Fort Benning, his heart went out of it, and the general shifted his focus to the fortification and rebuilding of as much of his fort as possible. Two helicopter mechanics had also survived the blast, though one died a decade later of an ailment none of the half dozen medics in the battalion could identify. The other, a first sergeant from Iowa, used two of the Blackhawks for parts to keep a third operational and ready to fly. A few times a year, most years, the general would fly some nominal amount of time to keep his skills somewhat serviceable, but by the time he heard the first of the radio broadcasts that would mobilize his army, he was flying more for nostalgia than for military readiness.

The primary benefit of having the Blackhawk on the march to Florida was obvious. The general was able to scout ahead to make sure the intended route was clear. In practice, it became a cumbersome exercise of short back-and-forth runs that required the army to camp near an open landing spot for the helicopter. On the outskirts of the town of Perry, a loss of hydraulic pressure forced the general down onto US-Highway 19, where he and the three soldiers riding with him had to spend a long night exposed in the open until the main army caught up to them. Once they did, the mechanic with a truck full of parts and tools was able to make the relatively straightforward repair of a kinked hose, keeping the Blackhawk operational for the mission, the chief of which was force projection once the army arrived at its destination. It was the general's hope and expectation that a show of military power would negate the need for another Harrisonburg.

Near Fanning Springs, the general came under relatively heavy small arms fire from a boat on the Suwannee River. Several rounds hit the landing steers, and two blew through the interior of the helicopter, missing the general and the controls by inches before lodging in the left shoulder of a 45-year-old corporal in the adjacent seat. It was the kind of wound that seemed superficial in action movies, but one that bled out the red-haired Michigander before the general made it back to the army and its medics.

The next day, when the army crossed the bridge over the Suwannee River and made it into Fanning Springs, they did so on high alert. In response to the dead corporal, the general gave his men a generally free hand to pillage what remained of the tiny town, and they obliged with enthusiasm.

With multiple sets of eyes on the map and the road ahead, the 198th did not make the same mistake as Georgie Pilsner. They marched directly to State Road 24 and turned right at the little hamlet of Otter Creek. Daylight was fading as they made the turn, so the army decided to make camp on a property with a large field and a handful of circa 1930 buildings that had once served as the Otter Creek School. In the later years of its useful life, the property housed a facility for adults with special needs before closing in the early 2020s due to disrepair. Subsequent to its closing, the school property was purchased by a yankee grifter who made a living as a bottom-tier Internet content creator. He had achieved some fleeting notoriety on the heels of a short-lived cultural phenomenon when America became fascinated with television shows about people buying abandoned self-storage units at auction, seeking treasure and profit. The soft-bellied, loud-voiced provocateur was the perfect embodiment of a culture in decline, delighting in the misfortune of others to expand his profile in an artificial world built on avarice, ego, and societal rot.

When the views for his videos about selling abandoned baseball cards, old coins, and scavenged family heirlooms began to dry up, the flim-flam costermonger moved to Otter Creek and began a series of petty feuds with the locals and the town council which he parlayed into more content for his channel. No artificial sleight or manufactured injustice was too small to hyperbolize into clickbait vignettes that cast the empty-suit mountebank in the role of social reformer. In a world skidding to the precipice of collapse, he was the perfect, pitiful fool, amassing a moderate following of viewers that drove him to increasingly petty lengths in the service of content, content, content. For a time, Levy County seemed to abide the outsider's indecency until, at last, the son of an older lady who was harassed and publicly lampooned by the inutile Ohioan defended his mama with a rope and a cypress tree. He had intended to burn down the old school as well, but gentility got the better of him. His commendable restraint meant the general and his staff now had a roof over their heads as they rested to make a 20-mile push the following morning for Cedar Key.

The army got a start at first light. The long stretch of slash pines and swamp water passed uneventfully, and they made it within a mile of the Number Four Channel by sundown. To preserve some element of surprise the next day, the army made camp in the Cedar Key Scrub State Preserve on the north side of State Road 24. The Blackhawk landed in the center of the road. In his tent that evening, the general went over the plans again with Major Lawrence, this time filling him in on details he had withheld four days prior in his office at Fort Rucker. To this point in the excursion, the major knew the mission was to march into Cedar Key to meet with other elements of the military arriving by water. It was only now that General Gill disclosed they were there to meet a nuclear-powered Nimitz-class aircraft carrier. The information hit the major at an odd angle, but his indifferent expression hid this fact from the general, who talked at great length about radio broadcasts with the verve of an artist and the conviction of an acolyte in service to a higher purpose.

The major lay awake for most of the night while the general slept free and easy.

The last time Georgie Pilsner was in Cedar Key was for the inaugural Cedar Key Shark Swim, an annual charity event organized by his buddy Thomas Buck to raise money for the Cedar Key School. A couple of hundred people were signed up to swim the half mile between the barrier island of Atsena Otie and Way Key, the main island of Cedar Key. Despite bold claims before the swim that he expected to beat the gifted swimmer Thomas, Georgie was nowhere to be found when it ended. It was assumed he had been picked up by one of the rescue boats, like so many others that had tuckered out on their way across the channel. Thomas, who had finished in a respectable ninth place, bested only by collegiate swimmers and seasoned triathletes, was just beginning to announce the winners when a flash of light reflected on the water.

"Wait!" Lida Marie Johnson called out, her half-size-too-small swimsuit moving further into the recesses of her butt as she pointed toward the main channel. "There's somebody out there."

And there he was, dauntless and imperial, commanding the waters and the wind, clinging powerfully to an inflatable unicorn raft and moving with godly gravitas toward the waiting crowd, who, recognizing Neptune in the mortal world, began cheering wildly as he doggie-paddled his vessel toward the shore. When the fever of the swimmers on the shore had pitched near euphoria, Georgie Pilsner slid onto the smooth, wet sand of the shore in the glory and triumph of dead-last place.

It was a memory etched into the island's history, one often retold thereafter in the joy of shared memories among friends and neighbors. In the first year of the new world, as the island faced a crisis of morale that threatened to dismantle the community entirely, the islanders decided to make the swim together again, a frivolity in defiance of a world set against them. Thomas and Hayes were locked in a dead-heat race for first place when once again a glint of light on the water intervened. Thomas stopped swimming, turned toward the light, and was sure he could see his old friend again, paddling toward him for all he was worth. When the light flickered out and the race was lost, Thomas despaired because he felt sure his friend, so close to the nation's capital, was dead.

As the friends now walked side by side from the fishing pier to Big Chief's office to meet the general, Thomas thought of that second light on the water, calling to him as hopelessly as the green light that beckoned Gatsby to Daisy's unreachable dock across the lake. The heaviness of that memory suddenly fell away because his friend improbably lived and had returned to him.

Benji Iverson was sitting outside the door to the chief's office when Georgie and Thomas arrived with the new mayor and Isaac Skipjack in tow.

"Everything good here, Benji?" Thomas asked.

"Pretty quiet," Benji replied, "Once he finally stopped yelling about that stupid helicopter."

"This is my old friend Georgie," Thomas said with a wide, warm smile.

"Shark Swim Georgie?" Benji asked.

"The very same," Shark Swim Georgie replied. He then followed Thomas into the office, saw General Clarence Gill sitting behind the desk, and calmly shot him in the face.

12

YOU CAN GO HOME AGAIN

Lizzy Fraydel refused to age. When she and Thomas Buck first met, passing buckets of water to each other in a long chain of islanders fighting against the Great Fire in the first year of the new world, she looked no different than she did when she was crowned as the Cedar Key School Homecoming Queen for the year 1990. Later, when they had fallen in love and built a life together in the new world, there were frequent jokes about the fact that Thomas would only have been a freshman during Lizzy's senior year. He was sure he would still have courted the ethereal high school royal, and she was sure that a fast-talking freshman had no shot whatsoever, however cute he may have been.

She was right, of course. They each had entirely separate lives to live. Hers manifested a thirty-year marriage to a good man that produced a sturdy Cedar Key son, every bit a confident waterman and captain as he took his late father's place at the helm of the birddog boat that ran the family clam farm. Thomas moved through the world with the ease of flowing water, but found in his life an immovable obstruction when it came to matters of the heart. Three failed marriages had convinced him that a cosmic deal was struck with the Creator or the devil on his behalf, trading heartache for the comfortable charisma that made the rest of his life so easy to navigate.

The path of these two disparate lives crossed at the handle of a bucket that moved water from the Gulf to the fire. Moving water is the animating force of all life on earth; the ocean currents, the ice and dew, the wet flesh of human bodies, the rivers, and the rain move in pattern and in chaos to force life past the trap of quiescence and death. So long as the water moves, life remains.

Water had moved Lizzy and Thomas together, and no force in the firmament or on Earth would ever pry them apart again.

Lizzy was in her garden, planting carrots and broccoli, when she heard a shot ring out in the direction of City Hall. The house she shared with Thomas at the corner of E and 3rd was only two blocks from City Hall, and she knew Thomas and Luke were there with the general. Cedar Key women are, above all else, Southern, which means they are seldom a single thing. A housewife might also be a bowhunter, a quilter, and a brawler. A schoolteacher might spearfish, rabble-rouse on Saturday night, and usher at church on Sunday morning. In Lizzy's case, the homecoming queen was a gardener, a clam farmer, and a rifle-toting demon if anyone threatened her man.

As soon as the shot registered to her as gunfire, Lizzy sprinted from the garden into the house, retrieved her lever-action Winchester, and ran toward the sound faster than a woman in her seventies had any right to expect. On her way, she passed several neighbor women similarly armed and heading for the trouble. The scene at the City Hall building was pandemonium. Everyone seemed to be yelling. Thankfully, Lizzy saw Thomas almost immediately, standing beside his son, who was trying to get the crowd under control.

Dale Warble was unmoored from himself as he screamed *Murder, Murder!* When that mantra began to lose its punch, he switched to *Traitors! Traitors! Traitors!*

The assembled crowd was not privy to most of the goings on since the helicopter landed at the park. They knew the fleet had set sail for the Number Four Channel and the Condition One had been signaled, but so far, no real reports had made it back to the people, aside from the wild story Dale was telling to anyone who would listen.

"Alright, that's enough!" Luke shouted. He climbed atop the four-foot-high brick and granite monument near the front door of City Hall that eulogized the nets stolen by an ill-informed mainland electorate. "We'll sort all this out. I'm calling an emergency meeting of the town council for one hour from now at the gazebo in the city park. I'll tell everyone what we know, what happened just now in the chief's office, and what we're up against at the channel. If we're gonna make it through the rest of this day, it's gonna take all of us working together."

Dale Warble was having none of it. "This is your fault!" he shouted. "They're here to help us, and you're trying to start a war."

William Buck lunged toward Dale, but his grandfather wisely pulled him back.

Luke replied with labored calm, "You'll get a chance to speak your mind at the meeting, Dale. There's a lot you don't know. City park, 2 o'clock, everyone. Put the word out and round up the other council members. Now I've got to talk to Mr. Hayes."

"Yeah, that's right," Dale mocked. "Best go ask the real mayor what to do."

This time, William could not be restrained from defending his father. He pulled free of his grandfather, took two giant strides toward the golf cart king, and thumped him in the nose so hard it knocked him off his feet and onto the concrete.

"Get up!" William shouted.

Dale grabbed at his swelling nose while he scrambled backward and onto his feet. "You all saw that. That big sumbitch hit me!"

The crowd responded as if they had seen nothing, and left to gather others for the meeting while Dale grumbled in slow retreat.

When things began to devolve in front of City Hall in the wake of the general's shooting, Isaac Skipjack returned to the Sawfish and his crew, feeling certain it was best to let Luke and the other islanders sort it all out. He had come to help, and he would be ready when the time came. As the afternoon began to drag on, however, Isaac paced the deck of his boat. Near the bow, he took notice of the missing houses along 1st and 2nd Streets that were taken by the great fire. The empty spaces gave him a line of sight well into the historic district, just far enough to make out the gray and red gable of a house that existed forever in his brain as a monument to a life, and a dream, deferred.

As he observed the David house on the 4th Street hill from so far away, Isaac was suddenly and totally overwhelmed by shame—the same private humiliation he had felt straining to hear Mark David's funeral ceremony back in the trees with all the other chickens. He turned away from the haunting gable and headed for the safety of the Sawfish's pilot house, but stopped short of stepping over the coaming. Against his will and better judgment, his body turned to the gangplank, crossed over it, and started up the hill to the gray and red house.

Isaac Skipjack was sixty-eight years old, still solidly built and honed by the sea into a hardened maritime toughness. He had worked his way through the enlisted ranks of the United States Coast Guard to become a decorated senior chief petty officer. He was a Boatswain Mate by training, the most rugged, demanding, storied rating in the sailing services, responsible for everything from navigation to seamanship to keeping the ship or boat afloat. He had led a crew of refugee Coasties away from the bombs that ended the world, through a costly and heartrending war, and into a new life on the river, and he had done so with the stolid, unflinching resolve of a brick wall. And yet, there he stood in defeat, frozen at the door of an old woman's house—the only building that ever felt like a home to him—gritting his teeth and trying to will an insubordinate hand to knock.

Just as he was deciding to turn and walk away, the door mercifully opened. Kinsey Buck, with her explosion of red hair, piercing blue eyes, and bright, toothy smile, stuck her head out the door and announced with comfortable authority, "Miss Bette says to stop slouching and get in the house. She made soup."

Isaac was eighteen years old when he stepped out of this house for the last time. Stepping into it again, seeing Miss Bette in the kitchen, sent him hurtling through time. Through the kitchen window, he could see the little tool shed where he had confronted Mark David about his father's killing. He would never forget the shock of rough cedar against his face when Mr. Mark threw him hard against the shed wall and pinned him there. He could feel the disrespectful words forming in his mouth again, and even now could see the pain in the powerful waterman's eyes as he offered mercy and a chance to take it all back. Worst of all, he could remember the warm sun on his face when he emerged from the dark shed and into the light of the day he left his family for good.

"Sit down, son," Miss Bette said without looking away from the woodstove. "Supper's ready soon."

Isaac walked a quarter of the way around the large circular table with the spinning lazy Susan in the middle, taking his regular seat as though forty-nine years had not elapsed since the last time it held him. Kinsey took a place across from him, knowing enough to sit quietly and let the moment develop. He was just beginning to take full breaths again when the 93-year-old woman turned and walked toward him with a bowl of redfish chowder. She was shorter than he remembered, but still moved with impossible spryness and was no less adorned with grace and power than when she presided over the big table with every seat full.

Isaac fumbled for words. "Oh . . . Miss Bette, I . . ."

"Hush, child, hush," she said, placing the bowl in front of him and carefully situating a spoon on a crisp white cotton napkin. "You're too skinny. You need to eat."

Isaac stared into the steam rising from the bowl, feeling his heart melting in his chest while he searched in vain for some possible thing to say that might excuse a half-century of inexcusable absence. When Miss Bette returned to the stove to retrieve a bowl for Kinsey, Isaac looked hopelessly toward his tablemate, who could only meekly shake her head.

"I don't know what to do," he whispered in defeat.

"Eat your soup," Kinsey replied. "She started making it the minute she heard your boat was at the pier."

Isaac ate his soup, and eventually the old woman joined them and ate hers as well. The silence at the table began to swallow everyone until finally

Miss Bette looked up from her bowl, smiling through tears she had thus far been able to hide.

"He'd be so happy to know you were home, son."

Senior Chief Petty Officer Skipjack dissolved into the air above the table, and a gangly teenage boy remained in his place, a spoon shaking in his hand and a face flush with regret, humiliation, and joy.

"I'm so sorry. I don't even know how to tell you how sorry I am," Isaac said in a faraway voice.

"No, sir. We'll have none of that," Miss Bette said, regaining her trademark composure. "You're here now."

"I came one other time," Isaac said without thinking. "But you didn't see me. I was too ashamed."

"You must have been," she replied with a wry smile, "to let the chickens gang up on you like that."

"You knew I was there?" Isaac asked in disbelief.

"Silly boy . . . I could barely hear the eulogy over the racket you and the birds were making. The whole island knew you were there."

"Oh," Isaac replied sheepishly.

"And we were all glad of it," she said as she looked toward the empty chair to her left. "Especially him."

Isaac put his face in his hands, closed his eyes, and let the memories in.

When he opened them again, he was eighteen years old on the deck of a clam boat, with a crisp November wind blowing through his hair as Mark David raced to the ramp with an enormous harvest ready for the holiday markets. Every November and December, orders for clams skyrocketed, such that a gold rush spirit imbued the last two months of every year. A farmer could generally sell as many clams as he could harvest for sixty straight days. This was the second or even third harvest of the day for most farmers, and everyone was struggling under the strain of exhaustion and cold.

As they neared the outside boat ramp returning from the Dog Island clam leases, a half-asleep captain of another boat turned suddenly toward them. Mark David reflexively yanked the wheel hard to port, narrowly avoiding being broadsided. When he did, water washed over the gunwales of his birddog, shifting the enormous weight of its cargo hard to one side and rolling the boat over as gently as a sleeping child. It was such a pleasant capsizing that neither captain nor mate recognized it was happening until they were both underwater. At the helm, away from the eighty full bags of heavy clams they had just harvested, Mark David was able to easily swim out from under the boat. Isaac's position near the power roller on the stern meant thousands of pounds of bags rolled over with him, pushing him to the bottom and pinning him there.

The ordeal was so non-violent and serene that Isaac was untroubled, even sedate, as he assessed his predicament. The weight of the bags was so thorough a restraint that his attempts to move registered only as muscle twitches that had no effect on the limbs they were meant to activate. The more ineffective his efforts proved, the more Isaac, waveless and tranquil, let go. It's true he could hold his breath a long time, with some on the island even suggesting he could challenge the infamous sponge diver Jud Bollins in a contest, but even a practiced breath holder feels the burning in their lungs when the air runs low.

Isaac never did.

As he settled into the soft, eternal mud, the faint yellow-green glow of the autumn sun—diffused through tannins from the rivers and un-told billions of Earth-sustaining phytoplankton—called Isaac to amniotic placidity and revealed his father walking along the bottom of the Gulf toward him.

Buddy Skipjack, unblemished and smiling, knelt in the mud.

"It's okay, son. I'm here."

At the surface, Mark David called out, but there was no Isaac. He dove under and searched for the boy for a full minute until his lungs were burning. After a quick, desperate breath at the surface, he dove again, this time making out of a pair of feet under a pile of clam bags. He pulled away bag after heavy bag until his breath and strength were spent. On the way back up to catch another breath, Mark despaired, feeling sure that too much time had passed.

"Down here," Mark shouted at the captain and crewmen of the other boat, who had been searching the water as well. "He's pinned under the bags."

For a moment, a boy with no father had two, loving him in equal, opposite measure, one calling him home to rest, the other fighting to pull him back into the joy and horrors of life.

When at last Isaac was freed, lying blue and lifeless on the deck of the other captain's boat, he could hear his father's voice calling still from the water and the wind.

For the rest of Isaac's life, after Mark David's Coast Guard training resuscitated him, coughing and pained, back into the living world, he would sometimes close his eyes and try to summon his father again. Occasionally, a man would appear, dressed in the clothes and face of Mark David, full-throated with Buddy Skipjack's voice, saying, "It's okay, son. I'm here."

The rough gravel of that voice was in his ears again when Isaac opened his eyes to a smiling old woman bringing him a second bowl of soup.

13

ANCIENT CHEMISTRY

Major Joshua Lawrence sat next to a fire outside his tent, waiting for word from his scouts. Since the general left in the Blackhawk earlier that day, the busy work of army camp life did little to relieve the stress of waiting for his return. The major had been opposed to such a garish display of force as the opening salvo of their interactions with the residents of the island. He had strongly advocated a small contingent of officers walking across the bridge to meet with town leaders, but the general was fixated on a shock-and-awe approach with the helicopter.

The poor sleep and long night reflecting on the general's state of mind let exhaustion creep up on the major as the day wore on. Over many years, the general had earned the trust and admiration of his officers and men such that Major Lawrence felt disloyal indulging doubts about his commanding officer and the mission. Still, only one man had ever heard the broadcasts that ordered the army to the march. Why had he not shared them with his executive officer? And there were only eleven aircraft carriers in the U.S. Fleet; even an Army man knew that. What were the odds that one of these was missed by the enemy when so much of the rest of the nation he had seen was destroyed? No tangible thing had occurred that was sufficient to undercut the general's credibility, but the major continued to wrestle with small details from the previous few months that nagged at his comfort. The fact remained, however, that General Gill was singularly responsible for the survival of the entire army, the major included. For this reason alone, the mission would continue. A scuffle between two of his men pulled the major's attention away, and he was glad to be distracted from his thoughts.

It was easier to soldier than it was to lead.

After the fight was broken up and both men had been reprimanded, shouting came from the ranks nearest the channel. Someone was swimming toward them. By the time the wet and freezing soldier made it across the channel and mud flats to the camp, his lips were blue, and his mind was rattled. Major Lawrence led him to the edge of his campfire and called for blankets.

"What happened, son? Are you hurt?" the major asked with genuine concern.

"I'm just cold, sir. I'll be fine."

The midafternoon sun had turned its back on the day and was beginning a race to the horizon. The temperature had reached its zenith, a crisp forty-eight degrees in a light breeze—cold enough to make the soldier's swim a miserable affair.

"What did you find out? What's the status of General Gill?" Major Lawrence asked.

"It was an older captain on the big boat that seemed to be in charge. He said they were talking to the general and would return him when they were finished.

The major's tone sharpened. "Did he say when that would be?"

The soldier's shivering was letting up.

"No, sir, just when they were done talking to him, but the head guy gave his word. I told him the general needed to be back here by sundown or we would come get him."

"I didn't tell you to say that," the major snapped.

The soldier fumbled his reply. "Yes, sir, I just . . . well, I wasn't sure they were taking me seriously and I—"

"You forced our hand," the major interrupted. "And maybe provoked a conflict we could have avoided."

"I'm sorry, sir. It just kind of came out. But they've got no right to hold him."

The major walked back his reprimand. He knew how much the men loved the general. "It's fine, son. I know you're just worried about the old man. I am, too. I'm sure they'll bring him back shortly."

"Yes, sir. Even when that captain was throwing me out of the boat, he was decent about it."

The major smiled briefly and then sighed long and heavy. "Just out of curiosity, what did he say when you told him we'd come get the general?"

"He said we'd better pack a lunch, sir."

"Very good," the major replied with a chuckle, before patting the soldier on the back and walking away.

While Thomas and Georgie waited in the E Street Library, catching up on a quarter century of missed time and keeping a low profile until the emergency meeting, Luke and his son William ran to the channel together.

The younger man pushed the pace a shade faster than his father could comfortably handle. By the time they arrived several minutes later, Luke was winded but determined. He sent his son to brief Big Chief and Rolf, with instructions for Rolf to hold the line and Big Chief to head to the park for the meeting. When William set out for the Croft's house, Luke blew an orange plastic whistle in a succession of three sharp blasts until Hayes finally saw him waving from the shore. Ryland Beecham and Gibbs Yardy maintained their position in the center of the channel as Hayes turned the *Cogency* and began an angled sail toward the new mayor.

"What's the word?" Hayes called out as he pulled up to the shore.

"All hell has broken loose," Luke replied in a slowing pant from the hard run.

"You've only been gone a few hours," Hayes replied.

"They've been eventful," Luke said with a little smirk that undersold the gravity of the situation. "Isaac Skipjack arrived in the Sawfish. It's tied up to the big pier."

Hayes was pleased. "I was hoping it was clear enough for him to see the signal. They here to help?"

"They are," Luke replied. "He brought a handful of other boats as well. But here's the wild part . . ."

"Oh boy," Hayes said flatly.

"Georgie Pilsner was with him."

"Shark Swim Georgie?" Hayes asked, with a kind of joyful disbelief in his tone.

"Yes, sir. My dad just about lost it when he saw him coming down the gangplank of the Sawfish."

"How did he end up with Isaac?"

"I think he took a wrong turn trying to come here and ended up in Suwannee."

Unease began to pry its way into the interaction because both men knew Luke had not run this far to talk about Georgie's return to the island.

"Well, get on with it," Hayes said. "What kind of hell has broken loose?"

Luke took a second to consider how to tell the story. "Well . . ."

"Just spit it out, Luke."

"I guess Mr. Georgie thought he might know the general we've got locked up in Big Chief's office. He didn't tell us how he knew him at first... just asked to go see him. He was calm as can be about it, and I didn't see any reason not to take him. I figured if he did know the general, he might be able to talk some sense into the old coot."

"Oh hell," Hayes said, perceiving the thunderclap that was about to come.

"My dad opened the door to the office and went in. Mr. Georgie walked in behind him, and without saying a word, pulled out his pistol and shot the general square in the forehead, deader than shit."

For the first time in their many years together, Luke saw a moment of unguarded distress in the old mayor's face. A less astute observer might have missed it, but Luke had inherited his father's hyper-observant nature when it came to the micro-expressions and mannerisms that make up human interactions. For a shadow of a half second, Hayes David was unsteady, and it hit Luke like a Kabuki-Kick to the groin.

The old mayor righted his internal ship as quickly as it had swayed off course. "Well," he pondered out loud, "we won't be able to stop a fight now. I gave my word to the folks across the channel that we'd return the general safely, no matter what happened."

"Oh," Luke replied, ashen-faced and slow. "That's a problem."

"There'd be no reason for them to deal with us in good faith now."

Luke said, "For what it's worth, I'm convinced they're here to do us harm no matter what."

Hayes nodded at Luke's analysis. "I'm pretty sure I agree, but what makes you think so?"

"I believe Mr. Georgie. Just after shooting the general, he told us about how the army out there destroyed his hometown back in Virginia. He says they killed almost everyone he knew and took everything they could get their hands on."

"Well, that makes some sense at least," Hayes replied. "And you think they are here to do the same to us?"

Luke nodded. "I do. But there's more to it than that. The general told us a wild story about radio broadcasts from the government that ordered him to march his army here to meet the Navy."

Hayes furrowed his brow. "The Navy?"

Luke continued, "Yes, sir. He said they were supposed to meet an aircraft carrier in the shipping channel."

"An aircraft carrier?" Hayes asked incredulously.

Luke added, "A nuclear-powered aircraft carrier."

"But that's not even . . . never mind. I've heard enough. We need to get the council together."

"I'm already on it," Luke replied with some pride in his voice. "We're meeting in the park in an hour. I came here to get you for it."

Nearby at the old Crofts house, Big Chief's militia continued their fortification work, but they had already made significant progress in converting the lush green yard and yellow two-story house into a dug-in fortress.

They might still be overrun when it came to it, but not without a costly fight.

Rolf and Big Chief were on the porch of the house when William arrived.

"Hey y'all," William said, as cheerfully as if it were Christmas morning and there was no army across the channel. More than anything else, the youngest of the Buck men was a joyful man. His life in the new world had been lived surrounded by the love of his parents and grandparents, and an island community whose lives were linked inexorably together. The Gulf provided almost everything he needed to survive, and the adventure that made him so effortlessly happy. He was unmatched as a fisherman by anyone in Cedar Key, and could hold his breath underwater longer than anyone, save for his uncle Jud. If there was a stronger brute of a creature anywhere in Levy County, no one from the island had ever met them. Because William Buck had no memories of the old world, there was nothing about it for him to miss, and no lingering post-modern malaise to weigh him down. He was formed from the water, birthed into it, and nourished by the prominent role it played in his life.

The three friends hugged, and William told them about the situation.

"Shark Swim Georgie really killed him?" Rolf asked in disbelief.

"Yes, sir," William replied. "You ain't gonna be able to use your office for a while either, Big Chief. It'll take some doing to clean up the mess."

Big Chief was more concerned with the implications of the killing than its physical reality. "That settles it then," she said. "They're coming. It's just a matter of when. We have to step up our efforts here."

Rolf agreed. "I'll get some fellas to roll Mr. Crofts' old truck and his wife's car out to the road to make another barricade. We need shooters along the ridgeline of the roof of this house, down in the mangroves, and in every hole we can dig before they come."

William added, "It'll have to wait till high tide later tonight, but we need the Sawfish and its big guns out there in the channel."

"Absolutely," Big Chief replied. "And I'll put a dozen of my guys on it with rifles."

"My dad wants you to come to an emergency meeting now in the park," William said to Big Chief.

"I don't think I should leave the line," she protested.

"The meeting's liable to go sideways," William continued. "He said he needs the chief there in case it gets out of hand."

"Shit, okay," Big Chief said.

"There's a group thinking we should just let the army on the island," William replied.

"Surrender?" Rolf asked disdainfully. "Bullshit we surrender," he answered himself. "I promise you'll I'll be dead before the first one of those fuckers sets foot on the island."

Big Chief replied, "I gotta admit I was worried how you would react to the army being here, Rolf . . . since you spent so much of your life in that uniform."

"That was a long time ago," the old soldier replied. "A long time of them not doing shit for us. The only army that matters now is on this side of the channel, and we've got more work to do to get ready for the fight. Head on back, y'all. I'll keep things moving here."

As casually as if they were discussing the weather, battle plans were being laid for a war that seemed certain now to come. A familiar fire stoked in Rolf's belly. He felt a raw, uncomfortable energy pumping in his chest. His mind was sharp and clear. Two decades of peace had been good for the island, but smothering to the old soldier. In the old world, the conveniences of modern life and the lack of danger and high calling in the daily routines of men had slowly worn away the masculine purpose that made them essential. Men became increasingly interchangeable with robots, artificial intelligence, and women, such that the ancient chemistry of their sex and the wild calling in their hearts was beaten out of them by polite society.

The army across the channel might yet destroy the island, but it had set the Angel of Death free.

14

ROUGH GRACE

Heff Webster had a family tie to Cedar Key, but he wasn't from there. His grandmother had married into an old island family and ended up with a grand Victorian house on 4th Street when her husband died. After a career in the Marines, Heff eventually found his way to the island, where he started a small roasted nuts company that he ran out of one side of a duplex on Gulf Boulevard, just down from the school. Heff absolutely loved nuts. He roasted the nuts himself and delivered them to shops around the island. Over time, he began doing a fair amount of business in nuts on the Internet and on a weekly delivery route throughout the Big Bend region of Florida. Before long, Heff became the Nut King from Perry to Chiefland to Homosassa.

The Nut King was a fit and competent man, but officious in the way many military men come to be after a long career in the service. The order and rigid hierarchy of the military doesn't always translate in the civilian world, especially in the wilds of Cedar Key. Heff's meticulous taskmaster approach was often at odds with an island culture built on individualism and rugged informality. He had a hawkish face and stern, deep-set eyes offset by a smile that was friendly and out of place. Within a single interaction, he could be warm and light, even funny, and somehow still imposing and unsteadying to those around him. This vague charisma was occasionally winning. He had been on and off the city council many times in the old world and the new, finding a solid base of support from a subset of the population, and fierce opposition from others. There were some crossovers, but in general, his base tended to be comprised of transplants and yankee ex-pats, with his most virulent opposition coming from the watermen and generational residents of the island.

To Heff's credit, whenever he was on the council, he took it seriously and showed up anytime there was work to do. The fact that he faced near constant pushback on his city initiatives stemmed from a military bearing that was easily perceived as condescension. Despite his polarizing nature, the Nut King had been reelected to the town council after a long absence in the same election that made Luke Buck mayor. The two leaders were as diametrically opposed as Caesar and Pompey, despite their cordiality at council meetings.

This cordiality would not last.

The other four members of the city council were already gathered at the gazebo in the city park when Luke made it back from the channel with his son, the old mayor, and Big Chief Hallie. A large crowd of islanders was assembled in a semicircle under the shade of the trees in the park, waiting for the meeting to begin. Thomas and Georgie stood quietly on the periphery of the crowd, while Dale Warble paced nervously nearby. The hulking Blackhawk helicopter sat ominously in the rear of the proceeding, no less intimidating in the soft afternoon sun than it had been when it first roared into the park. The presence of the terrible machine reminded everyone of the immediacy of the threat they were facing.

Luke took his place in the middle chair of the town council, flanked by two other members on each side, and said, "Pastor Willy, could you lead us in a prayer to open the meeting?"

The pastor's church had burned down in the Great Fire in the first year of the new world, but he and his congregation wasted little time converting a nearby surviving house into a new sanctuary. In short order, the church's worship services and Bible study continued, along with its service to the community. This trait had always been a hallmark of the Cedar Key Baptist Church, a fulfillment of Christ's instructions in the parable of the sheep and goats to feed the hungry and clothe the poor, instructions so often and regrettably overlooked by other congregations across a multitude of denominations in modern Christianity. In the old world, some fuss had been made, mostly in bigger cities, about prayers before government meetings violating the separation of church and state principle, but the Supreme Court ruled legislative prayer to be a permissible tradition, even if it was sectarian in nature. In Cedar Key, as in most other small Southern towns, the tradition was never in any danger of not continuing.

"Heavenly Father," Pastor Willy began as the crowd bowed their heads and closed their eyes, "we come to you today to ask for your grace and guidance in this, our hour of need. An army is amassed at the channel. Our small navy has sailed to meet it. If there are battles to come, we pray for your protection and favor, and for your wisdom and guidance to prevail. In your son's holy name, Amen."

Amen came the collective reply.

"Bullshit," Dale Warble yelled just after. "It's too late for God's wisdom now."

Luke replied in a stern but calm tone, "Dale, I told you that you'd get a chance to speak, and you will, at the appropriate time. After I lay out the threats and details as I see them, we will have a time for public comment, then the council will decide how we proceed based on the public's input. If that's not okay with you, then run on home and let the grownups handle the tough business."

Heff Webster chimed in, "I certainly don't see the necessity for your tone, Luke."

Luke replied instantly, "Feel how you'd like about it, Heff. Dale said our prayer was bullshit. I feel differently. He wants to take charge of this meeting, and I don't intend to let him. We'll run this meeting like all the others. Everyone will be heard."

"Let's get on with it then," Councilwoman Jonie Bartholomew said matter-of-factly.

Luke Buck stood from his chair and moved closer to his assembled neighbors so he could be heard more clearly. "I'll start by telling you everything I know, so we are all on the same page with the facts. Earlier this morning, that helicopter you see behind you was flown here by a man named General Clarence Gill. He said he was from Fort Rucker, Alabama, and was here with news about the war. He also informed me that he had men waiting at the Number Four Bridge for orders. Just as he and I began talking, we saw smoke rising in the sky from the direction of the bridge. I later learned it was Rolf who had initiated the Condition One signal and set the bridge on fire when an army of soldiers began to cross it. There are one thousand and twenty-four soldiers in that army, and they appear to be well trained and well-armed."

Audible gasps could be heard throughout the crowd.

Luke continued, "They have trucks with them carrying gear, and they're currently gathered on the mainland side of the Number Four Channel, just down from Leanna Beecham's place. We detained the general while we mobilized the fleet and sailed to meet the army. As we speak, the fleet patrols the channel, and Big Chief's militia has begun to dig in at the old Crofts house. Rolf has taken charge of that effort with the military precision we have come to expect from the Angel of Death. Isaac Skipjack responded to the Condition One and sailed the Sawfish from Suwannee to help."

Dale Warble, emboldened by a talk with Heff Webster before the meeting, and a developing alliance only the two of them knew about, shouted, "Tell everybody who else was on the Sawfish. Tell them what he did!"

Luke replied dispassionately, "I'm telling everything I know, and it'll happen a lot quicker if you can get a handle on yourself and pipe down until it's your turn."

"Sit your ass down, Dale, for Christ's sake," came a voice from the crowd.

Luke continued, "The general told us he had heard radio broadcasts from the United States government, ordering his men to Cedar Key to meet up with the United States Navy."

The crowd and even some of the other council members raised voices of disbelief, excitement, and shock in unison.

"There's more," Luke announced. "He said his orders were to meet a nuclear-powered aircraft carrier in our shipping channel."

The words were so outrageous, so far removed from anything anyone gathered there had expected to hear, that the net effect was a general silencing of the crowd.

"That was all he had to say about it. He then told me directly that if we do not allow the army onto the island, he would take it from us to continue his mission."

Finally, the island spirit broke through, and the undertones of resistance, always such a prominent part of the culture, could be heard in the grumblings.

"In response to this threat, I instructed my son William and others to round up saws and Jamie Mitchell's blowtorch and cut the rotors off that helicopter so it couldn't be used against us. I made that decision in the moment, without the counsel of anyone, because I believed it to be immediately necessary. We were having some trouble cutting through what Jimmy Mitchell says is titanium when the Sawfish appeared in the bay, and we all ran to meet it."

By now, Luke had the unwavering attention of every person in the park. There are few times in life when a moment is recognized as monumental while it's happening, but everyone seemed to feel the weight of what they were hearing.

"Before we get to the most serious part of the story," Luke said as he looked toward his father and Georgie Pilsner, "I need to tell you what I just learned at the channel first. While Mr. Hayes was patrolling the channel, the army sent a soldier in a kayak, flying a white flag, to ask about their general. Mr. Hayes told him we were talking with him, but gave his word we would return him when we were finished. The soldier then made what was either a threat or a warning and said that if we didn't bring him back by sunset, they would come get him. Is that how it all happened, Mr. Hayes?"

"It is," the old mayor said in a somber tone. "Best go ahead and tell the rest, Luke."

The cold air of late afternoon, which minutes before pricked at the skin and demanded attention, was muted now by the heat of the moment. Thomas put his arm around his childhood friend, and both men looked toward Luke with loving wonder. The little boy they both so loved, the one that had fought so courageously to live in the weeks after his birth with a congenital heart defect, the mischievous teenager that was half again too smart for his own good, the young captain who fought bravely in and on the dark waters of the Suwannee in the early years of the new world was a full-grown man now in every respect, standing before his neighbors in the face of unreasonable difficulty because the island needed him.

"Mr. Hayes won't be able to keep his word," Luke said.

The few seconds of silence that elapsed as he formulated his next sentence ticked by in geologic time as four hundred minds in the city park tried to work out how that could possibly be.

"Because Thomas and his buddy murdered him!" Dale Warble shouted.

"What?" Thomas said.

This time, Dale would not receive a gentle reprimand from the mayor.

Lizzy Fraydel sprinted toward the man in the backward hat and swung her elbow into his face with every micronewton of force her slight frame could produce. It made contact at the bridge of his nose, which split open instantly in a dazzling burst of crimson, while a ragged gash opened in the once and always homecoming queen's arm. Dale began to collapse, and Lizzy was upon him before he hit the ground, clawing and striking at his face, as their blood mixed together in the exchange. It took Thomas and Georgie to pull her away, both of whom took minor damage in the effort.

Heff Webster leaped to his feet, shouting, "Arrest her, Big Chief. That's assault!"

No one had ever been arrested in the new world, and Big Chief didn't seem inclined to start a precedent.

"It wasn't Thomas," Georgie yelled above the commotion. "It was me. I shot the general, and I'd do it again."

Everything seemed to stop. Dale stemmed the flow of his blood with a shirtsleeve. Lizzy fell away from her rage and sat calmly on the ground. Heff Webster retook his seat. Even the breeze seemed to sputter as all eyes turned to the brick outhouse of a man with the hillbilly Merlin beard.

"Do with me as you will," Georgie said. "But I promise I did you a service when I fired that shot. The dead general led that army at your channel into my hometown of Harrisonburg, Virginia, exactly eighty-three days ago, and used it to kill everybody I knew on Earth outside of this island. The bombs took my family on the first day of the big war. That piece of shit in the chief's office took everybody else. And for nothing. Because we were blocking the road they wanted to travel—our road. After they killed us, they tore apart our town as they marched away. I'm only still alive because they thought I was dead with the rest of the guardsmen who tried to hold the line. Once they were gone, I started walking this way while Harrisonburg was still burning, because the only human beings still alive who know my face are here in this park."

Georgie looked across the silent crowd, indulging in a brief scattershot of the happy memories he had made with many of the people there assembled, and peace descended upon him.

"Thomas had no part in the general's death. It happened from my hand alone, and I submit to the will of this council's judgment. Whatever the price, I'd pay it twice and do it over again with a clear heart."

In the candor of defeat, Georgie Pilsner radiated power, the picture of verisimilitude and the rough grace that can only come from spilled blood.

Even Dale Warble, in his humiliation, believed him.

Heff Webster could feel the tide of the meeting turning and stood to his feet in opposition.

"Even if all of that is true," Heff said in the stilted enunciation of performative leadership, "it doesn't preclude the possibility that the army across the channel is still, in fact, the American Army. Our Army. Are we not still Americans? Whatever trouble there was in Virginia, however that all happened . . . and how could we ever really know . . . if there's a chance the nation is still alive, are we really prepared to stand in its way?"

The emotional charge was draining away from the crowd, but Heff still had their attention. Turning to the diminutive councilwoman Norma Birder sitting to the right of the mayor, he said, "What would your dad say, Birdie . . . if he knew that one day we'd be having a meeting to decide whether or not to oppose the Army he fought so bravely for in the jungles of Vietnam? And those photographs on the wall of the hardware store, all those generations of island servicemembers that stood on our behalf in wars around the world . . . what would they say? My great-grandfather gave the last full measure of his devotion on a beach in Normandy, and I know he's rolling over in his grave right now."

Heff's words were somehow hollow and weighty at the same time. Had they not been diluted by twenty-five years of abandonment, spoiled by the rank negligence that helped to kill the world, the big ideas he sought to leverage would have overwhelmed a people as patriotic as the islanders he was trying to influence. As it was, they were hit or miss. Certainly, those of William's generation, all born after the fall, were immune to an appeal for a world they had never known. Even those around Luke's age, who had come of age in the full bloom of America's decline, found it hard to remember parts of the old country that could outshine the new lives they had crafted from its ashes.

The demographics were in Heff Webster's favor, however. The island birth rate was significantly lower than it had been in the old world, for a variety of pragmatic reasons, and Cedar Key had always trended older than the mainland. This put a solid majority of the population in the age range of those who had lived their formative years, and much of their adult lives, in the cradle of American splendor. For them, the big ideas were spiritual doctrine; the history and even the apocryphal myths of America were written on their hearts while rockets glared and bombs burst in the air above the unassailable ramparts of a nation favored by God Almighty.

There were no public comments. Even Dale Warble stayed silent. All the words that seemed to matter had been spoken. Heff called for a council vote on whether or not to let the army onto the island so they could wait for the Navy to arrive.

Luke Buck was the mayor, but as a member of the council, he possessed the same singular vote as the other four members. He had respectfully held his tongue while Heff made his case for capitulation, but he could no longer.

"You can't be serious, Heff. If we let them onto the island, they'll overrun us like they did Mr. Georgie and his neighbors."

Heff evoked the sniveling of parliamentary procedure. "We have a motion on the floor for a vote, Mr. Mayor. If you'd like additional discussion of the matter, we will need a motion to table the vote and another to reopen discussion."

Luke stared into the face of his rival, seeing the reanimated, cowering corpse of Nevil Chamberlain, and shook his head ruefully. "I vote against surrender. I vote to fight for our home. I vote for the island."

"So, that's a no then, Mr. Mayor?"

"You're goddamn right it's a no."

Jonie Bartholomew, whose family had been on the island as long as the Davids, did not unfold her hands or change her stoic demeanor as she said, "I vote no."

Karen Sherridan, who had lived in the two-story Craftsman-style house next door to Heff Webster since arriving from New Jersey two years before the flash, said so quietly that few could hear, "If there is a chance the government still exists, we have to do our part to help. I vote yes."

"I vote in the affirmative," Heff said in ministerial formality.

All eyes shifted to Miss Birdie. With the vote thus far tied, she fidgeted in obvious distress at the prospect of casting the deciding vote. "I'm not sure I can make this decision."

Heff replied, "You were elected to the council to make decisions. Yes or no, Norma?"

"I'll vote when I'm good and ready, and I'm not ready," Miss Birdie announced.

While an apoplectic Heff Webster paced angrily around the gazebo, Hayes David spoke up. "Maybe I can help, Miss Birdie."

"Order, order," Heff shouted back. "Public comment has ended. The councilwoman will cast her vote now."

Miss Birdie replied sharply, "I will not. If Hayes David has something to say, I want to hear it."

"You are out of order, councilwoman. Mr. David is out of order. The vote will continue."

As though Heff had not spoken at all, Hayes called out to the crowd. "How deep is our shipping channel?"

"High or low tide?" asked Little Chief Johnson.

"On the biggest king tide you've ever seen, how deep is the shipping channel, at its deepest point?"

"Maybe twenty-five feet, tops," answered Johnny Palasis, the former property manager turned mullet man.

Ian Rock, the aging waterman who still looked like Aquaman in his physical potency, added, "Even with a big tide, though, there are some parts that won't be any deeper than sixteen or eighteen feet."

Hayes' encyclopedic knowledge of ships underpinned the authority in his voice as he announced, "The average draft of a Nimitz-class aircraft carrier is 38 feet, loaded with gear and crew. Flat empty, it still needs 35 feet of water to float. No aircraft carrier is coming down the shipping channel. Even if it was deep enough, a blue water ship would never make it past Seahorse Reef to get to it. There is no more a United States Navy on the way to Cedar Key than there is an American Army at the channel. Those soldiers may be dressed the part . . . maybe they even used to be our Army, but not anymore. None of this makes sense."

No one holds elected office for fifty-one years if the community they serve doesn't fundamentally believe in them. Hayes David had his detractors, mostly folks with personal envy or some gripe unrelated to the man himself, and even a handful who irrationally hated him, but there were none among even these who doubted his integrity.

"I believe Shark Swim Georgie, and I think you should, too," Hayes continued. "And believe me when I tell you that I wanted to believe in the army out there. A part of me still needs to believe in America. You're going to think I'm making this up, but remember how we all had to sing *My Country 'Tis of Thee* in elementary school music class?"

Looks of recognition and nodding heads spread through the crowd.

"I always loved that song," Hayes said with a big, genuine smile. "It might even be my favorite. I catch myself singing it all the time, even now. *Sweet land of liberty, of thee I sing* . . . it just feels good to think about.

Especially in Cedar Key, where the folks who came before us are still such a part of how we live, the *land where my fathers died, land of the pilgrim's pride,* is a hard idea to turn loose of. But we've got to. It's long past time, no matter how much we miss it. I miss America like I miss my father, but this island is my country now. You are all my countrymen. Even you, Heff, you stuck-up dang fool. But you're on the wrong side of this, I promise. If we let that army onto the island without a fight, we'll lose it forever."

The old mayor's words landed like a bomb in the park, forcing his friends and neighbors to confront things they knew to be true but did not want to accept.

Heff was undeterred, announcing with calculated indifference, "If there is nothing further . . . Miss Birdie, are you ready to vote?"

"I'm not," the old woman said with a trembling of her voice that somehow evoked strength rather than indecision. "I'm sorry, Hayes. I think you're probably right about all of it, but I won't be the deciding vote that leads to violence. I just can't. I abstain."

Heff Webster intimidated, cajoled, and even pleaded, but to no avail. Miss Birdie had made up her mind. Deadlocked, the meeting adjourned, but most of the crowd lingered in the park. The various factions of the debate gravitated naturally together to discuss the way forward as the last of the day slipped quickly way.

At sunset, percussive booms and shrill whistling pierced the quiet evening as artillery rounds began to fall around the island, laying waste to everything they hit.

15

BAREFOOT AMONG THE DEAD

While the vote at the emergency council meeting was happening, Ryland Beecham was gutshot and dying alone on his mother's peninsula.

Gibbs Yardy had tried to stop him from going, but Ryland could not be moved. Every time he looked at the kayak on the deck of the Cogency, he grew more enraged at the thought of soldiers on the homestead his mother had meticulously designed and built. His head and heart were flooded with memories of family gathered beneath the shade of the giant oaks, singing around the firepit, netting mullet from the dock, eating extravagant meals together at the enormous handmade mahogany dinner table in the house. By the time he reached the dock behind the house, Ryland was immersed in the warmth of memories and energized by rage.

He moved quietly toward the outside staircase that led up to the main floor of the elevated house, crawled up it to keep from being seen if there were any soldiers remaining on the property, and slipped quietly into the side door. Just as Ryland was about to pass through the kitchen and into the living room with the enormous panoramic windows that offered a breathtaking view of the water on three sides, a behemoth of a soldier stepped around the corner and bumped into him. Both men were caught by surprise, and time seemed to melt into the marble tile floor as the synapses in both brains fired an all-hands warning to bodies that were briefly paralyzed before bursting into the desperate movement of survival. The soldier was easily a half foot taller and fifty pounds heavier than the lean waterman into whom he flung himself. Ryland let out a miserable wheezing sound as he hit the hard tile. It took the full capacity of his neck muscles to keep his head from smashing into the floor. The force of the collision was so great that it bounced the giant off the smaller man, headfirst into the custom oak cabinets Leanna Beecham had imported from Italy. The soldier's few seconds of disorientation as he tried to pull his head from a cabinet full of soup pots were enough for Ryland to get to his feet, scramble to grasp a Tora Tsuki Japanese cleaver knife from its magnetic holder near the stove, and swing it wildly at his adversary. The soldier, an Arizonan whose parents had immigrated from Argentina, had made it up onto all fours and was just beginning to back out of the cabinet when the heavy carbon steel blade chopped into his hindquarters, driving deep into the wrinkled asterisk of his asshole. It wasn't a fatal blow, but it was completely debilitating. In the uncontrollable spasm of his body's response, the soldier flipped unfortunately over in his agony, pressing his full weight onto the ten-inch blade adorned with elegant scroll work in the shape of a menacing tiger.

Ryland crawled toward his gun that had been thrown across the kitchen in the collision, slid the last few feet to grab it, and fired two fast rounds into the screaming, impaled soldier. A final, punctuated scream rolled into a soft whimper, then a faint clearing of the throat, and finally an almost prayerful silence.

The quiet reprieve was temporary.

The sound of the two shots from the .45-caliber Springfield brought a line of soldiers onto the long, canopied drive to the house. When Ryland saw them coming, he raced for the gun cabinet in the hall closet, entered the code to the mechanical lock, and retrieved a bolt-action .308 Ruger American rifle. Most bolt-action rifles of this style feature a three to five-round magazine, but this model held ten rounds, and the Beechams always kept three additional magazines full and at the ready. By the time Ryland made it to the wraparound porch and set up to start firing, more than a hundred soldiers were running toward the house. He supported the barrel of the rifle on the porch railing and chambered the first round.

Over the following two minutes, Ryland emptied all four magazines into the target-rich environment of the canopied drive. He and his best buddy Luke Buck were skilled, hyper-competitive marksmen who pushed each other to excellence as they hunted multiple days a week in the scrublands just beyond the army's encampment. Luke would never admit it out loud, but Ryland was the better shot of the two by a narrow margin. A lifetime of dedicated riflery culminated on the porch that day, as Ryland scored center mass hits on thirty-six of the forty rounds fired from the Ruger American. Dead army men were strewn all around the front yard of his mother's house when the last round was spent.

It was only then that Ryland felt the coldness in his hands and face and saw the blood running dark and free from his belly. He carefully leaned the rifle against the railing and sat clumsily into a wicker porch chair as Leanna Beecham walked barefoot among the dead in a flowing white dress. He smiled as she approached the house and floated up to the porch to greet him, then smiled again at the winter sun and died as peacefully as a spring morning.

The Howitzer M119 is a towed field gun that was widely used in the old-world American Army. Its ten-and-a-half-foot barrel fires 105 millimeter artillery rounds at a rate of six to eight rounds per minute for the first three minutes until the barrel overheats. Over a prolonged period of thirty minutes, it can safely average three rounds per minute of continuous fire and accurately hit targets up to twelve miles away. It is a remarkably versatile, mobile infantry-support artillery weapon that can be towed by nearly any military-grade truck and by many smaller four-wheel-drive pickup trucks. The army at the channel had towed a single Howitzer M119 from Fort Rucker behind one of its trucks, along with two full truckloads of its enormous rounds. As the sun began to near the horizon, Major Joshua Lawrence ordered his artillery piece to be positioned near the water's edge and readied for firing.

Georgie Pilsner left the meeting in the city park as soon as it ended, deciding, along with Thomas and Hayes, that he should go with Big Chief to meet up with Rolf and remain at the old Crofts house until the dust settled on the general's killing. Rolf ran to meet his old friend when he saw him walking up, and had enjoyed only a few seconds of a hearty hug before the sounds of rifle fire rang out from the direction of Leanna's peninsula.

"That's not from us, is it?" Georgie asked.

"It sure as shit better not be," Rolf replied. "I gave strict orders not to engage unless they're moving on the island."

The intensity of the firing increased, and Rolf could clearly discern two different calibers of weapons being discharged.

"What do we do?" Georgie asked.

"We stay dug in until we can't anymore," Rolf replied.

In two minutes' time, the firing abruptly stopped.

Georgie said, "Target practice, maybe?"

Rolf squinted his eyes and shook his head. "I doubt it."

A tense, silent half hour passed. The militia held. The vibrancy of the orange afternoon light faded quickly when the sun finally disappeared. A cool, calming violet hue moved across the water as the first artillery round boomed overhead en route to downtown Cedar Key.

The sound of the big gun awoke malevolence in the Angel of Death's mortal heart, activating an internal reserve of violent, focused energy.

"What the hell was that?" Georgie asked.

"Come with me," Rolf shouted as he turned and ran for the house.

The two men moved quickly up the stairs to the widow's walk, and Rolf borrowed the binoculars of the watchkeeper.

"Son of a bitch," Rolf said as he located the source of the firing.

"What is it?"

"Artillery," Rolf replied. "A fucking Howitzer... probably the 119, but I can't tell for sure."

"How many do they have?" Georgie asked worriedly.

"Looks like just the one," Rolf replied. "But one's plenty to hurt us bad, especially if those trucks are full of ammo."

The Howitzer continued firing at a furious pace. During his time in the infantry, Rolf had seen firsthand how devastating an artillery barrage could be, especially on an unfortified town. By the time the tenth round roared overhead, the old First Sergeant was visualizing hellfire raining down on his friends and could bear it no longer. He grabbed the rifle of the watchman to his left, sighted in the first of the soldiers manning the big gun, and put him down from above. Before they knew what was happening, two more artillerymen were down. The Howitzer fell silent as hundreds of rifles roared to life, sending a wall of lead in the direction of the big yellow house and the boats in the channel. The two watch standers dove into the stairwell, with Rolf and Georgie close behind.

"Fire, Fire, Fire!" Rolf called out as he ran through the house and made his way toward a foxhole in the yard. "If you can see the big gun, shoot anyone who gets near it!"

In the channel, Gibbs Yardy fell almost immediately. As he looked toward the sounds in the sky, the rifles on the mainland rang out, and the ruddy-faced waterman stepped painlessly and instantly into the next life. The rest of the fleet was shielded a little by the mangrove island behind which they were moored, but the boats were still taking fire.

The burly, hot-headed Joey Bannon, hero of two wars in the new world, took a round to his left elbow that tore apart the lateral epicondyle of his humerus bone and left a shredded extensor tendon dangling from the hole in his arm. The old captain absorbed the blow with a superhuman lack of alarm as he shouted orders for his crew to return fire and make ready to sail.

Sammy Canon, Jr., whose father had succumbed to the irradiated wind that overwhelmed his clam boat on the day the smokestacks fell, lost the pinky finger on his left hand as the Bushmaster AR-15 he was firing was hit by multiple rounds at once. Undeterred, the former star shooting guard from the Cedar Key School basketball team retrieved his rifle from the deck of Joffrey Sleedy's converted mullet skiff, assessed it to still be serviceable, and continued returning fire toward the mainland as blood poured down his arm.

Samantha Maye, a former marine who had helped to put down Little Don Meade's raiders in the Second Battle of Cedar Key, watched the great love of her life, the builder and brawler Bull Scott, toppled into the cold water by a round to his right thigh as he labored to unfurl the makeshift sail on his 19-foot Carolina Skiff. With no hesitation, the suspiciously bosomed first mate jumped overboard after her captain, crashing through knee-deep water and sinking into the thick, low-tide mud next to her man. Bull quickly reoriented himself and used his massive arms to pull himself and then his would-be rescuer back into the boat. Samantha freed the leather belt from around Bull's waist and used it as a tourniquet to stop the blood squirting from his leg in misty streams.

In addition to the seriously and trivially wounded throughout the fleet, a half dozen islanders were dead on the decks of boats struggling to set sail. It was impossible for the navy to see, but their return fire had felled a wave of soldiers on the mainland nearest to the shore. Darkness was spreading across the backwaters in the twilight between sunset and moonrise as all the boats finally began moving together in a tactical withdrawal from the punishing fire.

At the Crofts house, casualties were lighter due to the foxholes and other fortifications the militia had built throughout the day, but BoBo Hoffmann, the herbal enthusiast and old-world skydiving instructor, was shot through a single testicle in a wound that would have been utterly survivable with old-world antibiotics and basic wound care. Nurse Toni may have been able to help if she had seen him immediately, but BoBo fought on until an infection inevitably came, one that would eat away at his insides for nine hard days and then kill him. Silent, microbial enemies killed indiscriminately and randomly in the new world. For no reason at all, BoBo was marked for death while Joey Bannon, whose wounds were significantly more serious and similarly ill-tended, healed up just fine.

Once neither side could see the other, the firing slowed and eventually stopped as both sides took stock of their losses and settled in for a long night waiting for what awfulness was to come at first light.

When the artillery firing first began, many of the island's residents were just beginning to leave the city park. This put a fairly concentrated crowd on 2nd Street when the first shell landed nearby, taking out the old Fish Heads Sandwich Shop building on 3rd. Since they were being fired with no real targets in mind, there were some shells that landed harmlessly in the back canal or in vacant lots, but those that hit targets did so with a ruinous power that crumpled buildings and the morale of the islanders. The capability gap between a Howitzer and a deer rifle was as wide as the one between Spanish caravels and the dugout canoes of the Maya on the Yucatan Peninsula.

Terrified people ran and screamed into the twilight as the shells continued to fall. Hayes, Thomas, and Lizzy stuck close to Luke and William as they made their way to City Hall to seek what shelter they could.

"Get in, get in!" Luke shouted as he held the door open.

Inside, the windows shook with every exploding shell.

"What do we do, Dad?" William asked as everyone huddled in the clerk's office.

"We've gotta get in the fight," the new mayor announced. "We're good for nothing here."

The old mayor agreed. "I need to get back to the fleet. I left Ryland in charge, but there's no telling what they're facing in the channel."

Thomas said, "Rolf will hold the line at the Crofts house, but I agree we can't help from here."

"It's settled then," Luke announced. "I'm initiating Condition Two."

"You sure about that, Luke?" Hayes asked. "That's a big undertaking."

In another circumstance, even a mild second-guessing from his mentor might have wavered Luke's resolve, but underscored by a soundtrack of explosions outside the walls of City Hall, he did not hesitate to reply, "Yes, sir. Anyone that's not in the fight needs to be out of harm's way, at least until we deal with the artillery."

Thomas glanced at his old friend with a satisfied nod.

"Good," Hayes replied. "What else?"

Luke continued, "William, you'll stay here and lead the effort. I need you to find Isaac Skipjack and tell him to get the Sawfish away from the island. He should take it farther out in the bay so it doesn't get accidentally blown out of the water. Lizzy, if you think you can make it, get to Miss Bette's house. My wife is there. She'll be rifling up and trying to fight. Tell her it's critical she stays and helps you and the boy implement Condition Two. We've never done it before, so things are bound to go wrong. I need her cool head there to fix 'em when they do. There are three boats at the inside ramp you can use. I may be able to send a few more once I get a handle on the situation at the channel. Dad, Mr. Hayes, you're with me. We have to get to the fleet and Rolf and put together a counterattack. Big Chief and Georgie should have made it there already."

William protested, "Dad, no. I'm coming with you."

"I wasn't asking, son. I need you here."

The youngest Buck bristled at the order, not out of vanity or pride but for want of protecting his father.

Thomas understood his grandson. "We all know you want to be in the thick of it, buddy. But your dad's right. We need someone here to take charge, or Heff Webster will try to."

"Yes, sir," William replied. "We all know my mama and Miss Lizzy ain't got no trouble being in charge, but if there's any heavy stuff needs picking up, they can count on me."

"Attaboy, son. Give 'em hell," Luke said with a smile.

The close-knit group shared a knowing, happy laugh together—a quick indulgence in shared history and affection before the bad business waiting for them outside City Hall.

"We best get to it," Luke said regretfully. "But let's be careful out there, all of us. Look after each other. I need all of you to make it through the night."

There were quick hugs and *I love yous*, but urgency prevented the drawn-out lingering necessary for a proper Southern goodbye. Thomas whispered something in Lizzy's ear that made her smile from head to heart, then opened the door, and everyone headed out into the dark.

As they were parting in different directions, Luke called back, "Somebody hug Kinsey for me . . . tell her to try not to shoot anybody till I get back."

16

CONDITION TWO

On September 29th in the year 1896, a hurricane made landfall in the Cedar Keys, pummeling the archipelago with 125-mph winds and ten-and-a-half feet of storm surge. During this time period, much of the town of Cedar Key was situated on the barrier island of Atsena Otie, just across the shipping channel from the modern town's location on Way Key. The destruction on Atsena Otie was so thorough that it was almost totally abandoned in the immediate aftermath of the storm. A handful of the few surviving buildings were floated over on barges and set up on new Way Key foundations. Miss Bette's house on 4th Street was an Atsena Otie refugee, as well as the cottages along 1st Street that were largely destroyed by the Great Fire. By the early 1920s, the few remaining stragglers on the barrier island had died off or given up their homes. Remnants of the old town could still be seen in the twenty-first century on a walking path from the little beach facing the shipping channel to the cemetery holding the eternal remains of thirty-eight islanders.

In the twelfth year of the new world, a sickness laid siege to Cedar Key, likely brought in by mainland traders. Without modern diagnostic equipment, it was impossible for Nurse Toni to definitively identify the contagion, but its symptoms led her to suspect it was a variant of Hand,

Foot, and Mouth Disease, a viral infection more common in children in the old world but also contractable by adults. Flu-like symptoms combine with painful mouth sores and skin blisters in the classic presentation of that ailment, though the mystery bug that swept through the island also caused pronounced brain fog and abdominal distress, preventing a sufferer from getting very far from a bathroom for more than a few minutes at a time.

It was the diarrhea that most concerned Nurse Toni and her husband, the Coast Guard medic from Isaac Skipjack's crew. In the old modern world, diarrhea was little more than an annoyance, but throughout much of human history, it was a prolific killer. Children who came of age with computers in America would well remember in *Oregon Trail*, the first computer game of an entire generation, that diarrhea was way more likely to kill you than snakebites, drowning, or gunshots.

As the mysterious sickness continued to spread unabated, hysteria developed on the island. In an effort to fight back against the spread, two dozen uninfected islanders used repurposed birddog boats to haul load after load of salvaged building materials from damaged and abandoned homes across the shipping channel to Atsena Otie. They used them to build three dormitory-style buildings for quarantining the sick. The buildings and the protocol were crude constructions, but they gave the islanders something active to do in response to the threat. The 19th-century concrete water cistern was still usable on the barrier island, and over time, a windmill was constructed that called a long-dormant well back to life. In a few months' time, Atsena Otie began to take on the rough characteristics of a community once again. Around the time the construction was completed, the sickness left the main island as quickly as it had arrived, and there was never again an outbreak of it or any other illness serious enough to trigger a quarantine.

So that the construction wouldn't feel like a waste, the city council eventually did what governments do, and implemented official bureaucratic plans for the facility on the barrier island. After months of planning, deliberations, arguments, and votes, Cedar Key's second official emergency plan was implemented. Condition One dealt with intruders at the bridge; Condition Two was an evacuation plan for the main island in the event of any number of serious perils—illness, fire, insurrection, and, most pertinent to the present threat facing the island, enemy invasion.

After the meeting at City Hall, Lizzy made her way to Miss Bette's house as instructed, finding Kinsey there as expected, but also Isaac Skipjack, who had piled mattresses atop and around the giant dinner table to create a makeshift bomb shelter for Miss Bette.

"Lizzy!" Kinsey yelled as she ran to hug her mother-in-law. Kinsey's own mother was lost on the day the bombs fell, and their chaotic relationship had never been a close one. The loving calmness of Lizzy's way of being in the world had pulled Kinsey in almost immediately, and now, a quarter century on, the affection between the two women was immeasurably deep.

"Are you Isaac Skipjack?" Lizzy asked.

"Yes, ma'am," the senior chief replied.

"I've heard an awful lot about you. And I think I saw you at Mr. Mark's funeral. You were down with the chickens, right?"

Isaac, embarrassed, shook his head. "Yes, ma'am, that was me."

"I told you everybody knew!" came a laughing reply from the tiny woman under the mattresses.

"Yes ma'am, you sure did," Isaac replied meekly.

Kinsey didn't even try to hold back a deep belly laugh before clucking, "Buk buk, B-CAW!"

"Well, it's nice to finally meet you, Isaac," Lizzy said. "Don't pay these meanies any mind. They would've both sat with Nero and laughed while Rome burned."

Miss Bette stuck her head out of her shelter and said warmly, "I don't know if anybody's told you or not, but it's the end of the world out there. It has been for a long time. At some point, laughing is all you can do."

"Fair enough," Lizzy replied. "But we've got some serious business to handle."

Isaac said, "Sounds like artillery rounds out there. I'm not sure how much good a kitchen table and some mattresses would be against a direct hit."

"Agreed," said Lizzy. "The mayor has initiated Condition Two to get people out of harm's way."

"Oh Lord," Miss Bette replied in a tone turned instantly dire. "We've never had to leave the island before. It must be getting serious."

Lizzy said, "I think so, Miss Bette. Isaac, the mayor has asked for you to take the Sawfish out in the bay so it doesn't accidentally get sunk by the incoming fire. He says it's too important to risk until we take the fight to them."

"Absolutely. I'll head that way now."

Kinsey said, "I'll get my rifle. Let's get after them."

"Luke said you that's exactly what you'd try to do," Lizzy replied with a smile. "But he needs you and William to lead the evacuation across the channel. There are boats at the inside ramp ready to go, and he might be able to send a few more back to help."

"He's trying to hide me away so I don't get hurt," Kinsey replied in annoyance.

"That is something he would do, but I was in the room when they were laying out the plans. I think he knows what an undertaking this is going to be, and he needs someone he trusts to make it happen."

"Fine," Kinsey replied. "But I'm taking my rifle."

"Good," Lizzy said. "Your son is getting the boats ready. Let's you and me start spreading the word and helping people to the ramp."

"I don't think I can hold a rifle, but I got a revolver," Miss Bette said defiantly.

Isaac replied, "Best run get it then, and come with me. You'll be safe on the Sawfish, and I'll take you to the other island when they get everything sorted out over there."

Miss Bette's eyes filled with fire and purpose as she retrieved the revolver and filled her pockets with extra bullets. When Isaac took her hand, and they started for the door, the old woman had to push back against an upwelling of emotion that forced tears down both sides of her face.

Her second son had returned at last, and she knew he would take care of her.

Major Lawrence walked among his wounded and dead, taking measure of the losses sustained in the opening exchange with the island navy and the militia across the channel. There was a solemnity in his manner as he stopped to speak with each of the army's four company commanders to get their input on the performance of the men. As he took in their reports, he quietly made notes in a small notebook retrieved from the breast pocket of his uniform.

"Twelve dead and seventeen more out of commission in Company Four, sir."

"Thank you, lieutenant," the major replied. "Your men did well. It's hard to stand against an enemy you can barely see."

"Thank you, sir. No word about the general?"

The major was pained by the question, because he knew it was being asked throughout the army, and he didn't have a good answer.

"No," he replied gruffly. "Once they started firing on us from that house, I think it became clear they don't intend to send him back. The sergeant from First Company that paddled out to meet the boat captain in the channel stupidly told them that if they didn't return the general by sundown, we would come get him."

"That's unfortunate," the lieutenant replied.

"Yes. And since we don't have a way to physically do that, I felt like we had to use the artillery to send a message. That's a decision I made. It's why your men are dead, lieutenant. Given the circumstances, I think it's one I would make nine times out of ten, but it doesn't change the fact that we're worse off now than we were before we sent the first shell into that town. We might have to fight them house to house now if we want to get the general back."

The lieutenant felt immediately defensive of his superior officer, in the way that all men need to feel about the leaders they follow.

"You did the right thing, sir. And whatever it takes, we have to get the old man. You can count on us."

The instant acquiescence to a mission of such uncertain wisdom and value was hardwired into the lieutenant's training and the culture of his profession. It was easier for soldiers to fight and die, for even trivial reasons, if they were ordered to the killing by a man they respected. With few exceptions, the great societies of the world, across the wide expanse of human history, were built on the foundation of dead soldiers ground up by leaders in whom they found the thinnest of reasons to believe.

Major Joshua Lawrence happened to be a good man, with a reasoning mind and a heart unspoiled by the business of killing, but even he was caught in the mythos of military hierarchy. He was bothered but unbowed by the now seventy-nine dead and ninety-four wounded spent in an afternoon for a general whose connection with the realities of the world was at best frayed and at worst completely severed. The weight of this knowledge was carried by the major alone, however. Only he had been in the office at Fort Rucker to see the old man so moved by the meaningless static from the radio. Only he had been in the general's tent the night before to witness the discomforting fugue state enveloping an eighty-seven-year-old mind.

The major knew that when at last he was called to stand before his Creator, many years from now or maybe in the days to come, battling for an island that held no particular meaning to him, he would have to answer for the men that died at his command. As he walked quietly away from the Fourth Company lieutenant, he struggled to formulate what that answer might be, and yet, he was even then planning to send a hundred soldiers toward Sumner to bring him every boat, canoe, or kayak they could find to get his men across the channel to the enemy.

"Corporal, may I have a word?" the major called out to a soldier near the water.

"Yes, sir."

"Do you have a working watch?"

"I don't, sir, but we have a few with the company. How can I help?"

A lumbering waxing gibbous moon was rising over the backwaters, and its growing light was spreading across the camp. Major Lawrence looked at his own watch, then back at the corporal.

"It's 19:30 hours now. Beginning at 20:00 hours, I want one artillery round to be fired toward that island every hour, on the hour, through the night. Move the aim around a little to mix it up. Take this order to your company commander and have him administer it as he sees fit."

"Right away, sir."

"Tell him to keep the bulk of his company away from the Howitzer, and have the firing crew send the round, then run away from the gun as fast as they can. I want no more casualties tonight. And unless you hear the order from me, no one fires a rifle across the channel tonight. We might be here a while, and we need to conserve our ammunition for the real fight. You got all that, son?"

"Roger that, Major Lawrence. I'll pass the word."

"Very good, corporal. No sense letting the enemy get any sleep tonight."

By the time Thomas and the two mayors reached the channel, an almost full moon had risen, the shelling had stopped, and a nervous calm was settling over everything. As the yellow-orange light of the big moon slowly morphed into the silver hue that would grow in brilliance as it moved higher in the sky, the battlefield of water and mud between the island and the mainland took on a shimmering, dreamlike quality, thinning the diaphanous membrane between the living and the dead.

Big Chief and Georgie were talking on the porch of the Crofts house when they saw the delegation arriving from town. Rolf was still behind a rifle in a foxhole near the water, locked in and ready to fire long after the rest of the militia had relaxed.

"What's the word?" Big Chief called out.

Luke replied, "That artillery is hurting us bad. Kinsey and William are getting everyone who can't fight over to Atsena Otie until we figure out what to do about it."

Big Chief's family had been in Cedar Key since the late 1800s, so the thought of abandoning the island was as off-putting to her as it had been to her Uncle Hayes when Luke first announced the Condition Two.

"I guess it's the right thing, but I don't like it," Big Chief said.

"I don't like it any more than you do," Luke said defensively. "But we can't protect the island until we stop those big guns. Any idea how many we're dealing with?"

Georgie replied, "I think just one. The shelling let up when Rolf shot the three soldiers who were manning it. That's when everything went to hell."

Hayes said, "We could hear the rifles from City Hall. How bad were we hit?"

Big Chief replied, "We're still working that out. The fleet took more fire than we did here. They sailed toward Cedar Point and around the bend for cover, but not before they hit 'em back hard. Before it got too dark, we could see soldiers falling all over the place."

Hayes yelled down from the porch, "Rolf, get out of that damn hole and come help us figure out what to do."

There's only one thing to do, Rolf thought as he climbed out, but he had no intention of telling his friends.

"Bobo's nut-shot but alright," Rolf said. "I had to drag him into the house to get him to leave the line, and he fought me until all the firing finally stopped."

Luke asked, "Do we think the shooting is done for the night then?"

"Probably," Rolf replied, "But they'll sure as shit hit us again at daybreak."

As if it were written in the stage directions of an eye-rolling melodrama, a half beat of silence elapsed after Rolf finished speaking before the Howitzer across the channel ripped apart the silence of the silver-tinged night, firing a single shell high overhead toward town, eventually crashing into the old Shore Finds furniture building on 2nd Street. The islanders responded with a caterwaul of rifle fire in the direction of the blast as Rolf screamed for them to cease fire.

"We're wasting ammo we don't have to waste," the old soldier yelled along the line. "Hold, hold, hold!"

When the islanders finally stopped firing, they were surprised to hear a penetrating silence from the mainland.

"I'll get up to the roof and see if I can see anything," Georgie said.

"Shoot anybody who gets near the big gun," Rolf instructed.

"Why would they only fire once?" Luke asked.

Hayes said, "Maybe just to keep us on edge."

"Maybe," Rolf replied. "But we need to stay dug in and ready for anything that comes our way until we work out a plan to take out that gun."

"Agreed," Hayes said.

Luke, feeling displaced without a boat to command, said, "There's a canoe in the mangroves across the road near the FWC ramp. If I can find a paddle, I'll head back toward the Number Three channel and swing around to Cedar Point and see if I can find our boats."

"That's a solid plan," the old mayor replied. "I'll go with you."

The new mayor asserted himself with as much firmness as he could muster for his friend and mentor. "No, Mr. Hayes. If you try to come, then my dad will, too, and we'll have three guys doing a one-man job."

Thomas said, "You better believe I'm coming."

"No, he's right," Hayes interjected. "Luke's got this. There ain't going to be any fighting from the water tonight. We just need someone to take charge of the fleet and get it ready for first light. He's the one we want in charge. We should stay here and do what we can to help."

"Fine," Thomas relented. "But I don't like it."

"I'll be fine, Dad."

"I know you will. But be careful anyway, son. I love you."

The Bucks, for as many generations as anyone could remember, had rejected the world's determination to cultivate men who didn't talk about their feelings. When Thomas was a little kid, spending summers in Arkansas with his father, he had always delighted in the extended family's elaborate nighttime ritual when they stayed together at the cabin on the Spring River.

"Good night, I love you, see you in the morning," Grandpa Wig or Uncle Jim would call out.

"Good night, I love you, see you in the morning," came the exact reply from his Aunt Rita, cousins Paul and Lisa, his other uncle Adam, and his dad. One by one, without fail and in exact mimicry, everyone took a turn saying the line and waiting for the multiple replies before falling asleep in comforting Southern serenity. It was a silly, cumbersome tradition, but no matter the discord that may have transpired between them during the day, the Bucks would end the night with love.

"I love you, too, Dad," Luke said, habitually but sincere, as he turned and ran for the canoe before Thomas had a chance to protest further.

"He's good," Hayes said. "At least as good as us, and he moves a hell of a lot faster. He'll find the fleet and get 'em squared away."

"I'm sure he will," Thomas replied, failing to contain the inextinguishable worry of fathering.

Big Chief moved along the holes, barricades, and bunkers of the line, checking on every man and woman in her charge as the tense minutes rolled slowly by. Hayes and Thomas found rifles and held the line with the rest of the militia. Rolf was a ghost in the night, disappearing and reappearing throughout the compound and the house as he stealthily gathered supplies and worked his mind through the details of a reckless plan he was sure Hayes and Thomas would prevent him from implementing if they caught on.

Exactly one hour after the last shell was fired from the Howitzer, another burst from its long barrel, flying very nearly along the center line of State Road-24 as it whistled past the Crofts house.

Georgie got off two good shots at the flame-silhouetted artillery piece, which hit nothing of consequence, while Big Chief, magnificent in the moonlight, held the line together with her commanding voice and threatening aura. In the disquiet of that ordeal, a bantam figure pushed a kayak into the backwaters behind the far side of the Crofts house. He slung a rifle over his shoulder and slipped into the sleek, arrow-shaped vessel.

The entrance to hell is not a flaming gate; it's a trap door on the path away from God. While a thick school of mullet, fat with winter roe, rippled the moon-drenched water, Rolf's path revealed itself in the Number Four Channel.

The Angel of Death paddled into the bright, eternal night, moving silently toward the army on the mainland.

17

THE BOY FROM SUMNER

Elijah Meade was sixteen years old when Samantha Maye choked him unconscious in the early days of the new world. A handful of mainlanders from Sumner had waged a foolhardy campaign of vandalism on the island, and Elijah was caught in the act by the buxom Marine. The fires and ominous flags they set around Cedar Key were meant as a symbolic response to the islanders' devastating retaliation in the wake of Little Don Meade's raid that killed Folksy, their Episcopal minister. This retaliation left a pile of bodies around the one man they had crossed the channel to kill, and a deep, lingering resentment between the two communities.

Elijah had been locked in the same office where General Gill would meet his fate a quarter of a century later when Luke Buck and Hayes David, separately and of their own accord, each showed up with a bag of food and a plan to set the young vandal free in the night. When the current and future mayor realized they had both been on the same unsanctioned mission, an already strong affection between them was cemented into a lifelong bond. Hayes was so impressed by the young Buck's courage that he could no longer view him as anything but a grown man. It was on this occasion that he first tried to convince his co-conspirator to call him just

Hayes, but Luke—then as now—wasn't ready to lose *Mr. Hayes* from his life.

When Elijah paddled away from the beach at the city park, he was left with conflicting emotions about the island. He had helped to dig the graves of the Sumner dead on Shiloh Road, some that seemed deserved, and many he knew were innocents caught in a conflict in which they had no stake. The grim work left a mark on him, one that had faded little even twenty-five years later. Still, he was similarly affected by the kindness of the mayor and a boy who was only a handful of years older than him at the time. Surely, he reasoned when he thought of that night often in the years to come, these men had risked a great deal to help him. At the emergency council meeting earlier that evening, he had been paraded in front of an angry town still on edge from Little Don's raid and the murder of their minister. Until the mayor stepped in to calm their passions, Elijah felt sure he was headed for a noose. Throughout his adult life, he would see innumerable such examples of otherwise good people dissolving into a mob that could do unspeakable things when stirred up or frightened.

In the chief's office those many years ago, Elijah was a spindly, frail kid with an empty belly and a fearless heart. Now, as he stalked through the woods of the Cedar Key Scrub, leading a hundred armed Sumner men and women through the argentic night, he was a physically imposing man—broad-shouldered, lean-muscled, and powerful, with a face shaved clean each morning with a stone-sharpened knife, and bright, lustrous eyes that shone with an optimism the broken world had been unable to steal from him.

When the army from Fort Rucker first marched through Sumner on their way to the coast, fear spread quickly through the community. Elijah immediately mobilized the folks that served as its fighting force, albeit one that had never seen any actual fighting. They called themselves the *Swamp Foxes*, after the Southern cavalryman J.J. Dickison, hero of the Battle of Station Four and renowned for capturing the Union warship USS Columbine on the Saint Johns River. Following the precedent of their namesake, the Swamp Foxes trained relentlessly in guerrilla warfare tactics. Elijah knew that this kind of fighting was the only way they had any chance of withstanding an attack by a superior army like the one amassed at the channel.

The Swamp Foxes were most at home in the Cedar Key scrubland that dominated the area. This sandy, nutrient-poor land is a fire-dependent ecosystem that relies on the pattern of renewal caused by regular fires to sustain its life cycle. The stunted oaks, rosemary, shrubs, saw palmettos, and slash pines were a theater of operations in which the Swamp Foxes felt invincible. They blended into the terrain as comfortably as the scrub jays, gopher tortoises, and sand skinks that made their homes in a place most animals and people found inhospitable. As the 198th went about the business of setting up their camp, Elijah positioned his force around them in the scrub along both sides of State Road 24, where they dug into the terrain and watched from the trees.

There was no great story of how Elijah became a leader in his community. There wasn't an election or a public proclamation. He had simply lived his life in a way that made people seek his counsel; also, he fed them. After the ordeal on the island, Elijah found a way to let go of his anger and poured his efforts into learning how to farm. The soil in Sumner was better than it was on the island, but it still left much to be desired. With the intensity of a savant, Elijah experimented with the soil-enhancement techniques he read about in a book found on a shelf in the RV park clubhouse on Shiloh Road. By the time he reached his mid-twenties, he had turned sixteen acres of sandy scrub into a productive farm by mixing aged manure, fish scraps, and wood ash into the soil and covering it with the pine straw that was so abundant in the area.

In years when the harvest was abundant, Elijah would hitch a cart to his faithful donkey, Henry, and bring vegetables to the Number Four Bridge to trade with the islanders. Henry was the shortest, homeliest, most ill-tempered of Elijah's donkeys, but he was good under a heavy load, and Elijah felt bad leaving him in the field to be harassed by his enormous, domineering donkey-wife, Cinderella. The broodmare ass was easily a foot taller than Henry and twice as strong; he was powerless against her advances, and Elijah would feel a sinking in his stomach whenever he'd see Cinderella mounting Henry in a show of anatomically incorrect dominance, braying like an off-kilter washing machine into his twitching donkey ears.

Over time, Elijah began to notice a regular customer who came anytime he and Henry were at the bridge. She was disconcertingly tall, light on her feet, tan, and pretty. She always made a fuss about the donkey, sometimes trading fresh mullet or blue crabs for vegetables she would then immediately feed to Henry while she scratched his ears and spoke to him like a person. Elijah got a kick out of the tall woman's antics with the donkey, and he appreciated that she always brought him the freshest fish. By her third visit to his cart, he noticed the fullness of her curly hair and the mischief in her smile when she and Henry were discussing matters of importance. She had a way of being warm and mean and then warm again, sometimes within the span of a single sentence, such that Elijah never felt entirely at ease around her, but as their interactions continued over a humid Indian summer in the twelfth year after the smokestacks fell, he found that he was always sad to see her go.

Near the end of that summer, when Elijah had no more than a handful of scraggly vegetables ready for harvest, he awoke early and hitched Henry to an almost empty cart. They made the long walk from his farm to the Number Four Bridge while Isaac whistled and Henry swayed his head in time. When they arrived, Elijah rang the giant ship's bell at the end of the bridge, signaling the guards on the other side that he was there to trade. A series of bells along State Road 24 began to ring in succession, until finally a bell on 2nd Street alerted anyone that might be interested about a trader at the bridge. Elijah was the only one who ever used the bell anymore. Most just walked across the bridge, checked in with the guards, and made their way into town. Elijah had grown to appreciate a great many of the islanders, but something always kept him from crossing the bridge. Because the bell had become synonymous with Elijah and his donkey, the tall girl developed a kind of Pavlovian response to the sound and found herself dropping whatever she was doing to walk toward it.

"Am I the first one here?" the tall girl asked when she had made it across the long wooden bridge.

"Yes, ma'am," Elijah replied, looking away from her face.

She looked into the cart, then to Henry, and back to Elijah. "You came all this way with two sweet potatoes and a handful of okra?"

She had characteristically put him on edge, and though he was normally quick-witted and never one to back away from confrontation, Elijah found himself searching for a reply.

"Well, I just thought you . . . Or, I mean, somebody . . . might like them. I don't even need to get anything in trade. I just didn't want them to go to waste."

The tall girl had no intention of letting him off easy.

"You some kind of weirdo, Elijah?"

"No. What? Wait, how do you know my name? Come to think of it, I don't think we've ever really introduced ourselves. You spend all your time talking to the donkey."

"I know who you are, Elijah."

"Well, alright then. Hi, I'm Elijah."

"Yes, we covered that already," she said in a tone that was somehow shitty and encouraging at the same time. "So you walked . . . what, four, maybe five miles here with a couple sweet potatoes?"

"And the okra," Elijah replied with a little smile that was, to him, a Herculean effort at playing it cool.

"Well, Elijah, I've got six mullet. How many is a fair trade for the sweet potatoes and the okra?"

"Like I said," Elijah began with something approaching steadiness, "I just wanted you to have them."

"Me?" the tall girl asked, finding that she had lost the initiative of the interaction and was suddenly on her heels. "You brought them for me?"

"I did."

"Oh."

"Hey, what's your name, anyway?"

"I'm Hallie," the tall girl said. "I thought you knew."

"I didn't," Elijah replied. "But I like it."

Sharply, skeptically, Hallie asked, "Are you taller than me?"

"I think so, a little," Elijah replied.

"Good. That's good. It would never work otherwise."

"What wouldn't work?"

"Don't be silly, Elijah. You brought me sweet potatoes."

"I guess I did," he said. "And okra."

A probing, illuminating silence sprang into existence between them as they stared, unwittingly, into each other's eyes for the first time while marsh hens strutted nearby in the mud and belted their joyful, warbling nonsense into the wet air of August, while the future Big Chief and the former boy from Sumner fell intolerably, inevitably in love.

Henry's gnarled, crooked fifth leg, the one that drove Cinderella so crazy, hung in the dirt beneath him, as he smiled a buck-toothed donkey grin and he-hawed for sweet potatoes he knew would soon be coming his way.

In the years that followed, Elijah eventually ventured across the bridge, and Hallie stayed on the Sumner farm often enough to develop something approaching a green thumb, though neither ever considered moving away from their communities to build a full-time home together. This quirk did little to dampen their enthusiasm or lessen their commitment in any way; they loved each other, they loved their homes, and they were happy to split time between the two. After several years of transient romance, they were married at the exact midpoint of the Number Four Bridge, halfway between the island and the mainland.

Most nights, Elijah and Big Chief would have been together, on one side of the channel or the other, when the army marched through Sumner. Then, at least, they could have looked after one another. What had seemed the day before to be an inconsequential scheduling issue that would keep them apart for a single night had turned immediately into a crisis when the long column of soldiers appeared on State Road 24 and wedged themselves between the tall chief and her slightly taller husband.

Elijah had led his own soldiers into the scrub to silently flank the army, but his head and heart were elsewhere, crazed to find a way to his girl.

Georgie Pilsner scanned the field of view ahead of him from the widow's walk, trying to identify targets near the Howitzer. As quickly as a shell was fired, the gun fell silent and the artillerymen scattered. Admonished by the earlier calls to hold, he felt helpless to do anything but frantically scan. In the periphery of his vision, a dark shape emerged from the shadows and drifted into the water of the channel. Even a few hundred feet away, the Angel of Death was unmistakable in the kayak as it knifed through the water. It took only a few seconds for Georgie to work out exactly what was happening and turn for the stairs.

Hayes and Thomas were dug into a shallow foxhole, with their rifles trained on the mainland, when Georgie came thundering toward them like a bull moose.

"That crazy son of a bitch," Georgie said in a huff. "We've got to stop him."

Neither man in the hole needed further explanation, and both grew instantly angry at themselves for not having foreseen what was suddenly so obvious to them.

"He's going after that gun by himself," Hayes said.

"Goddamnit," Thomas said, shaking his head slowly.

"Why didn't he tell us?" Georgie asked.

"Cause that little shit knew we'd stop him," Thomas answered.

Hayes said, "That gun has to go, or we're as good as dead, but we should have made a plan for how to do it together. Rolf's got no shot over there by himself."

"We best go get him then," Thomas said. "There's a jon boat under the carport in the backyard. I'll pull it down to the water. Grab whatever you think we need and meet me there, Hayes."

"No way," Georgie protested. "Then we'll be down all three of you."

"He'd come after us," Hayes said in annoyance.

Thomas sighed as he turned to head for the carport. "He would."

Hayes quietly gathered two pocketsful of extra rifle rounds and a jug of water, taking care not to alert Big Chief or the others about their plan. The last thing they needed was to risk even more of their island friends, who would not be deterred from coming along. When he made it down to the water, he found Thomas already in the 10-foot aluminum boat, holding it in place with a paddle stuck in the mud.

"I scrounged up enough rounds for us to give 'em some hell, anyway," Hayes said as he loaded the rifles into the boat.

"I went ahead and sat in the back so you didn't pitch a fit about not being the captain," Thomas said with a smirk.

"Good call," Hayes replied in a deadpan honed to a hard edge over a great many years dealing with his snarky friend. "We won't be much help to Rolf if we sink on the way over. I don't like our chances if you're at the helm."

Thomas laughed through the tension. "Just get in and start paddling, captain."

Hayes had just sat down at the bow of the jon boat when Georgie appeared at the stern carrying a rifle and the pistol that ended the general's life earlier in the day.

"Georgie, no," Thomas said.

"Bullshit," Georgie replied. "I'm obviously coming."

Thomas was not unmoved by the gesture, but there was no way he was going to give in to his old friend's reckless loyalty. Rolf was his and Hayes' responsibility, and they were his; it wasn't required that Georgie march with them to the gallows.

"There's not even room in this thing," Thomas said in feeble protest.

"I'll sit in the middle," Georgie replied. "Besides, this'll square us up on the castle."

Thomas was undone by the memory of a world that seemed impossibly far away from them now. When the two friends were in their twenties, Georgie was nearing completion of a Master's of Fine Arts degree from the University of New Orleans. A culmination of this program was a semester abroad living in Ezra Pound's castle in northern Italy. Students in the program would study and write in the place where the great poet composed his 800-page chaotic masterpiece, *The Cantos.* Thomas had finished a soulless MBA program and made a little money in a real estate deal about the time Georgie was facing the absurd prospect of paying to study poetry in a castle. Giving his friend a little money to live the literary life for the both of them was a fruitful investment to Thomas, whose own writing dreams were kept vicariously alive through Georgie's bourgeois adventure in Europe.

"Don't be dumb," Thomas said. "We're square on that and a hundred other deals over fifty damn years."

"Then I aim to get a little ahead with this one," Georgie replied with a big, obnoxious smile. "We both know I'm coming, so get up already and let me in the middle before we piss the whole night away."

To save his friend, Thomas feigned acquiescence, getting out of the boat and into the shin-deep water. "Well, come on then."

When Georgie stepped into the water toward the boat, Thomas called on every remaining measure of flexibility in his aged body, as he raised his dominant leg and kicked his low-slung friend hard in the chest, knocking him off his feet and into the thick, binding mud where the water met the shore. On cue, Hayes began furiously paddling as Thomas pushed the jon boat toward the channel, leaping into it just as the water began to deepen.

Georgie, supine and struggling to catch his breath, could only watch as the little boat raced into the moonlight.

18

— · —

THE OLD KNOWLEDGE

Kinsey Buck was a red-haired comet in the night. She had already assembled three boatloads of islanders and was halfway to Atsena Otie when the first of the hourly artillery rounds crashed into the library building, erasing the life's work of librarian Nance Stephenson. It was not an incendiary shell, but the intense kinetic energy of its detonation sent friction-heated shrapnel through the few thousand volumes of books on the library's shelves, igniting them instantly and spreading flames throughout the battered building in a Bradburian torrent. The walls began to buckle, and the second floor collapsed into the first. The flames had done what the winds and flood waters could not.

Kinsey's first reaction was to turn back to help, but the older neighbors on her boat needed her care, so she begrudgingly continued toward the barrier island. Little Chief Johnson and his volunteers had just finished putting out the last of the fires from the initial wave of shelling and finally sat down at the firehouse for a break when the library was hit. They grabbed their buckets and gear and started running toward 2nd Street, but by the time they arrived, it was clear the library was lost. They shifted their focus quickly to containing the fire before it spread to adjacent buildings.

In addition to the bucket brigade, a key feature of fighting fires in the new world, the Cedar Key Fire Department had a homemade version of the hand pumper rig that came to prominence in firehouses around the world before the advent of steam and gasoline engines. Teams of men would operate levers that move dual pistons up and down, alternating between suction and pumping to create a continuous stream of water pumped from a nearby water source. The island's hand pumper was the creation of John Mitchell, the longtime head of the water and sewer service, completed just a week before his death. John had spent the bulk of his life doing the dirty work to keep the island's toilets flushing and its water running, even devising a solar-powered system to run the water tower for more than a decade after the smokestacks fell. It was his dynamite that took down the Number Four Bridge in the first weeks of the new world, protecting the island from invading mainlanders, and now his handiwork was continuing to serve Cedar Key long after his death.

The nearly full moon made the crossing to Atsena Otie easier than it would have been on a dark night, but it was still an ordeal to get twenty mostly elderly folks into and out of the small boats and navigate the trail from the beachhead to the barracks several hundred feet into the wooded interior of the island. While Kinsey led the operation, William was content to be the workhorse, lifting several less mobile islanders from the boats and carrying them without difficulty onto the beach. Alexis Studemeyer was only forty-five years old, but she had recently fallen out of a tree while hanging a clothes line and fractured her ankle in fairly horrific fashion. William had to carry the ebullient blonde lady the entire way from the boats. She had, of course, always been aware of the broad, muscled younger Buck, but aware in the way someone is cognizant of an oak tree in the yard.

As she draped herself about him for the ride, she was suddenly consumed with awareness of him as a man.

"I'm sorry for all this trouble," Alexis said disingenuously, feeling as unsorry about it as anything in her entire life. "Seems like it's taking forever for my ankle to get better."

"No trouble at all," William replied, oblivious as always to the subtext but finding himself suddenly overcome with the feminine smell of her hair in his face and the warmth of her arm on the back of his neck. "I sprained my ankle once, and it wasn't right for a year, no matter how much I rested it."

Alexis rolled her eyes playfully. "I've never seen you or your daddy sit still for more than a few minutes. Come to think of it, your grandaddy either. In the old days, when I was working at the café on 2nd Street, me and the other waitresses used to always joke about Thomas and Luke wolfing down their food so fast they barely chewed it and then bouncing out the door to do whatever it is you Buck men are always up to."

"We try to stay busy," William replied with a laugh.

When the elderly and infirm parade finally arrived at the barracks, William and Alexis were each sad for the trip to end.

"I guess I can make it from here," she said, demure as a ladybug.

"I best carry you on inside," the nervous, innocent giant said as gently as a lullaby.

"Well, if you don't mind," Alexis replied in a tone so breathless she felt sure William could see the desire tickling along the nape of her neck and rolling in little waves across her face and chest.

"No ma'am, I sure don't."

When at last he sat her down on one of the benches built into the barracks, he could not help but let his long arms slide along hers as he pulled away. With an impulse that surprised them both, Alexis grabbed a massive hand as it moved past her fingertips, and used it to pull William back to her, kissing him squarely and awkwardly on the mouth for three wet seconds that settled the matter between them for good. From then on, with little discussion about it, they belonged to one another, embarking on something less dramatic than a May-December affair, he being no more than March and she a vibrant September.

Aboard the cutter Sawfish, Isaac had just secured Miss Bette in the helmsman chair of the pilot house and pushed away from the pier when the artillery shell hit the library. Assuming more shells would be following, he assessed the direction of the wind, squared the spinnaker to catch it, and picked up speed as quickly as possible. Shortly, the Sawfish was passing Atsena Otie and making good time away from the main island toward Snake Key.

Making that kind of speed at night in the treacherous estuarine waters, even in the bright light of the moon, would have been a recipe for disaster for an outsider, but even so many years removed from his time working daily in the those waters alongside Mark David, Isaac could still look across the Waccasassa Bay and read the moving water like a nautical chart. As clearly as his last day on the birddog with the old man, he could see the mud flats, shallow banks, and oyster bars that made navigating outside the channel so treacherous, and the old knowledge was a comfort to him.

Shortly, the Sawfish made it a safe distance from the main island and dropped anchor in the shipping channel between Snake and Seahorse Keys. Isaac returned to the pilot house to check on Miss Bette.

"Everything okay, son?"

He closed his eyes for a half second, steadying himself against her words. The smiling, ageless woman sitting at the helm wielded an unfailing, elemental love over him, and in the shadow of his neglect, Isaac was powerless against it.

"Yes ma'am, we should be safe here."

Miss Bette smiled warmly and without worry. "Are they getting everyone over to Atsena Otie?"

"They were taking the first few boatloads as we were getting underway. There were others gathering at the dock. It's probably going to take several trips."

"Kinsey will keep 'em straight. That girl is plenty tough and she ain't afraid of anything."

"Sounds like someone I know," Isaac said with a grin.

"Oh, me?" Miss Bette demurred with an oblique look on her face and a little twinkle in her eye.

Seeing her there at the helm, ethereal in the moonlight filtering into the pilot house, energetically beautiful in absolute defiance of her age, calming like a hymn, Isaac gave in to nostalgia. He was transported to the front porch of the government housing the county gave him when his father died. He was patching holes in a cast net when Mr. Mark's truck pulled up to the stop sign on the street in front of his house. The truck stopped, then lurched forward a little, then stopped again. The windshield began to slowly fog up until it looked as though the seats might be on fire. The truck shimmied in fits and starts so forcefully that its suspension springs squeaked like an old door hinge. Worried, Isaac made his way off the porch to investigate. He had just begun to look into the passenger side window when it rolled down suddenly. Miss Bette's hair was crazy, and her eyes were beaming as Mr. Mark yelled out, "You some kinda peeping Tom?"

"Huh?" Isaac replied.

"Can't a man make out with his wife on the bench seat of his truck without some pervert looking in on him?"

"Oh . . . oh, God," Isaac said, red-faced and fumbling. "No, sir, I wasn't peeping. At first, I thought you might be coming to see me. But then it looked like something was wrong with your truck. I guess I thought you needed help."

Miss Bette, cool as the first day of March, cooed, "He sure don't need no help."

There were a hundred other stories about the surrogate family he abandoned that had played on repeat in his head for all these years. He was comforted by them, sometimes stalked by them, often wanted them to stop, and also wished there were a thousand more. A physical incarnation of this phantom life now sat in his chair at the helm of his boat, equal parts flesh and apparition, a reward and a punishment.

Isaac pulled himself from the memories and back into the urgency of the night, excusing himself to check on the crew and wait for word from Hayes or Luke.

When Kinsey and William had the first load of refugees settled into the barracks and a healthy fire started outside for warmth and light, they headed back to their boats and set out for more islanders gathering at the docks. One hour after the shell hit the library, another came whistling toward the island. Of all the events that had happened since the general's helicopter first landed in the city park, none was so calamitously improbable as the landing of the unaimed second shell fired into the night.

Just as the two transport boats sailed back under the Dock Street bridge, the whistling of the shell ended in the middle of the docks. MJ Keller and Cassie Pierce, beloved longtime servers at Fannie's Café, were so thoroughly blown apart and scattered across the water that no recognizable pieces of them were recovered before the fish and crabs carried them away. When the world ended, the core Fannie's crew stayed close; all four had been waiting on the dock to make the trip across the channel together when the artillery shell defied incalculable odds to blow them apart. Lisa Smithers lost only a leg but slipped away over three and a half harrowing minutes as she stared numb and frozen at the electric night sky while blood rushed Technicolor free from a femoral artery dancing wild in the smoke and fire. Head cook Angela Hernandez, whose soulful voice could often be heard throughout the restaurant as she sang sweaty R&B standards at the grill or prep counter, still had all her arms and legs and fingers and toes attached, but her head had ridden the outgoing tide all the way to Seahorse Key by the time her body was found in the mangroves behind the public bathrooms adjacent to the boat ramp.

A half dozen injured and screaming old people were strewn about the docks and in the water when Kinsey and William arrived to help.

The tired old moon, lazy but bright, pissed beauty in a shimmer across the night.

Luke paddled his wooden canoe behind the mangrove island where the fleet had taken feeble cover from the mainland fire, skirted around a line of oyster bars, and eventually emerged in the cut between Scale Key and Cedar Point. As soon as he cleared the staggered series of sandbars and emerged into the wider bay, he began to see a tinkling of metallic light in the distance. Judging that he was far enough away from the army to safely make noise, and not wanting to be mistaken for the enemy and shot, he called out to what he hoped was the fleet as he paddled closer.

"Don't shoot, it's Luke!"

His unease grew as he continued to paddle and call out with no reply.

"Don't shoot, it's Luke!" he yelled, over and over.

At last, a reply came from the direction of the bouncing light.

"Luke who?" asked a feminine, authoritative voice.

"How many Lukes do you think are out here?" Luke shot back.

"I couldn't say. At least one, I guess."

Finally, the voice and the sass registered to the only Luke in the Wacassassa Bay that night.

"Cousin?"

A perverse rolling of laughter spread across the water from multiple boats.

Samantha Maye called back, "Just keep paddling, Mr. Mayor. You found us."

Because sound travels so easily across the water, the fleet was further away than Luke imagined. It took several more minutes of paddling before he reached the boats. When he did, the scene he encountered was anything but a joke.

"Whoa," Luke said. "Looks like y'all took it on the chin."

"You should see the other guys," Jud Bollins replied.

"How are you lunatics making jokes?" Luke asked.

Lex Beecham replied from an 18-foot Grady White, "It's either that or crying. May as well laugh."

Beechams had always been as plentiful as sand gnats in Cedar Key, but the stoic Beecham in the boat, laughing to fend off tears, was unknowingly the last of his immediate family. His brother Ryland was dead in a wicker chair, and his mama's house was overrun; six of his shipmates were dead on the decks of nearby boats, and more violence was promised at sunrise. Against such an onslaught, the only available options were humor or collapse.

Luke pulled alongside the converted stone crab boat *Miss Jonya* and climbed aboard.

"Uncle Jud, help me get this canoe onto your boat. No sense losing it."

As they wrestled the heavy wooden craft over the gunwales, Luke thought of the underwater mission the two of them swam in the dark moving water of the Suwannee on the last night of the two-day war on the river so many years prior. The younger man had been able to swim faster than Jud, but the old-time sponge diver could stay underwater long after the young Buck was back at the surface, gasping for air. Two decades later, the older man was older still, slowing but stubborn, and his bond with the new mayor was as strong as ever.

"How'd they do at the Crofts house?" Jud asked.

"The place is shot up pretty good, but nobody's dead," Luke replied.

"Anybody hurt bad?"

"Bobo took a round to the boys," Luke said. "Seems like he'll be okay, though."

"Holy shit," Jud said with widening eyes. "His dick okay at least?"

"I didn't get a good look at it," Luke replied. "But I think he would've made a bigger fuss if it wasn't."

"I imagine so," Judd replied. "Six dead here, bout the same number wounded. Everybody but Daniel should be fine."

"What happened to him?" Luke asked.

"Shot in the chest. Jimmy Mitchell is taking him to Nurse Toni, but I'd be shocked if he makes it to the dock."

Luke said solemnly, "I hate that. He was a good dude. Took a while to get used to how he winks at you all the time, but he never backed down from a fight."

"That's a fact," Jud replied.

In fact, Daniel Solaro, head of one of the great clam families in the old world, had breathed his last breath, unlabored and serene, just as Jimmy's skiff sailed quietly past the Dog Island clam leases.

Shortly after the canoe was secured on the deck, the second artillery shell roared from the Howitzer, whistled through the night, and slammed into the docks at the inside boat ramp where the ladies from Fannie's had unluckily just arrived. The impact was so violent that the sailors in the fleet could feel it in their teeth all the way across the bay. Luke was jolted to action.

Yelling from the bow of the Miss Jonya, Luke said, "Here's everything I know. I just came from the channel. They got punched in the mouth, but everybody held. The general who flew the helicopter into town is dead."

"What? How?" came a voice from the other side of the fleet.

You're not gonna believe this, but Georgie Pilsner shot him in the face."

"The Shark Swim guy?" Jack Fraydel, Jr. asked from his nearby 28-foot Trembley.

"That's him," Luke said.

"How'd he get here?"

"Well, that's even weirder," Luke replied. "He showed up on the Sawfish with Isaac Skipjack, the Coast Guard fella most of us fought on the Suwannee. Isaac brought the cutter and a pile of Coasties up from the river to help us when he saw the bridge burning. Big Chief, Mr. Hayes, and my dad are working out how to stop that big gun. If they can take it out, my plan is for us to hit them with everything we've got just before dawn. I want the first thing that army sees when the sun comes up to be our navy and the Sawfish sending fresh hell their way."

A reckless, defiant cheer rolled from boat to boat, swelling the chorus of the deadly night, a prelude to the coming fugue at first light.

19

POCKETKNIFE

Tabby Lowery had been a Kentucky coal miner, a soldier in the United States Army, a Cedar Key bank manager, a clam farmer, and, most recently and of paramount importance to her, Hayes David's wife. As it relates to her husband, Tabby exemplified the Biblical example of wifely love demonstrated in the Old Testament by Ruth, the wife of the kinsman-redeemer Boaz from the Tribe of Judah.

In the Period of the Judges in the years leading up to 1300 B.C., roughly a century before King David's rule in Israel, the widow Ruth and her mother-in-law Naomi had each lost their husbands and were suffering through a famine with no means of support. Ruth, a Moabite Gentile, left behind her former family and life to follow Naomi to Bethlehem in search of food and support. Naomi's lands and possessions had all been sold off, and now both women were destitute. Ruth spent her days gleaning the fields of wealthy farmers, collecting the small measure of grains God had commanded be left in the fields for the poor and foreigners in the land. By happenstance, Ruth wandered into the field of Boaz, a close relative of Naomi's dead husband.

In the Hebraic tradition of the kinsmen-redeemer, a close relative is called to marry a widow and reclaim her ancestral lands to help continue the family lineage. Boaz was immediately taken with Ruth, lavishing her with even more grain than required by the law, but he stopped short of assuming the role of her kinsman-redeemer. In a move that was as dangerous as it was bold for the time, Ruth took the initiative, seeking out Boaz in the dead of night in a threshing house, sleeping at his feet, and asking him to marry her. Because of her virtue and loyalty to Naomi, Boaz was persuaded. He married Ruth, purchased Naomi's lost lands, and restored the family lineage through Obed, the son he had with Ruth. Obed would father Jesse, whose son David would go on to be King of Israel and sire a line that led directly to Jesus of Nazareth.

Ruth's loyalty to Naomi and her husband was rewarded and celebrated through the ages. In a passage Thomas often quoted when he officiated marriage ceremonies in Cedar Key three thousand years later, Ruth says:

> *Entreat me not to leave you,*
> *Or to turn back from following after you;*
> *For wherever you go, I will go;*
> *And wherever you lodge, I will lodge;*
> *Your people shall be my people,*
> *And your God, my God.*
> *Where you die, I will die,*
> *And there will I be buried.*
> *The Lord do so to me, and more also,*
> *If anything but death parts you and me.*

Tabby Lowery would follow Hayes David into the fires of hell, and by this virtue, she was naturally and powerfully connected to Lizzy Fraydel, whose commitment to Thomas was forged in the same crucible. Once

Lizzy had helped Kinsey get the word out about the Condition Two effort, she returned to her house on E Street, to the arsenal she and Thomas kept in the safe in the library, to gear up for the fight to come. When she arrived, Tabby was on the front porch in camouflage duck waders and a boonie hat, a rifle slung over her shoulder and another in her hands.

"I'm ready when you are," Tabby said, steely-eyed and determined.

Lizzy held up the rifle she was carrying with a smile and said, "Let me get my knife."

In the five hard minutes it took Georgie Pilsner to catch his breath after Thomas kicked him in the chest, the wet mud near the shore pulled him down more with each passing second. When at last the air began to fill his lungs normally, he was able to slowly work his head free from the mud and just make out the jon boat crossing the channel.

"You goddamned redneck!" Georgie yelled at his disappearing friend, furious as Napoleon when the rabbits held the field at Fontainebleau.

The mood on the little boat was understandably grave, but in one another's company, Hayes and Thomas had always felt elevated beyond the sum of their individual parts. Such an undertaking with anyone but each other would have seemed impossible to them both. As it stood, it was just another scene in the long story of their friendship, a story that required the willing suspension of disbelief to believe.

"What kind of gear did you round up for us?" Thomas asked as their paddles moved in coordinated efficiency through the glassy water.

"Maybe forty or fifty .308 rounds, a big knife, and a jug of water."

"What kind of knife?"

Hayes stopped paddling and held up a fixed-blade knife with a serrated edge on top and a cheap plastic compass built into the handle. "Some kind of Rambo-looking Chinese garbage. I found it hanging on a nail in the big shed."

"You find me one, too?" Thomas asked.

"I was in a hurry, and I know you've got one already."

Thomas said, "Just the little pocketknife your dad gave me."

"I'll trade you," Hayes said. "This thing couldn't cut a fart."

Thomas shook his head. "Hell no. If we go and get ourselves killed tonight, there's no way I'm telling Mr. Mark I lost his knife. He'd kick me into Purgatory if I traded it for that travesty."

"He would," Hayes said with a smile.

"Remember how he used to always pull it on me like he was gonna stab me?"

"I do," Hayes replied, remembering how his stern father was so often and so easily silly with his best friend.

"Did I ever tell you why that was?"

"No," Hayes said. "But I assume it was cause he wanted to stab you."

They shared a quiet laugh together, and Hayes began paddling again.

"Well, maybe," Thomas replied. "But one time, he flipped his knife open at me when we were grilling that elk Tabby shot on your New Mexico hunt. He really got me, too. He flicked his wrist so quick I didn't see it happening and nearly jumped out of my skin. I remember saying something like *Jesus, Mr. Mark, I just saw my life flash before me*. And he put his hand on my shoulder, serious as a judge, and he said *I only do this so you can see what'll happen if anyone ever tries to hurt you*. Then he looked me square in the eyes like he could have killed the whole world and said *I mean it, and don't you never forget it.* Then he folded the knife up and went right back to grilling the elk like nothing happened."

"That's a good story," Hayes said.

Thomas nodded. "And I believed him, and I never did forget it."

"My dad didn't say things he didn't mean."

"I know," Thomas said, fixated on the muted stars overhead as he paddled. "That's us too, right?"

"Huh?" Hayes said.

"I mean you and me. We're the *killing for* kind of friends, aren't we? Rolf, too."

Some version of this scene had replayed itself a hundred times in their lives. Thomas would push him to say a thing so obvious and true that it never needed saying, and Hayes would pretend to be annoyed about it.

"We're in this stupid boat together, aren't we? Hush up and paddle. We're getting close enough to the other side to be heard."

"Fine," Thomas whispered. "But you better share that jug of water."

Careful not to let Thomas see, Hayes leaned into the warm feeling in his belly and smiled. "There's enough for us both."

Just as the jon boat slipped out of his view, Georgie finally broke free of the mud. He was enveloped by its black, sweet stench, the smell of money to old world clam farmers dreaming always of a workable low tide. He took a few steps further into the water to scrub the mud off his arms and legs. As he worked to get clean, he kept walking further out to find more water. Before long, the still estuary gave way to the channel's moving water, and Georgie Pilsner began to swim.

In his ears, he could hear the wedgied Lida Marie Johnson shouting once again: *Wait, there's somebody out there!* He could see Tim Mueller, flopped like a toadfish onto the deck of a rescue boat, next to the girl with no arms who had bested him by a quarter mile. He could feel the cool white plastic of the inflatable unicorn he rode in majesty toward the beach, toward the cheering crowd, toward athletic glory denied him in his youth, onward to redemption and lifelong infamy as Shark Swim Georgie. Thus transported to the hour of his triumph, Georgie swam on once more, into the moonlight, unto the breach, stiffening the sinews and summoning up the blood to chase down his foolish friend in need. His thick-muscled legs kicked like a 2-stroke Evinrude, pushing him nearly on plane as he closed the distance between himself and the enemy shore.

Elijah Meade relayed instructions to his second in command, then slipped into the dark scrubland, heading for the shore. He had his tiny army ready to pin the big army between the channel and ninety-nine rifles aiming at them from the trees, but the one-hundredth rifleman could wait no longer to find his wife. In total darkness, Elijah would have had little trouble navigating the familiar terrain, but in the light of the almost full moon, he was able to run at nearly a full sprint through the slash pines and palmettos, bobbing and weaving with the practiced nonchalance of Ali rumbling in the jungle.

As he grew closer to the water, the patches of scrub thinned as large swaths of mud flat pushed in on the dry land. This configuration of poorly drained marsh extended for dozens of miles in both directions, providing a natural defense against developers in the old world that had thoroughly and wantonly torn apart much of the rest of the state. Elijah knew well the tricky, narrow path that would lead him to the water, and his pace quickened even more when he first saw light bouncing on the channel. His paranoia had been growing with every hour the army kept him separated from the Big Chief of his life.

At the water's edge, Elijah realized he was still carrying his rifle and made the snap decision to leave it, his boots, and everything else behind that would slow him down on the swim. The cold water was a salty, whole-body acupuncture as he ran hard and wild from the shallows toward the channel. To avoid a long slog through the mud and the possibility of being seen by the enemy, Elijah had taken a path through the scrub that led to a little stretch of sandy shore several hundred yards north of where the bridge had been. Candy Island was directly across from him, but he would swim at an angle back toward the missing bridge to miss a series of mangrove clusters until he could eventually turn directly toward the Crofts house. He knew the islanders would be dug in there as a first line of defense against invasion, and felt sure his wife would be leading the effort.

From his starting point, Elijah's disjointed swim would cover roughly three-quarters of a mile. This distance was not prohibitive for a man of his fitness and resolve, but against a tide that had turned and was beginning to come in from the open Gulf, and imbued with the stress of a missing bride and the possibility of being fired upon from the mainland, it would require the full measure of his energy and focus. Elijah found a rhythm in the effort, surprising himself by how quickly he covered the stretch from the shore to the scattered mangroves. When he made the southwesterly turn to start the kick toward the Crofts house, he heard a quiet splashing sound that had not come from his own movements. In an effort to locate the sound, Elijah stopped swimming and quietly treaded water to listen.

When his forward motion ceased, the splashing seemed to quadruple in volume for a few disorienting seconds before the solid mass of Georgie Pilsner crashed into him under the water.

The next several seconds were harrowing, violent, and almost fatal to both men, who had no choice but to assume the other was an attacking enemy. Elijah held the early advantage, grabbing the head of his torpedoing attacker and pushing it down hard under the water. If Georgie had not managed to chew a peach-pit-sized lump of flesh from Elijah's leg in the struggle, he would have certainly drowned. Elijah, reeling in pain and falling backward, was covered in an instant by his densely packed adversary, who swung three fast, jarring blows into his temple, darkening his vision and sinking him under the water toward the muddy bottom. After several seconds, he returned to consciousness and kicked for the surface. When he broke into the air above, he saw the other man swimming away from him.

"Hey!" Elijah called out.

"Piss off," Georgie called back, kicking hard and swimming with all his might.

Elijah, confused, swam in the other direction, feeling better as the distance between them grew. When he had made it halfway between the last of the mangroves and the fortified shore of the Crofts compound, an earsplitting percussion overwhelmed him, followed almost instanta-neously by a flash of light and fire so intense he could briefly make out the entire two-story yellow house and even the faces of the men and women in the foxholes ahead of him. The entire Gulf seemed to be rattling like a low-oiled engine. When it stopped, men were yelling behind him; some screamed. Here and there, a rifle fired. Elijah was too far away to see it, but he could hear the confusion in their movement. The clatter of army boots and the discordant hum of fearful men surging in confused, amoebic formlessness was haunting in the sharp contrast of the night. When at last Elijah reached the muddy bank on the island side of the channel, he collapsed exhausted on it, drawing in long, labored breaths as armed men ran shouting toward him.

On the mainland, Major Joshua Lawrence was punch-drunk and writhing in the dirt. A few feet away, a squat, scorched Angel lay still as Death, caught in the blast of leftover dynamite he himself had ignited. A quarter century prior, John Mitchell had used most of the same batch to blow up the concrete Number Four Bridge, separating the island from peninsular Florida and the broken world therein. The last few sticks from the old wooden box labeled *DANGER: HIGH EXPLOSIVES* in red stenciled lettering had gone off faster than they should have, but all two million joules of their expected energy burst forth as intended, summoning Erebus from the shadows in Planck Time to greedily pull the living into death. The Army's Howitzer and twenty of its men near the big gun lay in scattered, smoking pieces across the marsh and mud and moving water.

Hayes David and Thomas Buck arrived in time to see it all happen from the cover of the mangroves. As soon as they were in the open, running toward their fallen brother, the first of the rifle rounds tore through them.

20

ALL THE WORLD WILL BE IN LOVE WITH NIGHT

Even before their boats had fully come to rest, Kinsey and William were both in the water, first checking the bodies floating face down for signs of life, then darting like purple sparks in a Tesla coil between the wounded, performing a rough triage that separated the possibly savable from the hopelessly lost. More would-be refugees continued to arrive at the boat ramp, but the docks had been blown apart by the artillery shell. A panicked crowd began amassing in the parking lot beside the boat ramp.

"Over here, son," Kinsey yelled. "It's Miss Lena."

Lena Fines was the longtime manager of the café on 2nd Street in the old world. She and Thomas Buck had gotten off to a rough start when he was new on the island; his fast-talking and her abrasive personality had mixed poorly across the breakfast bar where he often sat to write and drink sweet tea. Lena had initially so disliked him that she threw away an important notebook he accidentally left behind at the bar, knowing full well it was his and that he would be back for it. It wasn't until many months later when Thomas intervened to stop a disrespectful customer from yelling at a server—dragging him by his collar into the parking lot and threatening violence if he ever treated one of the ladies that way again—that Lena warmed to the eccentric newcomer and apologized for the notebook. Thomas was by nature clinically unable to hold a grudge, so he just laughed it off and never thought of it again. Thereafter, Lena let her guard down, and Thomas grew to respect and even love a woman who was secretly kind-hearted, funny, and a fierce protector of her friends and the island.

"Is she dead?" William asked, assuming the worst when noticing the missing left arm of the body floating head-up in the still water near the shore.

"I'm not sure," Kinsey replied worriedly.

"I'm fine," Lena said, startling Kinsey so sharply that she let out a scream.

Through the shock, Kinsey managed a meek, "How?"

"I just had the wind knocked out of me. Help me out of this water."

An impossible sequence of physics and cellular dynamics had saved her life, when a white-hot length of jagged shrapnel simultaneously sheared off her arm and instantaneously cauterized the wound, sparing her the same fate as her friend Lisa Smithers, bled out and dead on a broken section of dock a few yards away.

"I've got you, Miss Lena," William said, scooping the old woman into his arms and carrying her to shore.

The welder and spearfisherman Harald Lett was also dead on the dock while his beautiful painter wife treaded water nearby, bloodied but calm. Keegie Word, the friendly but fiery former liquor store clerk, stood in waist-deep water halfway down the boat ramp, concussed and lost but not mortally wounded, while the restaurateur couple, Jordie and Shanda Keaton, were totally unscathed as they made their way out of the water.

When everyone who needed immediate attention had been tended to, Kinsey returned to the helm of her boat.

"As awful as this is," Kinsey yelled to her neighbors on the shore, "we need to keep moving everyone off the main island before more of those shells hit us. We'll move the boats as far up the ramp as they can go, and William will help you into them. We need to move now, quick as we can."

"Over here!" came a voice across the parking lot, near the outside boat ramp closer to the clam leases.

Jud Bollins and Luke Buck were waving their arms and running toward the crowd. The crashing of the second shell had brought the island navy home to help.

Luke saw his wife's red curls above the crowd and ran toward them with his insides tumbling. When able, he would, of course, feel the loss of his fallen neighbors in the water and on the docks, but even the thought of Kinsey being hurt had separated him from the practiced calm he tried to portray to the older watermen in the fleet. Seeing her there, radiant in the midst of catastrophe, regal in her command of the boat and the moment, overwhelmed the new mayor. He ran through the water and leaped over the gunwale to snatch his bride from the helm and into his almost deranged embrace, but suddenly could think of almost nothing to say.

"Kinsey, Kinsey . . ."

"I'm okay, Luke. Take a breath, honey. I'm okay."

"I knew you would be," Luke said, finding himself immediately steadied by her presence just as he had been when they first met on a foggy morning in the scrub half a lifetime ago. "But when this shell hit, it rattled our teeth all the way past Dog Island, and I nearly threw up thinking you might be caught up in it."

Kinsey replied, "If the boy and I had made it back here twenty seconds sooner, we would have been."

It was only then, calmed by the touch of his wife, that Luke was able to take in the extent of the carnage around him.

"My God," he said. "We can't keep letting them hit us like this. We have to stop their artillery. I was putting together a plan to attack them at first light, but I don't think it can wait till morning."

Kinsey said, "We can use the fleet to get everyone over to the barracks in a single go, then figure out how to take out that gun."

"The quicker we get everyone away from here, the better," Luke said. "I'll pack as many of our boats along the outside docks as we can fit, and you start leading everyone over."

Kinsey kissed her husband, lingering an extra few seconds to remind them both of what the coming fight was for, then Luke jumped back overboard.

"Son!" Luke called across the crowd when he made it out of the water and up the boat ramp.

"Yes, sir?" William called back.

"Get over here!"

Worried he had somehow displeased his father, William cut an aggressive line through the gathered islanders, twisting and shimmying as he proceeded in double-time toward him. When his boy arrived, Luke gathered as much of the massive man before him as his arms could hold, pulled him hard against his chest, and held on with every bit of strength he could summon.

"What's up, Dad . . . you okay?"

"Yeah, son. I am. You did good here. Thank you for taking care of your mama."

"She needs less taking care of than you or me, but I try to keep an eye on her," William said, smiling with a heart and belly full of warmth from his father's praise.

Luke had maybe never been prouder of his son, of the solid man he had so effortlessly become in the face of such hardship. William Thomas Buck had his great-grandfather's generous heart, his Paw-Paw's unreasonable optimism, his father's fearlessness, and an added measure of his own child-like but not childish wonderment with the world. The Buck men were getting better from one generation to the next, and Luke knew then, with perfect clarity, that he must destroy the army on the mainland, down to the last man if necessary, so that William could one day feel the edifying joy of a son in whom he would be well pleased. He would dam the moving water of the channel with dead soldiers if he must; in the countenance of his son, Luke understood the great purpose of his life at last.

There are many good reasons to die, but only love is worth killing for.

Love whispered from the mangroves for Hayes and Thomas to run toward their fallen friend. Neither man had an inclination not to listen. On a darker night, especially in the chaos following the swan song of John Mitchell's dynamite, it might have been possible, even probable, that Rolf could have been retrieved and dragged back to the boat without engagement, but in the light of a garish, agnostic moon that paid no worship to the plight of friendship or the armies of men, the night was splayed open like a gutted fish and everything could be seen.

Hayes and Thomas witnessed the explosion just as they arrived on the mainland, saw bodies and parts of bodies moving through the sky as effortlessly as feathers on a breeze. They had not witnessed the virtuoso killing concerto responsible for the dead soldiers already spread across the field in the moments leading up to the blast. All across the open stretch of ground ahead of them, the Angel of Death had arranged a bloody composition to rival Rachmaninov's *Isle of the Dead* in haunting atmospheric dread, or Penderecki's *Threnody for the Victims of Hiroshima* in screeching, microtonal despair, creating with his quiet, unyielding knife a work to stand alongside the great masters.

By the time the dynamite went off, Thomas had counted fifteen heaps of flesh in his field of view, and though his thoughts were scrambled by the force of the explosion, he felt reasonably sure there were half again that many more. In the Army, Rolf had been taught the Modern Army Combatives Program of knife-fighting, alongside standard rifle bayonet tactics, which emphasized lethal efficiency over the elegance of more formal martial arts. He naturally excelled in this training, using it to earn the Army's Combat Action Badge in recognition of his successful close combat in the Pech Valley of the Kunar Province in Afghanistan. The fighting there had been intimate and hateful, devolving from firearms to edged weapons quickly, and finally to clubs and rocks and fists. Sergeant Alvarez emerged from the ordeal sharpened to an edge his combat knife would envy.

The Army had taught him the tactics of his trade, but Rolf's killing magnificence came from within, from a lifetime of being overlooked and disrespected, from a hollow heart that had only begun to fill when he moved to Cedar Key and found in Hayes and Thomas a family so long and so painfully missing from his life. It was the threat to these men and to his island home that fueled Rolf's rage at the charlatan army undermining every core belief he had as a soldier. The retribution for their execration of honor lay in piles on the field his brothers would have to navigate as they emerged into the excoriating light of the moon.

Withering fire struck at Hayes and Thomas as they ran. Hayes was hit first but did not immediately fall. A scared soldier with shaking hands fired a round that ricocheted off the steel quarter panel of an army truck and tumbled across the top of the old mayor's chest, digging a shallow trench into his collarbone and removing a thumb-sized section of flesh from the front of his shoulder. The adrenaline flooding through him might have kept him from noticing the injury had not a little blood splattered into both eyes and momentarily blurred his vision. When it did, Hayes stumbled, catching himself with both arms to avoid hitting the ground.

The commotion caught Thomas' attention, who slowed and turned back to see if Hayes needed help. The turn placed him askance a trio of riflemen who fired quickly at him. Two of the shots missed badly; the third tore away a small section of calf muscle from his right leg and sent him tumbling ass over tea kettle, bleeding in the dirt. A shot from a perpendicular angle flew over Thomas and into Hayes' right shoulder, where it sent tiny bone fragments bouncing inside him before exiting through the scapula bone and the skin of his back. The kinetic force of this shot removed the old mayor from his feet and left him in a heap on the ground a few feet from his best friend. Suddenly, the shots seemed to be coming from everywhere at once. Hayes and Thomas' journey in the mortal world seemed certain to end then and there, and it assuredly would have if the heavens above them had not intervened on their behalf.

A cynic's view of the scene would have included the dispassionate science of that evening's meteorology. Since midafternoon, a cold front had been moving southeast from Pensacola Bay, bringing with it a line of dark clouds and frigid rain that were bearing down on the western coast of Levy County. At the moment of the fallen islanders' crisis, while illuminated as though they were on a stage to perform a scene from one of Thomas' plays, when the poorest marksmen in the enemy army could have picked them off without difficulty, the moon disappeared behind a towering cumulonimbus thunderhead, spewing cold blackness across the night. A poet might wax sentimental at the serendipitous waning of the moon, while the prayerful could easily see the hand of the divine. A fair judge of any kind would certainly find justice in the reprieve. Hayes and Thomas had lived their lives in service to the Gulf, and now its winds and currents were birthing a storm into which they might disappear.

"You dead?" Hayes asked, rolling closer to his friend.

"I don't think so," Thomas replied. "But we both will be soon if we don't get moving."

Rounds continued to hit all around them.

"Damnit!" Hayes called out as he was bitten through the boot by a shot skipping off the ground and rending a thin slice of ankle bone from him.

Another round punched a clean, tight hole in Thomas' button-down shirt, singing a tuft of underarm hair and melting flesh as it passed by. Stinging pain ran up his arm and neck in disproportion to the relatively minor wound.

"Come on!" Thomas yelled as he managed to get to his feet and pull Hayes up as well.

A steady peppering of rounds improbably missed them as they hobbled away from the last spot the enemy had seen them when the lights went out. The distance back to the cover of the mangroves was half as far as it was to reach Rolf, still motionless and maybe dead already. Zero mental energy was expended by either man in considering the direction they would travel; the Angel of Death was down, and they were going to get him.

Shortly after the moon's retreat, a bitter rain began to fall in heavy, intermittent waves. The blessing of the additional cover it provided more than offset its painful chill. Laboring on shot-up legs and feet, burned and bleeding, Hayes and Thomas moved slowly toward the direction they had last seen Rolf. The intermittency of the rain gave way to a steady downpour as clouds piled one upon the other over the land and water, saturating the perpetually wet land along the shore and turning the would-be battleground to mud with a dazzling speed verging on sorcery. Twice, both men lost their footing and fell; twice, they rose again and continued on. Through the dark rain, Rolf appeared in vague outline before them. He was sitting up now, trying to pull himself to his feet with his rifle.

"There he is!" Thomas called to Hayes above the percussion of the driving rain and the sound of rifle fire behind them.

Somehow, the old soldier regained his footing and began moving in jerky quarter steps toward Major Chamberlain, himself just beginning to recover from the blast that had incapacitated both men. The pitiful slow-motion parade continued as the rain swelled and the rifles rang out in a continuous wall of sound. Hayes and Thomas were gaining ground on Rolf, who was inching his way toward the major in grueling, stumbling rage. The asymmetric progress of the moving men and the triangular vector of their paths put all four on a track to convergence. As Hayes and Thomas grew closer to Rolf and the major, the grim details of their friend's condition took form in the haze and rain. Hayes called out to the First Sergeant, who was only just then aware that his friends had come for him.

Rolf shook his head in ghostly slowness. "I knew you'd come," he struggled to say in a shallow, raspy tone, as he turned toward his brothers. "You shouldn't have come."

Then they saw it. And they could not help but look away.

By the time the bombs fell, and the world finally ended, the sensibilities of the modern age had devolved so ruinously that there was almost nothing left for the wasted culture to exploit for sensation or titillation. Nothing was shocking anymore, even the vilest of violence, once covetously hemmed in to the battlefield, or locked away in the shellshocked minds of men who would never wish another human being to know or feel or see or taste or touch what they had borne in the savage warring work on which all civilizations are ultimately built and sustained. Death and dying had become no more gruesome than dogshit on the bottom of a shoe, and still, even to men hardened by the fall of man, the sight of their friend was momentarily more than they could bear up.

The right side of Rolf's face was undisturbed by all but time, and even in that regard, he seemed to be winning. He was only four years younger than Hayes and Thomas, but his Cuban genetics and small cherubic face had always belied his age, making him seem even younger. The line between Rolf's youth and his approaching death was not a metaphorical one. An upside-down L-shaped section of metal from the Howitzer's exploded barrel was lodged in his face, running vertical from just below his chin, though several shattered teeth and half a nose that hung on by a thin thread of skin near the bridge, where the jagged letter made its 90-degree turn left, through a liquified eyeball and out near the temple of his head.

Little bits of brain and life were dripping onto his charred, muscled chest, but still Rolf managed something approaching a grotesque smile as he said again, pridefully as he fell for good, "I knew you'd come."

21

IRREPRESSIBLE PROBABILITY

Neither of the first two armed militiamen immediately recognized Elijah Meade, lying exhausted in the mud. They were shouting at him, but in his exhaustion from the fight with Georgie Pilsner in the middle of the channel, Elijah was focused more on catching his breath than listening.

"I swear to god I'm gonna shoot you in the chest if you don't put your hands up," the aging former police officer Steve Lippolito shouted. He had served alongside Officer Biscuit in the old world and carried twenty-five years of misplaced guilt for staying behind to defend the home island instead of dying alongside his buddy in the Two-Day War on the Suwannee. As a self-imposed penance, he continued serving on the police force until his seventieth birthday earlier that year. When Chief Jank Edwins finally retired, Officer Lippolito hung up his gun as well. He had been retired for only a few months when the Blackhawk helicopter landed in the city park, and the militia was called up. When they called, he answered.

"Get my wife," Elijah managed when he could not summon the strength to raise his arms.

"Who's your wife?" asked Aaron Plumber, the overalls-clad moonshiner who had spent the year leading up to the flash hoarding enough silver to make him a millionaire on paper in the old world, and just a guy with several heavy boxes in the new.

"Elijah!" Big Chief shouted when she saw him on the bank. "Damnit, Steve, you segmented turd. Move! You've literally had dinner with us," she said, shoving him hard out of the way and hip-checking Aaron flat on his ass before diving so enthusiastically toward her husband that she knocked the wind from his already winded chest. Elijah wheezed and smiled, kissing his Big Chief frantically while they laughed and rolled together in the mud.

At the outside boat ramp back in town, there was little cause for laughter. To make room for more refugees, the dead sailors were removed from the decks of the navy's boats. There was no time for a dignified transfer of the fallen; they were laid on the sand by the water in the city park together, resting shoulder to shoulder as the Gulf whispered to them in the moonlight.

Westin Fines, the woodworker and furniture maker, was first in the somber line on the sand. Had his mother Lena known her son was one of the sailors arriving dead from the fight in the channel, she would never have consented to be taken to Nurse Toni's clinic to treat her severed arm. When the news reached her on the exam table, while the burned nub above her elbow was being tended, she tore the exam room apart getting out the door, and ran barefoot to the park. Big ideas about nations and armies are blasphemy in the face of a loving mother's anguish. She draped herself over the proud waterman who had brought pride and joy to her heart every minute of his forty-three years on Earth. She held him through the night, even when the freezing rains washed over them, squeezing his hand and singing *Hush Little Baby Don't You Cry*, imagining thing after thing that *mama's gonna buy* him, from an airboat to a compound hunting bow, to a new body that would pull itself up and walk back into life. Sometime in the small hours of the morning, the sand around Lena grew dark and red, as the imperfect cauterization broke free, a dehiscence of flesh and of the heart, a wound made mortal by despair.

When the morning came, they were gone together.

Cedar Key Sharks basketball star Ladio Lambeer, the terrorizing power forward, was next in line on the sand, then the baker John Martindello, the blue crabber Lyle Stewart, and the clam magnates Gibbs Yardy and Daniel Solaro—every one a hero to be lauded in island lore, each beloved and irreplaceable.

The losses were mounting, and Luke Buck's restraint was failing. "Uncle Jud, can you help make sure everyone gets over to the old island?"

"Sure, Luke," Jud replied. "Shouldn't take long with the fleet helping. Where you headed?"

"While the wind holds, I'm gonna sail Jimmy Mitchell's little skiff out to the Sawfish and brief Isaac on the plan. We need to get him moving this way."

Jud could see the strain in his young friend's eyes. The worry masquerading as resolve was as easy to spot now as it had been on the boat just before they both went overboard in the dark Suwannee during the war. Luke's father was pinned down in the Gateway Marina building with Hayes and Rolf, taking fire from Isaac Skipjack's Coasties barricaded in the nearby trees, and Luke was a coiled spring on the deck of the *Big Skiff Energy*. The plan to swim underwater from the main river, through the inlet to the marina, and along the boat slips to the shore, and then make a mad dash from the water to the besieged islanders had been foolhardy, daring, and entirely Luke's conception. In the years that followed, Jud thought often about how they should have been killed, and how easily and immediately he had acquiesced to the young Buck's bullshit smirk and reckless plan.

In short, he loved him.

He had served alongside Luke as a fellow boat captain for many years by then, had of course voted for him in the election, and felt sure he was the right man to shoulder the burden of leadership in its present, heaviest hour. The fact remained, however, that Luke had been thrown into the fire almost immediately after stepping into Hayes David's unfillable shoes, and the boy could be counted on to forsake all prudence in his effort to fill them.

"We're gonna get 'em, Luke," Jud said as he put a hand on the new mayor's shoulder. "But let's slow down a little and make sure there's enough of us left when we do for it to matter."

"Yes, sir," Luke said apathetically, having no intention whatsoever of slowing down, as he was turning to run for the skiff.

He had just made it across the parking lot when the last of John Mitchell's dynamite went off on the mainland, blowing the Howitzer to pieces, one of which was at that moment rapidly decelerating into the face and skull of the Angel of Death. At the boat ramps in town, the force of the blast made the falling artillery shell seem like a hiccupping church mouse in comparison. Even more than two miles away, the sound bore violently into the few hundred unprepared ears on the island, disorienting many to the point of collapse. The long stretch of water from the mainland to the outside boat ramp was a superhighway for the attacking sound, paving the way for its hard crash into the island. Any inclination for caution that Luke may have possessed, and there was little in the tank already, evaporated in the blast.

"Uncle Jud!" Luke called across the parking lot. "Take charge here and get everyone off this island now! Pick them up and carry them yourself if you have to. I've got to get to the Sawfish. We're not waiting till morning."

The rain fell in smothering waves. It so obscured Thomas' vision that he didn't trust the information streaming into his eyes. Mostly, he just didn't want to believe it. When Rolf fell, Thomas moved as quickly toward him as his injury and the mud would allow, forcing himself to put his face close to his friend to verify the awful image before him.

"Is he alive?" Hayes asked as he stumbled toward them.

"No," Thomas said, bereft of additional words in a way he seldom was.

"Well, damn," the old mayor replied. "That shithead did it, though. With the big gun down, we'll have a fighting chance."

Thomas could count the number of times he had heard Hayes curse on half of one hand over half a lifetime. Two curse words that close together were nearly as unsettling to him as the disconnected nose and missing eyeball of the soldier in the mud.

"Grab a leg and let's drag him back to the boat," Hayes said.

"You can barely walk," Thomas replied. "And I ain't doing much better."

Sternly, Hayes replied, "We're taking him home."

"You're right," Thomas said. "We got you, Rolf."

They had moved their friend only a few feet when a smaller caliber shot rang out nearby. Hayes turned toward the sound and could just make out

Major Lawrence firing his sidearm at them from a seated position against the bumper of a truck filled with artillery rounds that were now useless to him. Hayes started instantly toward the major, without regard for the significant hitch in his giddyap or the directness of his route toward the Sig Sauer P320 shaking in the hands of the army officer thirty yards in front of him. The major's head was still a mess from the blast that killed Rolf, and his vision was shoddy. Hayes was halfway to him by the time the second shot was fired, leaving the barrel at the moment of a tremor in the major's hand and missing wide by a horse length. The third struck the stumbling old mayor in his left thumb, exploding the nailbed and cleaving a third of the digit from the rest of his body. Thus reduced to one and two-thirds thumbs, Hayes nevertheless lunged for the major, crashing into him just before the fourth shot could be fired.

Hayes ripped the gun from the major's weakened grasp and spun it hard into his chest, letting the barrel crash into his ribs. He had every intention of firing the commandeered 9-millimeter until he saw the embroidered oak leaf insignia on the soldier's uniform.

"You're an officer?" Hayes asked.

"I am," Major Lawrence replied.

Hayes said, "In the Navy and Coast Guard, that oak leaf would make you a commander. I know it's something different in the Army, but I don't remember what."

"Major Joshua Lawrence, sir."

Hayes moved off the downed man and lowered the weapon.

"Major Lawrence, I need you to get a message to whoever's in charge here."

Chuckling at the improbable odds of their encounter, but not wanting to volunteer information that might get him killed, the major replied, "I believe I can do that."

Hayes said, "One of your soldiers paddled out to my boat under a white flag. He got a little smart with me, so I threw him overboard and made him swim back, and I don't feel bad about it."

"I know that man," the major replied. "And I've got the same trouble with him here."

Something nearing a moment of levity sat between them until Hayes continued, "But I gave him my word that we'd return the general safely to you, no matter what, once we were done talking to him."

"We got the message."

"I didn't know it then, or I wouldn't have said what I said, but by the time your man paddled out to my boat, the general was already dead."

"Oh," the major replied meekly, thunderstruck by the implication of what he had heard, unsure what to say next. Being forced to lead the army in the general's absence had shown the major how much of the responsibility of leadership he had ceded to the old man over the years. He had been an expert at enacting the general's orders, but found he was less enamored of the top job than he imagined he would be. However he felt about it, the interim position had just been made permanent.

"I don't know what all it matters now," Hayes began in a regretful tone, "but I'm sorry for it. It's a long story how it happened, and it wasn't one of ours that did it. Still, I gave my word, and I wasn't able to keep it."

"I appreciate you telling me," the major said with such a lack of discernible malice as to be off-putting.

Hayes continued unsteadily, "I figure I've got every right to kill you now on account of you were firing at us, and on double account for what your artillery has done to the island. And then there's my dead friend over there that blew it up."

"He did a lot more than that," the major replied sharply.

Working diligently to repress a satisfied smile, Hayes replied, "I thought I recognized his work on the way here."

"Well, get on with it then," the major replied, feigning gallantry in defeat.

Hayes shook his head. "No. What I'm gonna do is take your pistol and back away now. Maybe you won't credit a major's life high enough to offset a general's, but a major is all I've got to offer in exchange for a broken promise."

"Seeing as how I'm the major in question, your credit's good with me, sir."

"Good," Hayes said. "But if you so much as move until we're back to our boat, I'll come right back for you with a clear conscience."

"Fair enough."

"I don't know what was wrong with your general to make him think an aircraft carrier could get within thirty miles of Cedar Key before it ran aground, but I do know there's no navy coming to meet you except the one I'm bringing back here tomorrow, loaded down with every one of us that can hold a rifle. You sure better want our island bad, cause you'll have to kill every one of us to take it."

"Roger that," the major replied as Hayes turned and began stumbling toward Thomas and Rolf.

"Major!" Hayes called back through the driving rain.

"Yes, sir?"

"My name is Hayes David. I just thought you should know."

"Much obliged," the major replied.

Hayes said, "You'll see me again soon. I'll be right out front when the firing starts."

The major believed him; even wounded, the old man's presence was as calculated and commanding as it had ever been.

Hayes labored back through the mud, feeling weaker as he went. When he saw Thomas on the ground, leaning motionless against Rolf, with his hands dropped to his side and a narrow gaze fixed on some distant point in the falling rain, the old mayor went numb. The cold and the rain and the danger still between his present position and the safety of the mangroves disappeared as quickly and totally as a forgotten memory. The pallor of his buddy's face was the ashen hue of nearby death, and Hayes despaired.

"You okay, buddy?"

Thomas stared straight ahead.

"Yeah, I'm not feeling so good myself," Hayes said. "Okay if I sit with you for a minute while I catch my breath?"

Thomas turned his head slowly toward the old mayor and nodded.

The rain was slowing, but the moon was still locked safely behind a thick bank of clouds. Hayes began the tedious process of sitting, trying to accommodate each of the various injuries he had sustained in the night, along with paying the always rising toll of age and decrepitude. Halfway to sitting, a flimsy card gave way, and the whole house came tumbling down, landing the old mayor hard in the mud.

Thomas managed a sluggish smirk and a painful thumbs up when Hayes hit the ground.

"What are you laughing at?" Hayes asked. "You look like crap."

In haunting slow motion, Thomas managed to pull his shirt up a little, exposing the mangled meat of his gut, vindicating the irrepressible force of probability to them both—having miraculously and improbably escaped mortal injury from an army of high-powered rifles fired at him in the target-illuminating light of the moon, it was a haphazard shot from a trembling handgun, set loose in the darkness, that had finally stopped the momentum of Hayes' indomitable friend.

"No. No way," Hayes said, holding up his mangled thumb. "He wasn't even aiming, and he managed to hit us both. Ain't that something?"

Thomas drew in a rattled, shallow breath and said, "Best get a band-aide on that thing before it gets infected."

Hayes grimaced against the rising emotion. "You're right. And I'm worried you might need a couple stitches."

"I'd settle for bourbon," Thomas replied flatly.

"Well, come on then, we best get to Nurse Toni's or the bar before things get serious."

The old mayor tried to rise but could not.

"You first," Thomas said, choking on a belly laugh that squeezed a rush of blood into a dark pool on his lap.

Hayes replied unconvincingly, "Maybe a minute more. Then we'll get after it, buddy."

The minutes piled up, the clouds began to break, and the moonlight started a steady march toward them.

Near the pass-through wound from the rifle round Hayes had taken to his right shoulder earlier in the night, a tiny fragment of shattered bone was lodged in his subclavian vein just below the collarbone. Miraculously, it was holding back the mortal flood like the little Dutch boy with his finger in the dike. The physical confrontation with the major had wiggled it loose a little, and now the high pressure of a vein responsible for bringing blood back to the heart to refill with life-sustaining oxygen was pushing at the corners of the fragment, slowly working it free. Blood was spilling imperceptibly beneath Hayes' skin, subtracting incremental units of life from him as he sat. Without deciding to do so, or any memory that he had, the old mayor closed his eyes and drifted off.

A few minutes passed quietly in the waking world, but time dissolved behind the inside of Hayes' eyelids, as a lifetime of scattered memories projected on an endless field of screens covering the great expanse of his mind. He was standing with his fourteen-year-old chest bowed out at the helm of his first fishing boat, the one he bought with his own money saved from working at the David fish house, mowing yards, and patching nets. He was laughing at the ruined bathroom of his childhood home, the one in which his sister Lida Maria had left an enormous unflushed poop that was smeared across the walls, mirror, and floor by a cat-burgling raccoon that crawled through an open window in the night. He was packing up his desk on the joyful last day of his job at the island bank, knowing he would only ever work on the water thereafter. And finally, best of all in the delicate twilight of his sojourning mind, he was kissing Tabby Lowery for the first time again, discovering at last a love he knew would endure. As Hayes tried to pull her closer to him, an intruding sound roared into the memory, pushing away the small details of her face and the soft heat of her fingers pressing into the back of his neck. He squinted hard and tried to tether himself to the memory, but still the sound came, louder and more distinct.

"Wake up!"

With so much of his body's resources being marshaled into the fight to stay alive, Hayes' pain response was expectedly muted, such that it took several hard slaps to the face to eventually wake him.

"You'll either wake up, or I'll beat you the rest of the way to dying," came a familiar but not immediately identifiable voice.

"What?" Hayes managed faintly through a fog of memory so thick it muddled the already hazy lamina separating his finite life from the never-ending energy of life eternal.

A final hard slap brought the old mayor into the full bloom of his characteristic annoyance.

"Hit me again, and I'll shoot you in the face," Hayes said, squinting as his eyes finally focused on the figure standing over him.

And there Georgie Pilsner was, a granite rectangle of a man, phosphorescent in the half light of the moon as it danced in and out of wispy clouds chasing the tail end of the passing cold front.

"How?" Hayes asked faintly.

"How do you think?" Georgie replied. "I swam here after you sumbitches ditched me."

"But you're the third-worst swimmer I ever met," Hayes said with a painful hint of a laugh. "After Gainesville Tim and the one-armed girl."

"All right, yuck it up," Georgie replied. "But we've got to move. These clouds won't hold. I can't believe they haven't spotted us yet."

"Take Thomas first," Hayes said, with a thin timber of voice that was losing its definition.

"You think I didn't take my best friend first? He's already in the boat."

"Is he still alive?" Hayes asked nervously.

"He is," Georgie replied, "But he doesn't have much time if we don't get him to the clinic."

"What about Rolf? We can't leave him here."

"He's in the boat, too."

"You took a dead guy before me?" Hayes asked, forcing another painful laugh into his belly. "What'd I do to piss you off, dude?"

Georgie replied matter-of-factly, "Thomas didn't want to go without the two of you. I didn't think I could carry more than one of you at the same time, but turns out I was able to throw Thomas over my shoulder and drag the little one through the mud behind me with one arm."

"You wouldn't call him little to his face," Hayes said as he reached his arm toward Georgie for help. "But Thomas would."

"Let's go," Georgie said as he pulled Hayes up to his feet.

"I'll try to walk if you can just help keep me steady."

The dark shadows around them suddenly slid away in tandem with the passing clouds, sending a wash of moonlight sparkling across the muddy ground. As quickly as a flipping switch, the illumination summoned fire from invisible rifles still hidden from the light.

Already low to the ground, tethered to the Earth by meaty trunks, Georgie stooped even lower, pushing his shoulder into the midsection of the old mayor and flipping him over a muscled back as wide as the Eurasian steppe with little difficulty. Instead of running directly toward the mangroves and the boat, Georgie bolted for the nearest shaft of darkness, slipping into it as shots hit all around him on the ground. In a wide, dark arc, Georgie ran, nimbly skirting death with the classical ballet purity of Roberto Bolle leaping at the Teatro alla Scala. The piggy-backed Hayes held on for all he was worth as shots zipped by him like supersonic, kamikaze mosquitoes thirsty for blood.

In moments, they had run the bulk of the gauntlet, leaving only a twenty-yard stretch of open, moonlit ground to navigate to reach the break in the mangroves leading down to the tiny boat. Georgie stopped to catch his breath, and when he did a desultory shot found him in the darkness, entering his ankle at the lateral malleolus bone, tumbling and tearing through the connection between his fibula, tibia and the hinging talus bone, before exiting with jagged violence through the medial malleolus on the other side, all but severing his foot from his lower leg. Only a few strips of hairy skin kept the wide, lifeless foot connected to the pack-mule poet as he tumbled into the light, throwing the old mayor toward the mangroves.

"Keep moving!" Georgie shouted at Hayes, who somehow managed to make it up to his knees and crawl the rest of the way to the boat without being hit.

Georgie took another 5.56 millimeter round through his dominant right hand, with the cavitation effect of the bullet leaving a hole he could see through. His adrenal glands opened wide and flooded their magic elixir into his bloodstream, energizing him for the desperate crawl the rest of the way to the boat. When he reached the water, Georgie was shocked to see Hayes already in the boat, fueled by his own fight-or-flight chemical infusion, elevating him into a last gasp of spryness that would otherwise have been impossible.

Safely shielded from the rifles, Georgie removed his belt and used it as a tourniquet to stem the blood running free from the place where his ankle used to be. His already loose pants fell around his knees, and after three failed attempts to keep them up, he took them off and threw them into the boat. Bare-assed and lame, he dragged himself slowly into the boat at the stern, rocking the little vessel so violently that Rolf slid off into the water just as Georgie was fully onboard. In a move that Hayes found utterly impressive, George reached an arm overboard and snatched the fallen angel from the water as easily as picking a wildflower from a meadow, then began the painful, laborious process of paddling back across the channel with only one good hand available for the task.

"Nice work," Hayes lauded in a whisper, unaware that the little chip of bone had broken free of its subclavian mooring in the fall from the collapsing Georgie Pilsner. "Hard to believe a fella as strong as you can barely swim," Hayes said in a soft, teasing mumble while the adrenaline rushed away from him in a wave, and escaping, anaerobic blood darkened his skin as it pooled internally in places it was never supposed to be. His eyes closed fast and heavy, then he slumped over onto the deck. Here and there, Thomas shook and twitched as the four men teetered wobbly in the ten-foot aluminum boat.

The moving water of the growing tide continued to rush in, and the moon stretched forth again, as the living, dead, and dying floated into the light.

22

— · —

BREEDING LILACS

Lizzy Fraydel and Tabby Lowery walked briskly together down State Road 24, heading to the channel to join their men and get into the fight. When Rolf set off the dynamite that destroyed the Howitzer, they were roughly halfway there and were so unsettled by the force of the blast that they both lost their footing and fell to the ground. When the disorientation faded, they ducked off the road and took cover in the old Southern Star clam wholesale building. As they hunkered down, they could hear the rifle fire that followed, blissfully unaware that it was tearing holes in the men they loved as they ran from the cover of the mangroves toward the Angel of Death.

"I thought the fighting might stop for the night," Tabby said.

Lizzy gripped her lever-action rifle tightly and exhaled slowly. "Doesn't seem like it. We need to get down there before the boys do something stupid."

Tabby said, "That's a fact."

For time immemorial, women had been left to pay the tab run up by the poor decisions of men. Even good men, competent and thoughtful men like Hayes David and Thomas Buck, could seldom escape the evolutionary imperative for foolhardy action baked into the deoxyribonucleic acid script left by their ancestors for them to follow. Women are quietly the ultimate moral authority in most families because their strength endures, even and especially when their men march heroically or stupidly into death. Cedar Key women were the fiercest of them all, willing and ready to fight all comers, even the Gulf itself, to protect the home front.

In the shipping channel on the other side of the island, a legendary island woman was reminding everyone in her presence about her place in the present fight.

"I said no," Miss Bette repeated.

Luke Buck had made his way aboard the cutter Sawfish to brief Isaac and his crew. Rather than waiting until first light, the new plan called for the Sawfish to lead a midnight strike where the island would throw everything they had at the army, from as close in as they could sail the fleet, in hopes the element of surprise might shift the odds in their favor. Miss Bette thought the new plan was bold, and she wanted in, but Isaac was determined to take her to the refugee barracks as planned.

"The Sawfish will draw more fire than any other boat," Isaac protested. "You'll be safer with the others on Atsena Otie. We'll drop you off on our way out."

"I agree, Miss Bette," Luke added. "It's gonna be a real shoot 'em up. We can't risk you getting hurt."

"You boys finished with your speeches?" she asked.

"Yes, ma'am," they said in unison.

"Good. Cause I wasn't asking. I'm telling you that I'm going, so just get used to it. I'm ninety-three damn years old. I'm not gonna run and hide when the island's in trouble. Why would I? To stay safe a little while longer? How much longer do you think I have? Whatever that length of time happens to be, I do not intend to spend it anywhere but in my home.

At the corner of E and 4th. So I'll either fight now to keep them off the island, or I'll fight them on my front porch when they come. Either way, those bastards will have to kill me."

A punishing silence followed that overwhelmed Isaac and Luke while Miss Bette stared directly at them with fire in her eyes.

As though he were about to step into a briar patch, Isaac carefully ventured one last attempt at persuasion. "I can't help but think what Mr. Mark would do to me if I didn't try to protect you if I could."

The old woman tightened the muscles in her face and widened her stance unnoticeably to keep from buckling. She bit the inside of her lip until she could taste blood and gritted her teeth until they hurt, a ninety-four-pound Gibraltar standing against an invasion of feelings that threatened to betray her resolve. Still, the tears came, fast and free in two narrow streams down both sides of her defiantly beautiful face.

"I've spent the past twenty-five years thinking about him every minute of the day. Every morning, just before I open my eyes for the first time, I let myself believe he might be lying next to me when I do. Every single day, my heart gets broken again when I see the empty space where he used to be. Where he's supposed to be. You don't tell me anything about what Mark David might do. How dare you. I knew everything about that man. I could tell by the way he walked into a room how his day went. I knew what he was going to say or do before he even had time to start thinking about it. I'll tell you exactly what Mark David would do. He'd take the fight right to them. He isn't here, but I am, and I'll stand in his place. I absolutely will, and neither of you will stop me. If I get killed doing it, well then, fine. I won't suffer another day without him. Not another morning heartbreak. If you loved me, you'd put me out in front of everyone with a rifle and let me fight my way home to him."

Demosthenes himself could but wither in the face of such oration. Isaac and Luke, being just regular men, had no further arguments to make. Isaac began work to get the Sawfish underway, and Luke left in the fast skiff, racing toward the Number Four Channel.

Miss Bette sat at the helm in the pilot house and cleaned her gun.

Of the two, Thomas caught the most grief about failed relationships, on account of his multiple divorces, but Hayes was no less cursed in matters of love simply because he managed to stretch out a doomed marriage over the same length of time Thomas had cycled through three. For reasons as varied as their personality traits, both men had been on a long run of bad romantic luck when Thomas first arrived on the island several years before the flash, well before Tabby Lowery and Lizzy Fraydel would reveal themselves as saviors of the heart, the reward for every good thing either man had ever done in the world. In those early post-divorce days, Hayes and Thomas were making stereotypically bad decisions as they stumbled through premature midlife crises.

Thomas had met the slow-talking, obsessive-compulsive, overachieving mayor at a city council meeting and made a calculated decision to pursue a friendship with him. He could not have known then, as he embarrassed himself with a formal introduction to the town during the public comments section of the meeting—inviting everyone to a performance of his latest play in nearby Gainesville—how thoroughly the sharp-minded mayor with the aw-shucks elocution would factor into the rest of his life.

There was little initially to suggest a lifelong friendship would develop between the squared-away waterman and the big-idea writer whose contempt for details verged on zealotry, but they did have boats in common. Hayes, of course, preferred a spotless boat in perfect working order, one where people took their shoes off before boarding without being asked. All the switches, gauges, lights, and mechanical components would pass a scrupulous inspection on a Hayes David boat. Conversely, nothing in the nautical world delighted Thomas so immensely as a broken-down, leaking sieve of a boat he bought for cheap from some guy on the Internet, with an outboard motor as petulant as Holden Caufield and less likely to start than a Middle Eastern democracy.

For Hayes, a boat was a vehicle for adventure; to Thomas, the boat *was* the adventure, and he delighted in turning another man's garbage into the same garbage but with a clever name hand-painted on both sides near the bow, sitting like an avant-garde sculpture in his side yard on a trailer with bald tires that had to be aired up any time it was moved.

In his early days on the island, Thomas managed to run aground or outright sink so many ramshackle boats that his mainland buddy Barry Mitchem began calling him *Commodore Bottom*. Lena Fines, to her great delight, had once sabotaged Thomas' invitation to a group of skeptical ladies at the diner for a free boat trip by vouching for his character but repudiating both his boats and his captaining of them.

"He probably won't murder you," she said with a smile, "But I can't guarantee you won't sink or get lost at sea."

To Hayes' credit, he was always up for a trip on every new abomination Thomas would drag across the Number Four Bridge, but as an exercise in the relentless mocking that underpins all great male friendships, he wouldn't step aboard without wearing an obnoxious bright-yellow life-

jacket, the kind people buy in packs of four to meet Coast Guard require-
ments but would never actually wear.

So it was with the *Unsinkable Judith Jane*, Thomas' first birddog boat,
named after his mama. When he decided to become a clam farmer, as a
distraction from the oft-repeating and demoralizing image in his head and
heart of Annie driving away from him for the last time with his beloved
good boy Franklin looking back at him mournfully, Thomas was determined to find a real clam boat.

Many clam farmers, especially new ones, made do with skiffs or other
shallow-draft boats until they decided whether or not they would take to
underwater farming, but not Thomas. If he was going to be a clam farmer,
he decided, then he needed to have a proper clam farming boat. Birddogs
were hard to come by. Thomas spent weeks searching all over the state with
no success. He even took to stopping at any house that had a birddog in
the yard and knocking on the door to see if they were interested in selling.
Twenty-three icy rejections, more than one accompanied by a slamming
door, had not deterred him. Behind the twenty-fourth door, at a house in
Otter Creek that had two beat-up old birddogs in the yard slowly being
reclaimed by the Earth, Thomas struck paydirt.

"Excuse me, sir. I live over in Cedar Key, and I'm trying to start a clam
farm," Thomas said to the annoyed man who answered the door.

"They're not for sale," he said gruffly, before Thomas could even ask.

"I'd be willing to pay a premium. Are you sure you wouldn't consider
selling me your shittiest one?"

"I'll never sell either one," the man said.

From the back of the house, an angry woman emerged, sprinting toward the front door. "Yes the hell you will," she said. "I'm sick of watching

those things rot in the yard. You're not even farming anymore. Sell 'em both."

"Honey, no. I'm just not farming right now," the man said, balancing a pleading tone with his wife against the flaming disgust he had for Thomas.

"I'm sorry, friends, I didn't mean to cause any trouble. I think I better go," Thomas said.

"Not without one of those boats, you're not," she ordered, and suddenly Thomas and the defeated man were both scrambling to do what they were told.

"Fine," he said at last. "I'll sell you the little one, but it won't be cheap."

Thomas, beaming, would have agreed to almost any price in that moment, but by the time they had walked out to the boat, his late father's wheeler-dealer spirit asserted itself, and the 22-foot Trembley birddog left the yard for a thousand dollars less than the first quoted price.

On the twenty-two-mile trip back to the island, a wheel fell off the trailer, but Thomas was somehow able to safely pull the boat to the side of the road, chase down the runaway tire bounding into the swamp running alongside State Road 24, and lug it back to the trailer. A ratchet strap, an old hub from a random tire in the back of his truck, and the improvisational engineering skills of a poor Southern upbringing were all Thomas needed to get back on the road.

The faded white boat was painted a glossy navy blue, and Thomas hired an artist to scroll *Judith Jane* in bright white letters near the bow, an homage to his mama. He fitted the thirty-year-old Trembly with a twenty-year-old Johnson 2-stroke outboard, rigged a hydraulic steering wheel to fit into the wooden helm, and was working his new clam lease within a week. Even Hayes was impressed with the result and glad to see his buddy working the waters alongside him. The *Judith Jane* was six feet smaller than most of the other birddogs in the fleet, but it was also the fastest by a wide margin. Thomas generally ran it like a rented mule and put it up wet, so it came as something of a surprise that the old Johnson worked so well for as long as it did.

On a crisp and clear February morning in the waning hours of the old world, while Hayes tended to official city business on land, Thomas and much of the fleet were working the Dog Island and Corrigan Reef clam leases, on a glorious winter low tide, when a blinding light on the horizon incinerated the smokestacks across the bay, vaporizing more than a thousand people near them in a third of a heartbeat. As the heat and shockwave tore across the bay, the other boats in the fleet raced for shore, unwittingly sailing directly into the teeth of the irradiated wind. Thomas would have followed them into the radiation's gray embrace if not for a broken plastic oil nipple on his poorly maintained motor that left the *Judith Jane* stranded in the water. As the heat bore down upon him, Thomas crammed himself into the fiberglass dry box on the deck of his boat, closed the heavy lid, and waited in the darkness for death that did not come. The happenstance of the morning's wind direction marked his fellow captains and their crews for destruction, while the thin fiberglass walls of the dry box kept him absurdly, unjustifiably safe.

When Hayes rescued him later that day, Thomas was overcome with shame and guilt, having survived by negligence and chance alone while better watermen were left to suffer and die in gruesome slowness, withering to undignified deaths in the awful first week of the new world. Hayes refused to let his best friend indulge in self-pity while the demands of the new world were so immediate and unreasonable. He pulled Thomas quickly from his malaise, and they began the work together of reshaping the island, and eventually its boats, for a post-nuclear life.

Georgie continued paddling.

Of all the boats Hayes and Thomas had been on together, from the *Unsinkable Judith Jane*, to the venerable *Cogency*, the houseboat turned flagship *U.S.S. Blue Lang*, Luke's *Big Skiff Energy*, and innumerable bird-dogs, barges, pontoons, catamarans, and V-hulls, none were less auspicious than the ten-foot aluminum jon boat lumbering across the channel, paddled by a one-footed Virginian with a hole in his hand.

Near the middle of the channel, the moon's light seemed to be focused purposefully and directly on the little boat, with flanking dark clouds on either side casting darkness across the backwaters and the land.

"You fellas really ought to wake up and see this," Georgie said, letting himself imagine that his friends were merely sleeping off a rough night. "You'll regret it if you don't."

"Are we there yet?" Thomas asked miraculously.

"I thought you were gone," Georgie said, smiling because he could hear the smirk in his buddy's voice.

"I think I still am," Thomas replied as his arms jerked involuntarily and a hard hiccup filled his mouth with the taste of metal.

"You're fine," Georgie said. "We'll get you to the clinic, and they'll fix you right up."

"I was always a better liar than you," Thomas said.

Georgie tried to think of something clever to say, but could only manage a frustrated nod. Hours later, when the moment was lost forever, the perfect response invariably came. *Every good story is some kind of lie* would have consecrated the moment in fine literary style had not blood and exhaustion overtyped so much of the scene already.

"Yell at the mayor and see if you can get him up," Thomas said.

"Mr. Mayor!" Georgie yelled. "Wake up!"

"Hit him with the paddle," Thomas said with a smile and a little building strength in his voice.

Georgie whacked Hayes in the side of his leg with a surprising amount of force for a one-handed blow.

Hayes' eyes popped open inside a motionless body, and he said, "I sure thought your buddy and me were friends, Thomas. But this dude is having a big time beating the crap out of me tonight."

"Alright, y'all just keep talking," Georgie said, relieved. "Stay with me a little bit longer. We're almost there."

Suddenly, both men rebounded. Hayes pulled himself up to a seated position, and Thomas managed to reach an arm around Hayes' neck for the kind of awkward side hug he had come to expect from his old friend.

"I was talking to my dad," Thomas said, wide-eyed and alert.

"Pretty sure you're dead then," Hayes said. "I didn't see my dad any-where. I was just taking a nap in a little boat."

"Nobody's dead," Georgie said. "Everybody's making it to the clinic."

"I don't think Rolf's gonna make it," Thomas said, laughing blood into the boat.

In the terminal lucidity of those last moments, when any man could be excused for cowering before the long night, with its Reaper reaching out for them from just beyond the moonlight, there in the narrow crease between the heavens and the Earth, defenseless in the terrible silver glow, the old friends chose laughter.

"There's something wrong with both of you," Georgie said, before joining the laughter.

Hayes smiled at the brave Virginian. "Thanks for coming to get us, buddy."

"Sorry I kicked you, brother," Thomas added.

"I would've done the same to you," Georgie replied, no longer able to stem the sadness rushing over the gunwales and into the boat. "We'll call it even on the castle."

"Even and a little more," Thomas said in a quiet, failing voice.

The wave of spontaneous energy had crested and was racing away from them now. A few moments of silence stretched into a full, eternal minute. Hayes was slumped over again, and Thomas' arms hung low at his sides.

"Luke . . ." Thomas said with tears in his eyes, staring toward the shore. "My boy."

Hayes smiled, thinking of the Buck men, his friends, and drifted away.

Thomas tried to reach for the old mayor's hand, but the last of his strength was gone. With another breath or two, he would have said I love you, but their fathers were calling, and Hayes already knew.

23

—·—

UNRAVELED

Major Joshua Lawrence was never going to be an architect or a banker or an artist. From his first day on earth, his family legacy determined that he would be a soldier. His mother's maiden name was Chamberlain, and her family covetously protected and proclaimed its military lineage back to the Revolutionary War, where Ebenezer and Henry Chamberlain were documented to have fought in some of the bloodiest battles in the nation's war for independence from the British Crown. The most impressive feather in the Chamberlain military cap, however, was the Hero of Little Round Top during the Battle of Gettysburg in the Civil War, General Joshua Lawrence Chamberlain.

Major Lawrence was the third Lawrence to be named after the great general, each preordained for military greatness, none but the major ever rising above the rank of captain, and all failing to bring glory to the family commensurate with their namesake. Of the three, the major was the most similar to his four-greats grandfather in temperament and education. General Chamberlain was a professor of rhetoric, oratory, and modern languages at Bowdoin College in Maine when the young nation's fraternal war broke out. He was famously fluent in nine languages besides his native

English tongue—Spanish, German, French, Italian, Greek, Latin, Arabic, Hebrew, and Syriac.

Bookish and reserved, General Chamberlain had no formal military training when he was commissioned as a Lieutenant Colonel with the 20th Maine Volunteer Infantry Regiment, and held the rank of full Colonel during the Battle of Gettysburg. On the second day of that battle, Colonel Chamberlain and his men held the left section of a rocky hill called Little Round Top. A superior Confederate force, the 15th Alabama, was charging up the hill toward the position held by the 20th Maine, whooping the bloodcurdling Rebel Yell as they came. Running out of ammunition and recognizing the significance of holding the hill after the Union Army's defeats thus far in the battle, Colonel Chamberlain ordered his troops to fix bayonets and charge down the hill at the rebels, executing a wheel maneuver that turned his troops into a swinging hinge and trapping the enemy between two fronts. The audacity of the maneuver caught the rebels off guard, and they were driven off the hill. During the battle, a Confederate officer fired a revolver at Colonel Chamberlain's face but missed from close range. The colonel forced the officer's surrender at the point of his sword, and he kept the revolver for the rest of his life.

Many historians point directly to Colonel Chamberlain and the 20th Maine as the element that prevented a disastrous route of the Army of the Potomac at the Battle of Gettysburg, one which could plausibly have led to the loss of the war. For his heroism under extreme duress, Colonel Chamberlain was awarded the Medal of Honor and eventually promoted to Brevet Major General. He was present at Appomattox Courthouse when Confederate General Robert E. Lee surrendered the Army of Northern Virginia to Union General Ulysses S. Grant. Ever a man of honor and decency, General Chamberlain earned additional historical fame for ordering his troops to *carry arms* as a salute to the surrendering Confederate soldiers.

For Major Joshua Lawrence, with a connection to a man of such god-like qualities and achievements, no amount of personal valor could ever live up to his name. Still, he was generally the most literate and thoughtful in any command in which he served. He could not claim to speak nine languages, but he was fluent in English, Spanish, and French, and could manage a little German and Italian in a pinch. He had not been a West Point man like the dead general that had led his army to the channel, but he had graduated third in his class from Norwich College in Vermont, formerly the American Literary, Military and Scientific Academy, with a Bachelor's Degree in Strategic Studies, and a Master of Arts in Military History. For the modern age, Colonel Lawrence was every bit the scholar-soldier, and if not the equal of the great man for which he was named, he was certainly a respectable addition to the family's military register.

If the world had gone on living as it had before the bombs fell, there is every reason to believe the major would have risen to the upper echelons of Army ranks, though only the major himself knew that his heart had been drifting away from the allure of military glory for years leading up to the collapse of the nation he had dedicated his life to serving. As the new world dragged on, the drudgery of military life had grown increasingly intolerable. On the march to Mount Weather, at least, there had briefly been a reason to believe in the general's unbelievable mission. If some chance remained that America endured, the call of his family's legacy might have reinfused his life with high purpose once more, but from the moment the major saw the empty hole where an impregnable fortress should have been, his continued service to the army was merely a function of habit and routine, one increasingly devoid of honor.

So it was that Major Joshua Lawrence, still nursing the physical effects of a concussion and the emotional aftermath of his encounter with Hayes David in the freezing rain, decided he would follow the example of the great Nez Perch Chief Joseph and *fight no more forever*. He had been complicit in bringing the army so far from its home for such a pointless and ignoble purpose. In the general's office after returning from Virginia, the sounds coming from the receiver had been meaningless, incomprehensible noise, and the major knew it. The general had disappeared into the noise, possessed then by the static in the speaker and in a lost world that no longer needed soldiers to fight for it. With an idea as big as America thus unraveled, it was easier for the general to hear orders than it was to hear nothing, and it had been shamefully easier for the major to keep on majoring than it was to wake the general from his dream.

He was now suddenly and painfully aware that the chain of command was a flimsy defense for his lack of opposition to the general's delusions. It's true the major had no idea how deep the water had to be to float an aircraft carrier, or what the depths around Cedar Key happened to be, but in his gut, he knew none of it made sense. The blood of his soldiers, and of the old boat captain who could have killed him but did not, was now soaked into hands that had always felt more comfortable holding books about war than the instruments of it.

With the rain stopped and intermittent moonlight beginning to set in around the camp, Major Lawrence had a fire started and assembled the officers and men to relay the news of General Gill's death and his decision to withdraw back to Fort Rucker.

In short, the announcement went poorly.

Word of the general's death sent the men, especially, into a furor. The officers made a show of trying to settle them down, but most had the same misgivings about the major's order as the enlisted men. Major Lawrence was the only formally trained officer left in the army. The handful of company commanders were all enlisted members of the 198th Battalion who were commissioned and promoted over the years by the general himself, thereby increasing their radical devotion to him. This unfortunate truth meant there were none among the officers or men with whom the major could cogently discuss military strategy, so his attempt to relay the specifics of why their numerical advantage was mitigated by the terrain and lack of boats was quickly drowned out by shouts to avenge the general's death.

"Company commanders, front and center!" the major ordered in his most commanding voice, feeling like a stage actor rather than a leader of men.

The three captains and one lieutenant made their way toward the major as their men continued to shout and rage.

"Gentlemen," the major began. "Are we going to have a problem here? You will get your men in line and restore military order or—"

"Or what?" the lieutenant interrupted.

The three captains, similarly bristling at the major's orders but lacking the nerve for outright insubordination, stood in stunned silence.

"I came here to fight because the old man told me to," the lieutenant said.

"The old man is dead," the major snapped back. "I'm the senior officer now, and I'm telling you we're leaving."

"Fourth Company's going nowhere until I tell 'em, and I ain't telling 'em nothing until that island pays."

With time to think through the decision, it's possible the major would have backed down, but with the demands of the moment so pressing, all the soldier that remained within him rose to the fore. In a dazzling move that seemed to be the result of years of practicing, because in fact the major had been practicing it in the mirror since he was a young second lieutenant, the Sig Sauer was drawn so quickly from his holster that its barrel was square against the mutinous junior officer's forehead before he had any possibility of reacting.

"Arrest this man, captains," the major ordered.

The entire scene was playing before a captive audience of killers, lit dramatically by the moon and fire, and racing toward a denouement to rival the Ides of March.

"Sir, please, put the gun down," one of the captains pleaded.

Major Lawrence stood firm, even as Fourth Company broke ranks and rushed toward him in a wave.

Just as the last of the would-be refugees were being loaded into the navy's boats for the short trip to Atsena Otie, a line of men and women that did not need or wish to be evacuated, and were neither members of the navy nor the militia, began to arrive in the parking lot, ready for service. Kinsey Buck sounded the alarm and ran from house to house, relaying the call to arms. Islanders of varying ages and fitness for combat began mustering, arbitrarily and sometimes laughably armed with everything from old deer rifles to shotguns, hunting bows, machetes, and knives. Jimmy Mitchell, who had been stranded on land when Luke took his skiff to meet Isaac Skipjack on the Sawfish, arrived back from his house wearing a steampunk aesthetic backpack contraption he claimed to be a flamethrower he had built in his barn. No one had cause to doubt him, and likewise no one wanted to stand near him in case he actually tried to light the thing.

At the front of the ragtag formation, working with surprising success to establish something resembling order, was a rejuvenated Heff Webster. After a little time to lick his wounds from the repudiation suffered at the emergency council meeting, the oft off-putting but nevertheless tireless old Marine had made peace with being wrong about the army at the channel, and had shown up to fight alongside his neighbors. Of small towns, William Faulkner famously said that, "People everywhere are about the same," but this had never been especially true of the island, a place where folks loved even those they didn't especially like.

Throughout its history, Cedar Key had been a repository for the wayward, the self-determined, and the damned. A principled bureaucrat like councilman Webster often found himself a few beats out of time with the island's impenitent song, but he nevertheless continued to work as he saw fit to serve his neighbors, even when they sometimes vigorously opposed the service. A lesser man would have given in to bitterness long ago; Heff Webster persisted, and in the present effort, his Marine Corps training proved useful. At his side, Dale Warble did what he could to amplify Heff's direction to the crowd, and in short order the two self-appointed leaders had arranged seventy-two non-soldiers into a passable formation.

"Nice work, Heff," said Denny Gall, the former owner of the Steaming Clam restaurant and the café on 2nd Street.

"Thanks, buddy," Heff replied with a performative casualness to mask the dopamine surge accompanying the compliment. "We might make a fighting force yet."

Kinsey arrived back in the parking lot, winded from the running but by all accounts ready for a fight.

"What's the word?" Heff asked. "Where are we needed?"

Kinsey replied, "The plan had been to hit them with everything we have at first light, but Luke doesn't think we can risk waiting until then. The Sawfish and our fleet are going to sail toward the channel as soon as everyone who can't fight has made it over to the old island. For now, I think we should all get to the Crofts house on foot as quick as we can and meet up with Big Chief and Hayes and my daddy-in-law to see where they need us. There'll be room on the Sawfish and our boats for some of us when they get there, and the rest can join up with the militia."

"You heard the lady," Heff announced to the crowd. "Let's move out!"

The citizen soldiers followed Heff and Dale into the night, rag-tag but determined, as the boats in the fleet set out with refugees for Atsena Otie. Luke Buck passed the fleet in the shipping channel on his way to meet up with Hayes and his dad to relay the new plan for an all-out nighttime attack. If the Sawfish and its 50-caliber machine guns could lay into the center of the army as they camped, the rest of the fleet could split into two flanking forces on either side of the cutter and unload everything they have from oblique angles. He would talk with Big Chief and Rolf about leading separate forces to attack on land from Leanna's Peninsula on one side and the scrub on the other.

The younger Buck had a head full of steam and a mind racing with details that needed to be handled to give the island the best chance for success. As he made his way past Dog Island and began the turn at Cedar Point, he could not help but feel that he was finding his footing as a leader at last. He could also not have known how irreparably his world would break over the next half hour, how unmoored he would soon become by a little boat overloaded with death and men he loved.

All fathers die; some die badly and too soon.

The several minutes between Dog Island and the Crofts house would etch themselves into Luke's mind and heart from then on; as he made a smooth, fast turn into the narrow inlet and dodged the series of sandbars that had hung him up more than once in his early years as a captain, the world was still full of possibility, and despite the coming battle, despite the numerical advantage of the enemy, despite the losses the island had already sustained, some sequence of events were possible that would lead to liberation and victory, to a trial by combat that would prove him to be the man he always hoped he was and feared he could never be; everything was possible until the fast skiff made its way to the shore in front of the Crofts house, where already Lizzy and Tabby were in the water and wailing, where Big Chief sat on the bank with her head in her hands, where the smothering smog of death had blotted out the beauty of the night, where his father and his mentor were strange approximations of themselves, hollow and sad in the embrace of death, bloody and spent like the last dollar of a paycheck that had not kept the lights on—muddled, ruined memories of the men they had been.

24

— · —

INFINITE ENERGY

Fourth Company's lieutenant was the least squared away of the four company commanders, as evidenced by his inferior rank and the fact that he had been commissioned at the same time as the other three. The gangly, sandy-headed Oklahoman had made captain around the same time as his colleagues but was busted down by the general after twice showing up to muster piss drunk on moonshine. He had made the hooch himself in the woods near the Fort Rucker barracks and supplied it to the rest of the company in trade for all manner of goods and services.

When the general began to lose his connection to the day-to-day operation of the army, while he slipped deeper into the delusion of radio broadcasts and orders from a government that almost certainly no longer existed, the lieutenant leaned into the army's collapsing standards of discipline and decency. Most of the burned buildings in Harrisonburg that Georgie Pilsner encountered when he emerged from the fog of injury and began his walk to Cedar Key had been set by the lieutenant. The men of Fourth Company quickly began to emulate their commander's malfeasance such that by the time they reached Fanning Springs on their way to Cedar Key, they were little more than marauding vandals. As they marched away, the small riverfront community was as decimated as Baghdad when Hulagu Khan and his Mongol hordes sacked it in 1258.

When the major drew down on the insubordinate lieutenant, the men of his company immediately rushed forth, not for sentimental attachment to the angular, pockmarked Oklahoman, but in rebellion against the order Major Lawrence sought to reestablish. In the absence of virtuous leadership, all armies are destined for devolution and brutality. It was as true of Ivan the Terrible's Oprichniki torture squads as it was of Pol Pot's Khmer Rouge and the more polished depravity of the twenty-first-century regimes and governments that killed the world. The general's abdication of leadership had given his soldiers an unrighteous taste for blood that could not be removed from their mouths without force—force a single man with a handgun could scarcely wield against them.

In the two-and-a-half to three seconds it would take the Fourth Company soldiers to reach the major and his company commanders, a range of options still existed that would have spectacularly different effects on the following several hours, and indeed the rest of the lives of every man present. The three captains could have intervened to help establish order, but they did not. The soldiers in the other three companies could have intervened to stop Fourth Company from their attempted coup, but they stood as fixed in place as Terra Cotta Warriors in a mausoleum. The major could have shot the lieutenant and fired into the charging soldiers to shock them into withdrawal, or taken him hostage at gunpoint to coerce his men to stand down, but he exercised none of these options.

In less time than it takes for a good deep breath to make its way into and out of a body, the major's lifetime of studying military history and strategy led him to conclude the battle was already lost. No additional killing, counsel, or instruction could save his army. It was in its death throes at the Mount Weather hole and slipped away for good outside a Virginia courthouse when the Shenandoah Home Guard fell to an armed mob. By the time its corpse left Fanning Springs, the meat and honor had been stripped fully from its bones.

The moon was high overhead, and his heart was broken as the major lowered the gun and returned it to his holster. This was no longer his army, and these were no longer his men. A moment later, the Fourth Company wave crashed over Major Joshua Lawrence and tore him asunder.

Luke's memory of the scene at the shore was one to be locked away and hidden, but the boat ride preceding it became a geodesic marker of a time when he was the son of a living father, when William had a Paw-Paw, and the Buck men would live forever. In the moments before he first saw the little jon boat, Luke was fixated on the battle plan he intended to present to Hayes and his dad. He had formulated it in the aftermath of the artillery's destruction of the docks, when the sight of his dead neighbors had filled him with seething rage.

There was no room for rage when he saw the men in the boat, only love. Luke's love for his father was an ever-fixed mark, unchanged by the bending sickle of death, unaltered by the ruined visage of the man that sang him lullaby versions of Counting Crows songs to soothe him to sleep when he was a baby, that taught him to play golf and the guitar, to love history, rifles, old boats, and Cedar Key; such a love could never be transmuted to rage or hate and could no more cease to be than time or the First Law of

Thermodynamics or God. Love is an infinite energy that can never die, once it's been created, once it's been given away.

Luke would reformulate his battle plan, unhurried as a lullaby, focused as a father's prayer for a sleeping child, to kill every soldier across the channel possible, because he was Thomas Buck's son, and William Buck's father, and his love would bear out even to the edge of doom.

First, he would join Lizzy in the water, where she was leaning into the little boat to hold his father and kiss his face and sob. They held him together until he could feel the old woman's heartbeat in near-time with his own, could feel joy poking at the edges of the grief because his father had at last been thoroughly and perfectly loved by a woman such as her. When Luke was seventeen years old, he had accidentally seen his father staring quietly into the empty closet where Annie's clothes had been after she drove away for the last time. He had witnessed him carefully and unsuccessfully crafting a front of strength in the aftermath to protect his son from turmoil. Luke had secretly hurt alongside him as a lasting love continued to stay just beyond his father's reach.

But then there was Lizzy, beautiful as azaleas in bloom, solid as a kept promise, fighting a fire in a bucket line alongside his father, loving him almost instantly forever. He was overcome with gratitude for her as they froze together in the water.

Big Chief and Elijah carried Georgie from the boat, who touched Luke's face as he passed and said, "He was calling for you, Luke, at the end. He was looking toward the shore and calling for his boy. I paddled as hard as I could to get him to you, but I didn't make it. I'm sorry."

Luke kissed his old friend on the top of his bald head and said, "Thank you for trying, Mr. Georgie."

"Of course."

"Do you remember what my dad always said we had to do for him if he died?"

"Send him up like Billy Crud," Georgie replied.

"Yes, sir. We're going to do exactly that," Luke said with a far-off light in his eyes.

"Perfect," the battered Virginian replied with a smile.

"What does that mean?" Lizzy asked through her tears. "Who's Billy Crud?"

"I'll tell you all about it soon," Luke said warmly. "There's so much to do. We need to get started."

Several members of the militia pulled the little boat onto the shore with the fallen heroes still inside.

"Can we get something to cover them up for now?" Luke asked. "I don't want everyone seeing them like this. This is no way to remember them."

"Remember who?" William asked from several yards behind him.

He and his mother were just arriving from downtown with Heff Webster and the rest of the islanders who had come to join the fight. Before Luke had time to answer or turn to stop his son from going further, a wild, confused howl tore through the night, laying low everyone in its path, as Thomas Buck's grandson ran toward the boat and fell alongside it on the ground, a feral giant toppled like Goliath by a gruesome tableau he was not equipped to process. William reached out to touch his Paw-Paw but stopped short, paralyzed with indecision and pain, then turned back to seek in his father's face a comfort that could not be provided. No moment in Luke's life would ever hurt him more, and yet, as his son struggled before him, never was he more aware of his own father's love, rough-hewn and constant, unyielding in physical death, exalting in it even, because it would not and could never die.

Luke joined his son at the boat, and the three Buck men sat quietly for a long while together.

An orgiastic tangle of soldiers beat the major into a frenzied, intimate death. When it was finished, a pair of Fourth Company sergeants threw the body into the fire. While the major slowly burned, the lieutenant surveyed his men with beastly satisfaction, writhing like the prophets of Baal in ritual to a false god—corybantic, untethered, and lost as they celebrated a victory so pyrrhic it would cost every man involved his immortal soul.

The three captains from the other companies shrank before the lieutenant, suddenly elevated by a coronation of blood and loyalty that outstripped the adornments of rank.

"Captains!" the lieutenant yelled above the ruckus. "Any objection from you gentlemen about staying put and taking this island?"

Meek, non-verbal affirmations came from all three.

"Excellent!" the lieutenant replied. "Let's let the men enjoy a little fun tonight. In the morning, we can make a siege plan. We've got 'em cut off. They ain't going anywhere."

At the lieutenant's order, several marked artillery shell crates were retrieved from one of the army's trucks and brought to him.

"Open them!" the lieutenant called out excitedly.

When the top was pried off the first box, a cheer went up from the men. Even as the moon began to slide behind a new wall of clouds, enough light found its way into the crate to dance through the glass and clear liquid of moonshine bottles piled three rows abreast and four bottles deep. A Dionysian hootnanny kicked off that filled the estuary with sounds of revelry, perverse in the flickering moonlight of the blood-soaked night, drifting in and out of periodic violence, chest-thumping self-exalting speeches, and every variation of the dishonorable, prurient, and obscene.

Across the channel, the watchstanders on the widow's walk took in the scene with amazement. With the naked eye, they could see the fires and the wild movement of men, could discern from a distance that something had changed within the army, but through the binoculars, the details were shocking. A man was burning in the fire, and all around him, other men cheered. As the night dragged on and the bottles of moonshine were drained, the levee of military order gave way completely, and the basest impulses of the killers took charge of the night. Lingering petty feuds exploded into a wave of fights that left bloodied men stumbling along the shoreline. The tenor of the sound racing across the water and the images inside the binoculars were discomforting and foul, equal parts celebratory and threatening, Saturnalia without the symbolism, a Gomorrah so depraved that not even Lot's wife would turn back to look at it—against trees, in tents, and on the wet open ground men pushed themselves into other men, slicked with spit and spoiled by blood and shit while fires burned and the moon, hiding its eyes from the degradation, disappeared for good.

As disorder spread through the army, the lieutenant decided to make Leanna Beecham's house on the peninsula his headquarters. When he discovered the sprawling wrap-around balcony on the second floor, he took up residence there on a comfortable patio loveseat a few feet from the fallen

Ryland Beecham, whom he left slumped in the wicker chair where he died early in the evening. Thus ensconced, the lieutenant summoned the three other company commanders via enlisted messengers, then stretched out in luxurious repose while he waited for their arrival. The bodies of the soldiers Ryland had dispatched were still littered across the yard and driveway. The lieutenant had stepped over several on his way to the house. When he saw the rifle leaning against the railing near the dead islander, he nodded his head in admiration.

"You did all this alone?" the lieutenant asked.

Even in the quietude of his defeat, Ryland was magnificent. His eyes were open and fixed on the killing field he had created in defense of his mother's home, and his heart, cold and dead now for hours, was nevertheless still bursting with a love so pure and violent the interloping lieutenant felt diminished by his proximity to it.

When the captains arrived and found the lieutenant on the balcony, he pointed at the chairs around him and motioned for them to sit.

"Time was against us when we thought the general was still alive," the lieutenant began. "Now that he's gone, I don't see a reason for us to get in a hurry. The major had planned to send a hundred men back toward the mainland to find boats we could use to cross the channel. I'm going to make it two hundred. With even ten or twelve boats, I think we could get enough of our boys across to take control of the island. I don't think we'd even have to kill that many before they just gave up."

"They fought pretty good as far as I could tell," the Second Company captain replied skeptically.

The Third Company captain added, "I lost sixteen men before we even knew what hit us. These aren't regular civilians. It'd be a mistake to underestimate them."

The lieutenant asked the remaining captain disdainfully, "How bout you? You as scared as these two?"

First Company's commander replied defensively, "Nobody's scared. We're just saying we ought to be ready for a real fight."

"Fine," the lieutenant replied. "It'll be a fight. Or it won't. It doesn't matter. They killed the old man, and they've still got our helicopter, and I'll be damned if they don't pay for both. Get back to your men and pass the word for them to settle in. We might be here a while."

Luke Buck was called to the widow's walk in time to witness the chaos unfolding on the mainland before the last of the moonlight flickered out and mystery reappeared in the darkness. Based on what he had seen in the binoculars, he decided to delay implementing the new battle plan until the partying was over and the soldiers were as drunk and exhausted as they were going to get, then hit them shortly after they all passed out for the night.

Luke descended from the widow's walk and gathered the militia to begin preparations for the attack.

"We need to pull the Crofts barn down, a board at a time. We need as much of that dry old wood as possible. Heff, can you grab ten or twelve others and take charge of that effort?"

"Sure, Luke," Heff replied. "But what's the wood for?"

"I promise I'll fill everyone in shortly. Jimmy, can you get my dad and Mr. Hayes and Mr. Rolf out of the boat and covered up on the ground? We're gonna need that boat, your skiff I sailed here, and one more small boat for my plan. Can you round up some volunteers and make that happen?"

"I'm on it," Little Jimmy Mitchell said.

"Thanks," Luke replied. "The rest of y'all, let's huddle up and go over the land portion of the plan."

"Got any work for a couple of has-beens?" came a voice from just behind the crew that arrived from town with Heff Webster.

Retired Police Chief Jank Edwins, arthritic and limping from a deteriorating vascular issue, looking like a worn-out old mule but steely as ever as he rested his hands on twin six-shooters holstered on both hips, smiled as he stood alongside retired Fire Chief Bob Roberts, white-haired and wild-eyed with a fire axe on his shoulder.

"Absolutely," Luke replied warmly. "I'll take all the chiefs I can get."

Luke relayed the details of his plan, assigning leaders for each portion of it, and finally revealed the purpose of the three boats and the barn wood.

"You're definitely Thomas' kid," Dale Warble said, shaking his head. "That's some weird shit."

"It's perfect," Lizzy said.

"Uncle Hayes would love it," Big Chief added.

"Rolf, too," said Kinsey.

In the building darkness, an eastern screech owl underscored the electric peril of the night with its shrill descending whinny and evil, even-pitched tremolo as the Coast Guard Cutter Sawfish sailed quietly into the channel on a massive full moon king tide. The Cedar Key Navy followed close behind, blooded, nimble, and dexterous, ready for the fight to come.

25

—·—

THE LAST GREAT STAND OF CEDAR KEY

In the several years leading up to the fall of man, a cultural phenomenon emerged in the United States known as *Florida Man*. For a long while, the nation remained fixated on the wild times, misadventures, and criminal enterprises of Florida ne'er-do-wells, miscreants, and outlaws as they invariably ran afoul of the law and wound up on the news. The news stories would always begin with *A Florida man...*

A Florida man kidnaps a scientist to make his dog immortal.
A Florida man throws a live alligator into a Wendy's drive-through window.
A Florida man is arrested for selling golden tickets to heaven he got from Jesus behind a KFC.
A Florida man tries to rob a bank after paying a wizard $500 to make him invisible.

The nonstop parade of unbelievable stories coming out of the Sunshine State captivated the nation's attention and held it for many years. There seemed to be something in the water or sweltering heat turning an entire state into an asylum. In reality, the phenomenon derived most of its energy from the state's Sunshine Law, which made arrest records publicly available immediately after they were filed. Lazy journalists only needed to monitor the public records for a seemingly endless supply of clickbait stories that were guaranteed to draw a wide readership.

Thomas Buck initially hated the entire Florida Man mythos because, in his view, it focused on the low-hanging fruit without taking the time to dig into the systemically weird and wholly original soul of a swampland culture that infiltrated the characters in his plays and books. He spent a year mocking all things Florida Man, and turning up his nose at every new story, before giving in and writing a Florida Man play out of spite that debuted off-Broadway in New York City to wide acclaim before sold-out regional productions back in Florida. Resolved that he could not hold back the flood of all things Florida Man, he had determined to write a substantive, character-driven play that brushed aside the trappings of shock culture and probed toward the inner workings of the place and people he so loved. Despite his best efforts to elevate the genre, his play nevertheless included a homemade sex robot, a corpse reanimated by hard lemonade-fueled hallucinations, and a conspiracy-theorist rap about 9/11 being an inside job. At its heart, however, like so much of Thomas Buck's writing, was a father-son story. With wiener jokes, a ghost, and a country cemetery near the black waters of the Peace River, the story shone a disinfecting light on the multitude of powers, tender and brutal, that love can assert over human beings.

The primary connotation of love is happiness and light, but light without darkness is a hellish repetition of blank space. Because love is the opposite of hell, it must necessarily be a spectrum from bright devotion to black death and all points in between. Within the *in between* lies the sum of all human joy, conflict, achievement, and defeat. Thomas' Florida Man play was a treatise on the *in between* of love, told silly and profane to help the medicine go down smoother.

In the theater world, playwrights learn they must be able to sell their play in the time it takes for an elevator ride by developing a one or two-sentence summary that will elicit immediate interest in the story. This elevator pitch is called a logline.

The logline for the play *Florida Man,* by Thomas Buck, was the following:

A Florida man digs up his dead father to give him the proper Viking funeral he always wanted.

After he buried his father in a pine box at the cemetery near their house, Billy Crud, the main character in the play, became increasingly haunted by his late father's frequent demand in life that he not be put in the ground or in a crematorium under any circumstance. The elder Crud was debilitatingly claustrophobic. He wanted to be drenched in gasoline, floated on a boat into the middle of the river, and set ablaze with a flaming arrow. He talked about Viking funerals so often that Billy began to tune it out. He couldn't actually be serious, Billy reasoned, and such a thing was almost certainly illegal anyway. And yet, as the weeks passed after the funeral, he grew agitated to the point of constant distraction that he had failed as a son to honor his father's dying wish.

William Crud, Sr., was a heartless reprobate whose meager love was willfully destructive to those it touched, and still, Billy decided to dig him up. A mishap with propane tanks turned the Viking funeral from a dignified slow-burn to an explosive affair that rained down bits of the elder Crud across a wide swath of the Peace River. The old man was free of the hole, and his ghost was satisfied at last, even as the alligators, gar, and snapping turtles feasted on Crud meat for days to come. No such satisfaction would ever come for his boy; even this final act of outrageous service had failed to close or even reconcile the distance between the Crud men. The hole in Billy's heart remained as empty as the robbed grave of a negligent father.

Luke Buck had thrived in the sunlight of his father's unfailing love; even though Thomas had mostly been joking about being sent up like the character in his play, Luke was taking no chances. The barn was being torn apart for the fuel of its desiccated wood, and three small boats were gathered together along the shore. The new mayor's battle plan would marshal the dead to fight alongside the living.

Thomas, Hayes, and Rolf would go up together.

It was just past 4 AM when the camp across the channel fell finally silent. The three captains, clinging to some semblance of duty and military bearing, stood watch as their haggard men stumbled into tents or fell asleep in the open. They had found their sense of duty too late to save the major, maybe too late to be worth anything at all. The chill air of the small hours stung alongside their guilt as they walked through the camp surveying the feckless army, rendered inert by the lieutenant's ascendancy.

In Leanna Beecham's sprawling manor house, the lieutenant was sound asleep on thousand thread count Egyptian cotton sheets and goose down pillows, dreaming of the last girl he kissed in Oklahoma before he left for the army. Katie Spelacki was the second baseman on their high school softball team, a year younger than her soon-to-be soldier boyfriend but twice as smart. She was four feet, eleven inches tall in shoes and every bit the fiery sparkplug stereotype a person of her stature was expected to be. She was dwarfed by the other girls on the softball field, but was a sure glove and had exceptional range in the infield. Her tiny legs moved at such a furious pace that she was always the fastest girl from either team in any game they played, flitting between the bases like an electric current. She was a perennial batting average leader based almost entirely on her skill in laying down drag bunts and turning on the afterburners such that few fielders even attempted a throw to first. She had not only been the future lieutenant's last kiss, she was his first and also his only. Once, she had turned a corner in the hallway at school and discovered him leaning in to kiss Molly Wallace, the meaty third baseman on her team, beside her locker. Katie took two running steps toward her, leaped into the air, and punched the dump truck of a girl square in the left eye. As soon as the diminutive ninja hit the ground, she kicked her boyfriend hard in the long, thin penis that had been in her hand in the front seat of his pickup truck just the night before. He fell hard to the ground alongside his would-be paramour as tears welled up in his eyes and he turned green around the gills.

"Get up, crybaby," Katie said, reaching out her tiny hand, pulling him to his feet, and walking away with him hand in hand.

The lieutenant had a satisfied smile on his face as his dream skipped ahead to the angry, territory-marking sex the tiny girl had visited upon him when school ended later that day. It was the first time for either of them; neither had any idea what they were doing, but Katie surrendered to the wet rage and managed to steer the event from lusty violence toward a rough approximation of care. It was needy and it was unhealthy and it was love.

The lieutenant had this dream several times a month. It had become a psychological waypoint, a marker from a time before the rigors of Army life and the nation's collapse. Whenever the world was especially dangerous or fearful or seemed to be set against him, the lieutenant was sure to see the dangerous, fearful face of Katie Spelacki in his dreams that night, comforting him in her unsettling way, kissing him clumsily and rough, taking from him the burden of all responsibility except to follow her lead. She was over him now, with her face pressed close against his ear, but the voice was out of place and foreign. He shook his head to try to shake the dream back on track, but the voice grew louder and more jarring. He put his hands over his ears to drown out the unfamiliar sound, but it was too late; the comforting illusion of sleep was ended.

The lieutenant awoke to see Big Chief towering over him, a foot taller than the girl from the dream, her eyes nitid with the twinkling of death, and a dopey, incongruous grin on her pretty face. He made almost no sound at all when she pushed her grandfather's buck knife into his neck and held her hand over his mouth as he drifted quietly away.

The preliminary steps of Luke Buck's battle plan were now underway.

Big Chief and fifty militia members had been dropped off by the navy on the southern shore of Leanna's peninsula, where they were tasked with quietly clearing the big house and grounds of enemy soldiers, then forming up for a flank attack of the army when the signal was given from the navy that their frontal assault had begun. They made light work of the three other sleeping soldiers in the bedrooms down the hall from the lieutenant and found no other soldiers on the grounds. It was Big Chief herself who found Ryland Beecham in the wicker chair on the balcony. Even in the midst of the adrenaline and tension, she stopped to examine his proud face and vacant eyes, remembering the girlish crush she had always had on him, and the way she would ride her bike down to the outside boat ramp when she was a teenager, hoping to catch a glimpse of him shirtless at the helm of his birddog. She had seen death before, but never someone she knew well and never this up close. She wasn't frightened by it. Ryland's curly blonde hair and big hands, and the sneaky smile still pressing at the corner of his lips filled in the blank spaces in her perception of how the battle might go with personal, human details, and they steadied her resolve for the work ahead.

On the army's northern flank, Little Chief and sixty islanders were dropped off at the edge of the scrub woods and had similarly formed up in silence to await a signal from the navy. Elijah Meade had ridden with them, then ran a half mile through the scrub to find his own forces still hiding in the trees. A dozen of the island's best shots remained at the Crofts house and took up positions on the widow's walk and roofline. The moon's retreat behind the wall of clouds meant they would only be able to sight in targets once Hayes, Thomas, and Rolf joined the fight.

At the water's edge, three small boats were piled high with barn wood, sticks, and dried cabbage palm fans that would burn nearly as fast and easily as gasoline. In the center of each boat were crudely constructed supports that took on the unintended appearance of crosses, especially once the fallen islanders were strapped to them. Three non-functioning rifles were rounded up and lashed to each man for visual effect.

William asked, "We gonna use Joffrey Sleady's bow to set the fires?"

"No," Luke replied. "You were just a baby, but we actually tried something like this a few years after the smokestacks fell. There used to be a fella on the island named Jimmy Bluff who lived in that weird little house across from Fannie's. Even though he came here from Chicago, he was an alright dude, and my dad really liked him. He fell off the roof of his house and into the canal that runs under the little bridge there. The fall wasn't even that far, but it was low tide, and he stuck face down in the mud and suffocated before anyone knew he was in there."

"Dang," William said. "He wanted a Viking funeral?"

"Not really. But another guy named Shroeder had coincidentally died that same day."

"What got him?" William asked.

"Not sure, but he had to have been a hundred years old."

William was trying to piece it all together. "And Shroeder wanted a Viking funeral?"

"He just didn't want to be buried. The plan was to burn him in a big fire on the beach, but someone suggested it'd be better if we did it out over the water. Then Jimmy's wife, Mary, heard about it and thought it sounded nice. So we spent all day making rafts, piled 'em up with wood, and set them out from the outside boat ramp. We were out of gas by then, but somebody found a little jug of kerosene to make flaming arrows."

"I bet that was awesome," William said with excitement in his voice.

"It would have been," his father replied. "Except the wind kept putting out the fire on the arrows before they made it to the rafts. We shot every arrow we had, maybe twenty of them, and not one was able to get the fire going. It was a blow-out winter tide, and it was racing out like a river. By the time we shot all the arrows, the rafts were halfway to Seahorse Key."

"What did y'all do?"

"We just sang 'Amazing Grace' and watched them drift out to the reef. I like to imagine they made it all the way to Playa Escondido and scared the crap out of some Mexicans when they came floating up."

"Whoa," William said.

"Yeah," Luke replied. "So we can't take a chance with arrows. We need your Paw-Paw and Mr. Hayes and Mr. Rolf's help in the battle. Every second the army is distracted and freaked out by the flaming men coming at them is a few more seconds for us to lay into them with the 50-cals from the Sawfish and every other gun we can put on them. We need every advantage we can get to offset how many more of them there are than us."

"How are you gonna light 'em up then?" William asked.

"You're gonna help. You and me and Uncle Jud are gonna swim the little boats across the channel, light them on fire, and then haul ass underwater back to the fleet to join the fight. We've got masks and fins to help, but it'll still be a slog. You up for it, son?"

"Absolutely. Can I push Paw-Paw across, and you take Mr. Hayes?"

Luke had thus far into the night held his composure to an almost unreasonable degree, but the force of his son's simple request overwhelmed his emotional defenses, staggering him to one knee as tears came fast and heavy.

"You okay, Dad? I'm sorry, I didn't mean to upset you."

"No . . . no, son. I'm good," Luke replied. "Your Paw-Paw would love that. And I love you for wanting to do it."

Luke's self-doubt as a father, the doubt that all parents have about their parenting—the constant, nagging worry that their own failings will hurt their children—disappeared into the darkness. He knew then that his son would be okay, no matter how the night unfolded. In William's devotion to his Paw-Paw, Luke saw the closest thing a man can get to immortality; in the heart of his grandson, Thomas Buck lived on. Luke Buck would also never die, even if the following few hours plucked him from the mortal world. And if William were to fall alongside him in the coming fight, he would live forever, too, within the never-ending, indestructible energy of love.

Just before Luke, William, and Uncle Jud entered the water to start the swim across the channel, Lizzy climbed into her husband's boat, unfazed by the strangeness of his action figure pose atop the pyre that would burn him away from the world. Earlier in the evening, as they were heading in separate directions from the City Hall building while artillery rounds were still landing around them, Thomas had whispered something into Lizzy's ear that took away her fear and worry in an instant. It was an affirmation they had developed for one another, a three-word question and a three-word answer to remind them, no matter the difficulties, dangers, or uncertainties they may be facing, that they were never alone.

"You and me?" He had asked her.

"You and me," she lovingly replied, sure as the sunrise, solid as a stone wall.

Now, with her face pressed close to his, Lizzy prepared her man for the fight to come.

"Listen up, honey. It's about to get wild out there, and you and the boys are gonna be right out front. I know you'll hold the line for as long as you can. I'll be with you, like I've been all these years—these wonderful years, Thomas."

She kissed his face and rubbed her aged hands through the small patch of hair remaining on the back and sides of his head, while her tears ran in streaks down both of their faces. She lifted his eyelids so he could see her and said sternly, "Now I'm not asking like we usually do; I'm telling, because it's the truest thing I know."

Lizzy pressed her lips gently against the ear of her immortal husband, in the fullness of her feminine authority, whispering, not with the power of the wind, or the earthquake, or the fire, but with the still small voice of God, "You and me."

Reliving the glory of their dark swim in the Two-Day War on the Suwannee, Luke and Uncle Jud pushed their boats forward and began the slow, arduous kick across the bay. The younger, stronger, fitter William swam his Paw-Paw's boat as easily as if he were pushing a rubber ducky around a bathtub. A central worry about Luke's plan was that guards on the mainland might detect the arriving boats before they could be ignited, spoiling the surprise and effect, but as all three made it two-thirds of the way across the channel and their anchors were gently lowered to the bottom, the darkness had grown so luxuriously thick that the three captains standing guard remained oblivious to their arrival. The swimmers struck ferro rods into the tinder and dried cabbage palms, waited a few moments until the fires kicked off in earnest, then turned and swam like hell for the fleet. Before they made it halfway back, the dark night had fully capitulated to the burning and the light.

The fire raged all about the three friends in the little boats, illuminating their determined faces into the haunting glow of demi-gods in the world of men, as they burned but seemed not to be consumed, indestructible as Shadrach, Meshach, and Abednego, radiating power from a floating Golgotha, penitent thieves sanctified by the greater love of the savior, righteous, mythical vanguards to rival Huitzilopochtli, Odin, and Mars, fathers, sons, and husbands, lamps unto the feet and light unto the path ahead for the people they loved and would continue to serve even through their temporary transmogrification—their bright and burning final victory over the paper tiger of death.

The second Luke, William, and Uncle Jud made it back to the fleet, the Sawfish's 50-caliber machine guns opened the gates of hell and sent a leaden army of demons toward the army's camp. The first three to fall, in near-perfect synchronization, were the final remnants of the army's spoiled honor, the three captains who were opposed to the major's death but had not intervened to stop it. While the army lay incapacitated by the lieutenant's abdication of order, the three captains had been standing guard in their stead, but were overwhelmed so quickly by the Sawfish's guns that they had no time or opportunity to command their companies.

Signaled by the burning islanders and the roar of machine guns, the rest of the fleet trained their fire on the tents and the disheveled men crawling out of them. As the army wilted against the fire from its front, Big and Little Chief's forces enfiladed them from both flanks. A wonderous suffering sprang up like a desert flower in the heavy rain of small and large arms fire as soldiers fell by the dozens where they slept and stumbled and ran. A third of the army was killed or wounded in the first two minutes. Five minutes later, their number was reduced by half. In the vanguard, Rolf's face melted enough that the Howitzer fragment fell out of it and his bindings burned through, slumping him down into his boat, but Hayes and Thomas, boiling from the inside and ghastly, nevertheless stood firm, firing imaginary rounds from broken rifles and demoralizing the terrified enemy.

Small pockets of soldiers began to form up behind cover and return fire. Denny Gall fell in the first wave, when a 5.56 round tore through the near center of his heart, ending his life in a painless, bloody millisecond. Adam Bud, who became the proprietor of the Island Hotel and Trident Lounge when his stepfather Andy Bear retired in the waning years of the old world, fell seconds after Denny, gutshot and briefly suffering until enough blood ran out to numbingly usher him into the next life. Little Chief took a grazing blow to the pisiform bone in his left wrist that stung like a hundred wasps, but he was right-handed and continued to fire his rifle through the pain. In a wild move, Heff Webster ran from the trees toward the concentration of soldiers that were hitting his team the hardest, firing accurately at an almost inhuman pace, killing a half dozen of the enemy before twenty rounds hit him at once, ending the gallant, foolhardy charge. Dale Warble took three shots to his right arm, which fell limp and useless at his side. He could no longer manage a rifle, but stayed in the fight with a revolver commandeered from James Custard, the former city works employee who was shooting a thirty-ought-six deer rifle from a prone position and systematically picking off exposed soldiers still making their way out of the tents. Mel Beecham, the 6-foot-five former air traffic controller turned clammer, fought ferociously alongside his fetching, five-foot bride Angie, a real estate dynamo in the old world and a sailmaker in the new. Mel stood at least a head above most of the militia, but despite the temptation he no doubt provided as a target for enemy riflemen, he was somehow unscathed in the battle. Jimmy Mitchell managed to get his flamethrower working, and immediately set both his legs on fire. In a feat of Olympic dexterity, he was somehow able to remove his flaming pants and continue the fight in his underwear.

Steady, carefully-aimed rounds from the widow's walk and roofline of the Crofts house dropped soldiers in a rhythmic cadence while the rifles from the boats in the fleet—positioned in a semi-circle behind the flaming vanguard—fired so furiously that a continuous wall of sound and death came from them. The Sawfish's machine guns worked with the blithe efficiency of an assembly line in a candy factory, cheerfully fabricating the destruction of the enemy army in a steady wave of moving metal. Isaac Skipjack split his time between shouting orders to his Coasties and working to keep his body positioned between the army and the berserking Miss

Bette as she skipped along the deck of the cutter, firing her forty-five caliber revolver toward the mainland, each time nearly losing her footing from the recoil and laughing maniacally. All around, the music of the dead and dying rang out like a marching band in a small-town parade, sometimes out of tune and time but familiar-sounding in a far-off way—the ancient warring song of all mankind.

In a perfect scenario, when visibility was ideal and Luke Buck's plan could be implemented without the passions and shortcomings of human beings, the island's losses would have been far fewer, but in the white-hot chaos of battle, the citizen soldiers could only do the best they could, nevertheless losing their bearings often in the smoke, low-light, and frightened confusion that attends the business of killing. Thankfully, no one could have known it was happening, and certainly no single person could have judged that they themselves were culpable, but several islanders fell from friendly fire misdirected in the night.

The menacing army that even several hours earlier had seemed too ferocious for clam farmers, fishermen, artists, and old folks to resist was now evaporating like morning dew. After a particularly devastating volley from the fleet, as Luke Buck shouted orders in the wild magnificence of a man draped in the mantle of his high calling, when thirty soldiers fell at once, the remaining army turned tail and ran like the Prussians fleeing George Washington at the Battle of Trenton. They had made it no more than fifty yards when Elijah Meade and a hundred Sumner riflemen emerged from the scrub and cut them to pieces.

By the time the firing stopped, only five of the original one thousand and twenty-four soldiers that arrived on the march from Fort Rucker were still standing and able to surrender. Forty-seven were grievously wounded and would die over the next several minutes to hours. Another dozen had sustained injuries from which they would ultimately recover, and nine hundred seventy-two lay dead on the field or in the yard and house on Leanna Beecham's peninsula.

The guns of the Sawfish and the rifles on the boats and in the trees fell silent. Hayes, Thomas, and Rolf burned straight on through till sunrise, when a warm, reassuring light filtered across the Wacasassa Bay and the island fleet sailed for home.

26

MOVING WATER

Nurse Toni and her Coastie medic husband, HT Morgan, put in several long days and nights caring for the wounded islanders and the soldiers from the defeated army. Those soldiers who surrendered were given bags with several days' rations and escorted all the way to Otter Creek with instructions to never set foot on State Road 24 again under penalty of summary judgment and death. As the wounded soldiers regained their health and strength, they were each escorted away under the same conditions. Within a few weeks, the last of the soldiers were gone, and the island began its recovery in earnest.

In total, just over ten percent of the island's population was lost in what would come to be known as the Third Battle of Cedar Key, following the first in 1865 and the second in the early days of the new world when invading Meades were put down on the little bridge in front of Fannie's Café. No Cedar Key residents lost their lives in the first battle; the second resulted in a single islander death, the Episcopal minister Folksy Phillips, but in the aftermath of the third, forty-four islanders were dead, and ten more had wounds that would hobble them for the rest of their lives.

For a cost so high, Luke Buck became increasingly convinced the island deserved more than just an ended threat. His father, his mentor, and so many of his friends had spilled blood for the home they loved, and the new mayor determined that this blood would purchase something worthy of its cost. When the bombs fell on the cold morning of the flash, America and all the nations of men failed as surely and spectacularly as the '85 Red Sox or New Coke or the Ford Edsel. In a bastion of patriotism like Cedar Key, hope for the survival of the nation held on for more than two decades, being only finally extinguished when a remnant of the American Army made war on the island. If some vestige of the old nation remained somewhere out on the mainland, the islanders had no further use for it.

A formal declaration of secession was drafted and presented at an emergency meeting of the city council, where Dale Warble took his seat for the first time to replace his friend Heff Webster, and every islander—man and woman, young and old, healthy and infirm—came to vote in a referendum on the severing of ties to a big idea that had once so thoroughly raptured their hearts. The unanimous final vote for independence was a repudiation of the iniquity and avarice that killed the world, a unified statement that an America without the virtue of the founding ideals was no better than a tinhorn dictatorship and no more useful than a pet rock or a set of teats on a rank boar hog.

We hold these truths to be self-evident, Luke Buck wrote in the founding document, *that the island is created unequally from the rest of the world, that it is endowed by the Gulf with certain inalienable blessings, that among them are the mullet, the moving water of the tides, and a channel that separates it from a broken world.*

The old flags came down. New ones went up. *My Country Tis Of Thee* was still sung, along with the other old songs, but their words were changed here and there to herald the new nation, the Republic of Cedar Key.

In his father's library on E Street, Luke Buck began the work of writing the history of the great battle, from the moment the Blackhawk appeared in the sky above the city park, to the day the last of the enemy soldiers were exiled from the island for good. Since the earliest days of the new world, he had been writing the island's history because he could not bear the thought of so many great stories being lost to the vicissitudes of memory and time. His father had taught him by osmosis to care about the past, not just the wars and the great men and women, or the rise and fall of empires, but also the human stories of everyday life that found a way to carry on in the midst of upheaval, cataclysm, triumphs, failures and the sometimes unbearably long stretches where not much happens at all.

Luke had manned a shovel for four straight days to help bury his fallen neighbors in the cemetery. The chickens penned in the back had griped and crowed the whole time, and twice a big osprey overheard, as an offering to the dead or a mockery of the living, dropped a live mullet among the diggers, always with an unbothered *cheep-cheep-cheep* and not the frantic, wavering squeal of alarm or unease. If it had been a month later, the sand gnats would have made the work unbearable, but in late February, the chill air was still keeping them away.

Just before an islander was placed in a newly finished hole, Luke would retrieve his father's notebook, the one he used to jot down ideas for future books or plays he intended to write, and in it he would record his neighbor's name and everything anyone could tell him about them. Sometimes the information would only fill a short paragraph, and sometimes multiple pages were needed to take it all down, from the basic facts of their birth and death and their old world jobs and education, to their new world endeavors, their favorite things, the art or music they made, who their closest friends were, and how they fought and fell in battle. Luke's field journal became a repository of the raw data he would use to flesh out their place in the history he was writing. Over time, after the dead were all buried and the hot memories of the battle had cooled, even folks who had not fought the army began to call on Luke for the sole purpose of telling their stories for his journal, and he was always happy to oblige them.

Luke was able to write much of his best buddy Ryland's story from his own experiences, finding in the task catharsis punctuated by moments of melancholy and great loss. Often, the sight of his wife Kinsey's wild red hair would transport him back to the day he and Ryland first met her while hunting in the scrub. Kinsey had beaten them both to the deer all three had been tracking, and from then on, she seldom lost any of the frequent competitions the three friends cooked up to help pass the time. In Kinsey's steady, uncomplicated affection, Luke's memory of Ryland was constantly refreshed, and he found he loved his wife all the more for it.

Rolf's entry in the journal was aided by the recollections of a dozen islanders who knew him well, and to their stories Luke added an account of how the Angel of Death had taught him to quick-draw a cowboy gun and disable an attacker with a knife, and a sentence about how deeply his father and Mr. Hayes had loved him.

Eventually, Luke finished the ten full pages of notes about his friend and mentor, Hayes David, but not without breaks of a full day or more in between each heartrending section. From the nautical knots his father refused to learn but Mr. Hayes had taught him so effortlessly, to their fishing trips to the secret shark hole in a creek off the Wacassassa, to the long walk they had taken together while the votes were counted that make him the first new mayor in fifty years, Luke's memories of the old mayor were an ever-present comfort as he went about the difficult task of leading a new Republic into an uncertain future. For the rest of his life, whenever doubt or self-recriminations would gather in the corners of his mind, Luke would pull himself from their grasp by thinking of the night he stood outside the door of the City Hall building with a bag of food under his arm, determined to set young Elijah Meade free in the night, in defiance of the town council. While he worried whether it was right to do a thing he knew to be right—at the crisis of his indecision—there was Mr. Hayes, with a bag of food under his arm as well and a proud hug for his principled young friend. As Elijah paddled away into the night, the mayor told his best friend's son, who had only ever called him Mr. Hayes, that the *Mr.* was no longer required—they were equals now and just Hayes would do. Luke continued to call the great man Mr. Hayes for the rest of his life, and for as long as his own memory held, Mr. Hayes was who the old mayor would always be.

Rather than making a recordkeeping entry in the journal for his father, Luke Buck wrote his dad directly into the history. There was no chance his memory of the elder Buck would fail because their lives were intertwined like the roots of a thicket, tangled like the mangroves that built the Florida coast and shield it from the wind and surge; from Luke's first breath, father and son had defined themselves in terms of one another. Notes in a journal would feel like a betrayal. When the time came to write his father's story, Luke had only to think of his own life, and there, unwavering at its center, was Thomas Buck, with his arms outstretched, saying *this is my beloved son, in whom I am well pleased.* Even after the Transfiguration of the pyres in the little boats, when the mortal elements of the three men were burned away, leaving only the spirit of a loving God in their places, still Thomas was his father as plain and sure as the day he was born, unmistakably as he will yet be when at last the universe expands itself out of existence. He and his father were a single life, a solitary light crafted from the same bag of stardust, inseparable as light and shadow.

Luke took a break from writing, and as he was looking through the books on his father's shelves, Lizzy arrived from town with Georgie Pilsner, still crutches-bound but beginning to move around mostly on his own.

"How's the history coming?" Georgie asked.

"A little more to do before it's all caught up, but I'm making headway," Luke replied.

"I've been trying to work up the nerve to come here," Georgie began with trepidation in his voice.

"Why?" Luke asked. "We go all the way back, Mr. Georgie. You were literally at the hospital when I was born. You don't need any nerve with me."

"I want to tell you about your dad."

"I can't think of anything I don't know about him already," Luke said skeptically.

"So that you have the full story for the history . . . I need to tell you how he died. How he was at the end."

"Oh," Luke said quietly.

"I can come back if you're not ready," Georgie said, looking down. "But I think he would want you to know."

"No. No, now is good. It's important to get the story right."

Georgie made no effort whatsoever to forestall the tears, leaning into the teeth of the heavy emotion, saying, "Thomas was my oldest friend.

When the world ended and the years started piling up, I never stopped hoping I would get a chance to see him again before we both got too old for it to matter. When I left Florida for Virginia, I never looked back for anything but your dad."

Luke said, "I'm glad you were with him at the end. I know he was, too."

"I'm glad, too, Luke. I need to tell you the rest of the story, but it hurts, and I'm struggling."

"This was a good start," Luke said as he put his arm around the old poet. "As long as you don't think you'll forget it, we'll do a little at a time over as many days as it takes. I'll enjoy looking forward to seeing you, Mr. Georgie. We've got all the time in the world."

To the relief and delight of everyone on the island, there unfolded a long stretch of not much happening at all. The water moved in and out of the estuary as it always had and would; the sun rose and set, the days ran together, and the months began to slip by. Lizzy and Tabby grew closer as they helped each other through their grief. William and Alexis were married in a month, and she was pregnant in two—a blushing, forty-five-year-old first-time mother. The helicopter in the park was torn apart piece by piece for scrap and salvage, and to put the memories away for good.

Yonder all before the island lay a vast expanse of time and possibility. Luke continued writing the history as it unfolded, and a Constitution for the new Republic, with ink and lead in scribbled handwriting on scraps of paper that could not hope to last beyond a generation or two. The temporal nature of human affairs was more acute in the new world, but hope and love continued to make the doing worth doing. For as long as they could, the islanders would live with and for each other, on little sandheap keys dangling like a string of pearls into the ancient Gulf that would ebb and flow beyond the last trace of humankind.

In the end, the Gulf remains. It is loving, indifferent, hateful, and kind; oblivious to the lost age of man, flowing in and washing out, wearing away the brief, defenseless land, mixing with the rivers and the rain, it streams away from the protected harbor of the once and fallen Americas, around the wide, dead world, and back again.

Moving water is the last song on Earth.

Acknowledgements

Special thanks to Heath Davis, the real life Hayes David, a friend to Thomas Buck and to me. When a friendship is worth writing three novels about, it's a valuable thing indeed.

G.M. Palmer is a smart, thoughtful, demanding, infuriating, gifted editor. I owe much to him for the success of the Cedar Key novels, and I'm looking forward to working with him until we're both too old and stupid to do it anymore. Thanks, brother.

To the dearly departed Mrs. Iris Cole, the unimpressible high school English teacher that told me I should give up writing and focus on golf or playing the saxophone, this book, like all of them, is fundamentally for you. In the bright light of your disapproval, I loved you, and I love you still. Rest easy, sweet(ish) lady.

The real life Lizzy Fraydel continues to be the stabilizing force that makes it possible for me to write a book every year. If anything ever happens to her, I'll be lucky to write a few greeting cards every now and then. I'm grateful to her in ways immeasurable and essential. In my life, she has been the still small voice of God, the magic behind the stories.